ORDER OF SEVEN

ORDER OF SEVEN

BETH TELIHO

branches & ink
Press

ORDER OF SEVEN

Cover Design by Seedlings Design Studio
www.seedlingsonline.com

Typesetting by Atthis Arts LLC
www.atthisarts.com

Published by Branches & Ink Press
www.branchesandinkpress.com

ISBN: 978-0-9861577-0-7 (paperback)
978-0-9861577-1-4 (e-book)

To Jim,

Because twelve years ago you wrote *I believe in you* on a sticky note and left it on my desk, and you never stopped.

1

Introduction

My older brother, Nodin, remembers more than I do. But I have something he doesn't.

I have the dream. A snippet of life before our adoption; a single event played over and over while I sleep. Hundreds of times, I've woken up with a scream in my throat and a name on my lips. The dream is always the same. Pounding drums. A tribe surrounding a fire. A night that starts as a celebration but ends in panic and chaos.

Now the dream is changing. For the first time, it's revealing new details. Nodin says it's a suppressed memory trying to reconcile itself in my subconscious. I think it's more than that.

I think it's trying to tell us something.

Mom and Dad were always open with us about our adoption. They made sure we understood that once we were both adults, information would be available to us if we wanted to learn about our biological parents. Two weeks ago, I turned eighteen and, at our request, Mom gave us the paperwork. There wasn't as much information as we had hoped for, but what we did learn was disheartening.

In the right column, a box labeled *Biological Mother* had one word typed inside: *Deceased*.

The rest of the page has more blank spaces than filled, but the most obvious are our birthdates. The case worker at the facility told Mom and Dad these weren't provided and they could choose birthdays for us. Nodin was around three years old, they said, and because he was taller, probably a little older than me. Mom decided my birthday was November 2nd, in honor of her father's birthday, and Nodin's approximately eighteen months earlier, April 21, 1991.

Ian and Elaine Bennett, our adoptive parents, flew to

Johannesburg, South Africa, in February 1994 and signed the papers to make us legally theirs. They kept our birth names, Devi and Nodin, which I've always thought was cool. They brought us home to Odessa, Texas, where they loved and nurtured us. We lived in a safe neighborhood, went to good schools, attended church on Sundays, and had family dinners every night around a table overflowing with as much laughter as food.

We could easily leave things as they are, but Nodin and I want to know what happened the night I relive in my dreams. We want to know what two white children were doing with a dark skinned native African tribe. We want to know how our mother died and why we were given up for adoption. But there's another reason we want to explore our roots: our paranormal abilities.

My brother Nodin can feel and influence the emotions of others. I find myself sometimes aware of things before they actually happen. Intuitive sensitivities are not common, yet we both possess them. These gifts—if you can call them that— are poorly understood and certainly not accepted in society as a whole. We suspect the only way to fully understand our abilities is to find our family.

I'm in a woman's lap. We're sitting on the dirt ground, across from a fire. The earthy smell of sage dominates the air. Embers spit high and fast from their log nest, snapping an arc of light as they go. The woman braids my hair. My pudgy toddler hands play with the tassels at the end of my dress. It's dusk. I can already see the moon, faded by the orange creamsicle sunset.

Dark skinned men sit with us, completing our circle around the fire. Their faces are decorated in bold stripes of black and white paint, making their appearance more mask-like than human. Each has a drum in their lap which they beat in unison; a quiet, slow rhythm. They wear strips of red cloth around their waists. Thick gold chains hang from their necks and ankles, dancing with the yellow and orange reflections of the fire.

The women are beautiful. Shortly cropped hair frames ebony faces with high cheekbones and full lips. One eye is encircled with intricately placed swirls, dots, and dashes of bright blue, yellow, white, and red; each woman with their own unique design and color palette. They stand on the outskirts of the circle, smiling, moving to the rhythm of the drums. Like the men, they wear a red wrap around their waist, but theirs continues up over one shoulder, leaving a breast exposed.

A man wearing a bear mask stands at the head of the circle holding a tall, decorated stick. He's dressed differently than the other men. He wears a vest of reeds, interlocked with beads and feathers. The skin on his arms and legs is covered in yellow paint. I stare at him, suspicious I know who he is and hoping I'm right.

I love him. I trust him.

I look at the man sitting directly to my left. He doesn't have a drum, and is wrapped in a brown hooded robe, leaving only his face and hands visible. The whites of his eyes glow and there's something unnatural about his jet-black skin. His strange eyes peer at me, making me uncomfortable. I wiggle in the woman's arms under the discomfort of his stare. I want to stop looking at him, but can't.

The drums beat louder and faster. The man with the bear mask tilts his head to the sky. All eyes are on him. The air is electric with anticipation, but for what I don't know. I squirm again, uncomfortable with the noise. The woman squeezes me, tussling my hair. I know she is trying to comfort me.

I don't relax.

The bear-masked man holds his stick out in front of his chest. The drums cease, creating instant silence. The man looks directly at the woman holding me and points his stick in our direction. She nudges me to stand.

I hesitate.

He booms, "Mandah."

I stand, wobbly in the knees, with the woman's hand at the small of my back to support me.

With his stick still pointed at me, his deep voice reverberates through the air, "Dakahn manyan mah pih tah nili hasi."

Gasps pierce the silence. I hear his words repeated, fluttering around the group. Eyes wide with wonder and awe gaze upon me, and arms reach out to touch my hair and face. The creepy man next to me is nodding, smiling. I'm confused by all the attention, but am certain of one thing: this ceremony is for me and I've been given a name.

In an instant the energy changes. A scurry, a commotion, and then shrieks break out. Happy faces transform to panic. Men take defensive stances, shouting from all directions. The creepy man moves toward me and the woman. I scream and look for the bear-masked man. He's gone.

The woman shoves me into the arms of another. As I'm pulled backward, I see the creepy man dragging the woman away from me and lay eyes on her for the first time. Her skin is not black, but brown, like milk chocolate. She wears a dress of yellow leather with tassels on the end, just like mine. Long braids of brown hair fall past her shoulders. There is terror in her eyes.

I wake like I always do. Like I have a hundred times: clutching my sweat-soaked sheets, face damp with panicked tears, calling out a name. A bastard name with no identity. *Nami.*

2
November 12, 2010

"**H**op in," Nodin shouts from the window of his blue Ford Bronco.

I just finished a four-hour shift at the university bookstore and he's giving me a lift since my heap-o-shit pickup-truck is in the shop, again. Bad timing, because tonight we have special plans.

My brother and I both attend the University of Texas of the Permian Basin. I'm a freshman, without the slightest idea what my major will be. Nodin's a sophomore. With his grades he could have gone anywhere, but I feel like he opted for the flat, dry lands of Odessa he dislikes so much just so he could stay near me.

Nodin is following in our dad's footsteps, studying archeology. Dad's been the professor of archeology at UTPB for twenty-four years. My mom earned her Master's in art history there. She ran a gallery in town for more than a decade, but retired after they sold our house to move a little outside of town where they could have some land. Horses are her new hobby.

"Thanks again for the lift." I wince as vibrations from my tree travel through the ground into my legs, summoning me to it. A demand, not a request.

I've spent hundreds of hours in my tree's branches, connecting to its energy, experiencing sensations so mind-blowing everything else in life seems dull, or muted in comparison.

It doesn't happen with any tree, just the one in the backyard of our childhood home. I receive visions there, sometimes of events that haven't happened yet. Like when I knew Nodin was going to fall off his bike and sprain his wrist a week before it actually happened, or how I knew Aunt Lily was pregnant before she announced it. Other times, the vision is from long ago or feels like déjà vu.

There's no ignoring the tree's calling. Not just today, but ever. The longer it takes me to respond, the more punishing the calling gets. But I can't always bolt the minute I feel it. I have school and work, for fuck's sake.

Sensing my tension, Nodin leans forward and makes eye contact. His brows lift with understanding; he knows I'm being called by the tree. Nodin is an empath, which is the term for the type of intuitive ability he has. He's highly sensitive to his surroundings, particularly other's feelings. As a child, being in public would make him physically ill. It took years of practice to control the emotions that threatened to overwhelm him. But there's no one he's more in tune with than me.

"I need to take you to the tree now?" he asks. It's more a statement than a question.

"Yeah. Just drop me off and I'll call you when I'm ready, okay?" I pat the cell phone in my jacket pocket. I don't carry a purse. I prefer to keep things simple.

He turns the car toward our old house, the one we grew up in, just a few miles from the college. His shoulders relax and his hands loosen their grip on the steering wheel as he sheds my anxious feelings.

"Are you excited about Baron and Ben coming?" I ask.

In his youth, Nodin endured months of intense traditional therapy and testing to find a reason for his emotional distress. One day, after a particularly harrowing group session where Nodin fell to the floor and vomited, a doctor discreetly handed Mom a card for a place specializing in children with paranormal abilities: the Center for Intuitive and Sensitive Children, or CISC.

Two weekends a month, Mom drove Nodin all the way to Dallas to see Steve Beckman, a therapist at CISC, where he was first diagnosed as an empath. They trained him on how to manage the emotions he absorbs, and taught our parents ways to help accommodate his extra sensitivities, like keeping rose quartz in his room and smudging the house with sage. Not all parents would've been that open-minded. I have to give them props.

At CISC, Nodin met other kids with sensitivities, two of which became life-long friends: Baron and Ben. Ben, a psychic, has visited Nodin countless times over the years. I've never met Baron, but I've heard stories about him. He can see and manipulate energy. A shaper, trained as a healer.

Nodin smiles. "Yes. I can't wait to show Baron around here."

"So, I finally get to meet the famous Baron Latrosse. Why has he never visited before? Is he too good for Texas?"

He glares at me in response, blond brows furrowed over his blue eyes. Even knowing Nodin my whole life, the ice-blue color of his eyes is always striking.

"Don't look at me like that, there's nothing I can do about it," I snap, knowing what his look means, and then feel bad. He can't help experiencing what I feel. I normally wouldn't get so irritated by it, but the calling makes me edgy, or as Nodin would say, an itch with a B.

"I'm not. Chill out," he says, scowling.

"What's your deal, then? You look stressed." His hair is a mess, but not in a trendy way, more of an Einstein-I-haven't-slept-in-a-week way.

He waves away my question, his eyes never leaving the road. "Play nice tonight when you meet Baron. Okay?"

"*Play nice*? What the hell does that mean?"

Nodin sighs. "You can be little intense sometimes. Just relax. Try to be friendly."

"I'm *always* friendly." I'm more than a little taken aback. "I didn't have any trouble making friends with Ben."

He looks at me, incredulous. "You met him when you were nine. And incidentally, he was my friend first, before he became so close with our family."

I stare at him, trying to decide how to respond. I feel defensive. But he's right. I have acquaintances, but no close friends.

His shoulders sag as my hurt feelings drape over him like a wet blanket. "I'm sorry. I didn't mean to make a big deal out of it. It's not your fault," he admits.

"Then whose fault is it?" I ask, looking down at my hands.

"Not who. What." He shoots me a quick glance. "Your ability. It consumes you. You're disconnected from everything else. That's not a judgment. It's just the way it is."

"So I'm narcissistic and cold?"

"Not at all. You have a huge heart, Devi. You're just not used to sharing it." He looks at me with a little smile. "You're a rookie."

I would argue, but in a lot of ways he has more insight into me than I do, and frankly, I'm too tired: the tree's calling is kicking my ass. Another band of energy zips through me like an electric eel. I clench my jaw and lean into the vibrations. When it passes, I decide I'm done with analyze-Devi-hour and change the subject.

"Why didn't Baron and Ben ride here together before? Seems like common sense with both of them living in Oklahoma."

"Well…" Nodin hesitates.

"They're pretty tight, aren't they?"

"Oh yeah. Real tight." He pauses. "Ben's only had a license and his own wheels for about a year. And Baron, well, Baron is pretty busy being a healer."

Ben's mom would fly him down in the past, or sometimes they'd make the drive together. His dad died in a plane crash a month before he was born. It's always just been him and his mom. He's so close with our family he feels like a brother. At times, a protective one, especially where I'm concerned. This can sometimes be great, and sometimes highly annoying.

Nodin pulls the Bronco in front of our old house. "He's really let the landscaping go, huh?"

"Guess so." The sight of the front yard reminds me of when a For Sale sign stuck out of the ground. It seems like a lifetime ago they sold the house, yet the panic and depression remain a lead weight in my gut. Mom and Dad don't know about the tree. No one does, except my brother.

I do have a vivid memory from when I was about five years old. I was climbing down from high in the tree and Nodin was waiting for me below. As soon as my feet touched the ground, he took me by the shoulders and warned me not to tell Mom and Dad about the tree.

"It will be too hard on them," he said. This was on the cusp of them trying to find out what was wrong with Nodin, before they knew he was an empath or had even heard of CISC. "No one can know," he said.

When you're five and your older brother who you idolize tells you to keep something quiet, you do.

As the years went by, I saw how hard our parents worked to understand Nodin's intuitive abilities and what they sacrificed to ensure he had the support he needed. He was right. I couldn't add to their burden. I spent years secretly researching, but never found anything closely resembling the connection I have with my tree or the visions I receive from it. Despite the frustration of not understanding my ability, combined with the crushing isolation of keeping a secret this big, I've never told a soul.

Mom and Dad were confused and upset by my sheer panic about the move, too much for Nodin's comfort. He used his ability to distract them. He only influences others' feelings when it's in their best interest. I'm the only person whose feelings he's unable to manipulate.

"What's up with the eight foot fence? How long's that been there?" he asks.

"A couple years. Turns out Joe doesn't appreciate a certain girl trying to sneak in his backyard to get to her tree."

Nodin's brows rise.

"He wants me to have to go through him," I say.

His eyes fix on mine for a few seconds before he sighs and looks away. "I guess you better get going."

I pull a hairband out of my jeans pocket and put my hair into a ponytail at the nape of my neck. I never know how windy it'll be up there.

3

TRANSCENDENCE

I crunch through fallen leaves to Joe's front porch, teeth clenched, muscles quaking. It knows I'm here. I feel like a junkie. What I need—what is mine—is at this house. *His* house now. I knock on the door. Like an addict, I'll return over and over for my fix. But first I have to talk to Joe and go through the niceties and wait an eternity to get where I need to be.

Joe opens the door. "Here she is, here she is." A wide grin erupts a landscape of wrinkles across his tan face. The pissy Chihuahua he holds under his left arm—whom I secretly refer to as Assface—bares his teeth. Joe wears the same faded T-shirt and baggy cargos I see him in every time, just a different version. Grey shoulder-length hair is tucked behind his ears.

"Hey there," I say.

He beckons me inside. "Come on in, young lady. Come on in." Assface snaps his teeth.

I turn sideways to avoid the jaws of crazy-paws and shimmy past them. I'm gripped by rattling pulses for a few seconds, my mind a swirl of hot red lights. It ebbs and I resume walking to the family room. Joe, of course, is oblivious.

The house looks so different I no longer associate it with the place I spent my childhood. It's more like a storage warehouse than a home. Glass cases filled with meticulously cared-for possessions line the walls. Large, pregnant bookshelves sag under the weight. Every available surface and corner is stuffed with shipping supplies. The blinds are almost always completely drawn, making the house a cave. Joe calls himself an artifacts dealer. More of a hoarder, if you ask me. But what the hell do I know?

Joe's collections seem to go through phases. His current obsession is gemstone skulls. They supposedly have healing properties, and he thinks they're fascinating. I think they're creepy.

I preferred the arrowhead phase, which only rivaled the Nepalese artifacts phase in longevity. The most interesting thing to me in his house is the mountain of junk that never finds its way to the trash. Packing peanuts litter the floor, empty food containers pile a foot high on his coffee table and never less than five used coffee mugs occupy the little remaining table space.

Joe is lonely. Claims to have no real friends or family. He never goes on trips over the holidays. He told me once he does most of his buying and selling over the Internet, although he does frequent a few salvage yards from time to time. He knows I will always return and he takes full advantage by squeezing as much conversation out of me as possible.

We are two people completely dependent on each other. He needs me for companionship. I need him to access my tree.

He sits in his recliner, tucking Assface next to his thigh. "I didn't expect you 'til Sunday. I have something special to show you. I just got a new skull in—she's a beauty." His light blue-grey eyes sparkle. "This one's made of moonstone, hand crafted in Chile." He reaches beside his chair to retrieve a box, then pulls out a wad of blue tissue paper. With long, thin fingers he carefully unwraps a milky skull about the size of a large marble. "Isn't she stunning?"

I nod.

He holds it out to me. A grey strand of hair falls in his face. Assface sends a warning growl as I take the skull from Joe and roll it around in my palm. It's cold but feels nice. There's something oddly reassuring about its weight. "What's it supposed to do?"

"Ah," he says and holds up a finger, eyes flashing. "I'm glad you asked. It's supposed to balance energy and be good for circulation."

I grin, thinking that skull couldn't touch my energy field. He tucks the stray hair behind his ear and I notice he's wearing a new ring. It's silver and turquoise and looks enormous on his thin finger. He's always donning new jewelry, apparently a fan of Native American stuff. I feel another wave of energy oscillate toward me. I brace and it shatters through me, leaving my ears ringing.

"You okay?" He squints with a tilt of his head, like he always does when he's worried about me.

Since he's witnessed me wincing more times than I can count, I had to tell him I'm lactose intolerant and my stomach always hurts. Not a brilliant excuse, but I don't always have the luxury of time to think of awesome lies.

"Yeah, I'm fine." A nativity scene on the coffee table catches my eye. It's small and colorful. "What's that?" I ask, and immediately regret it. I fell for it. It's obviously been placed right in front of me in hopes it would strike up conversation. I just ruined any brevity this visit might have.

His brows arch high. "Ohhh, that's special. It's hand-carved out of ancient petrified wood in Honduras, just delivered this morning. And look." He leans forward and picks up one of the animals. "These are pigs, rather than sheep like we're used to seeing."

I'm reminded of the time Joe told me he was agnostic. I was younger then, maybe fifteen. I didn't understand what agnostic meant until I looked it up and learned it's not a disbelief in God, like atheism. It's the opinion that the existence or nonexistence of God is unknowable.

I reach for the Virgin Mary figurine and inspect the tiny details of her burgundy robe. "Why are you buying nativity scenes if you're agnostic? You kind of have to believe in God to believe in Jesus."

He sits back in his chair still holding the tiny wooden pig and smiles. "Ah, but the very reason I study religions is based on my agnosticism. The reason we need stories such as those in the Bible, or the Koran, or the Tanakh, is because no one *really* knows anything, and since it's impossible to know, we have faith, and faith is dependent on stories passed down from generation to generation, giving mankind hope and direction." He puts the pig on the coffee table. "The power and necessity of stories is the one thing I do know for sure. That's my religion."

It's the most profound thing I've ever heard. It never dawned on me religion is based on stories, or that one is not more right than the other. I'm about to ask him another question when the calling grips me again. When I look up at him, he's got that concerned look on his face.

Joe sighs. "I know. You want to get to your tree. But just one more thing." He scoots Assface into a crate on the far end of the room, shuffles down the hall, and returns with an envelope which he offers to me.

"What's this?" I take it from him.

"You'll see." A smile widens across his face.

I open it, trying to keep my hands steady. It's a birthday card. Inside, wrapped in a tiny square of green tissue paper, is a tree of life charm.

"Happy eighteenth. Sorry, it's a little belated," he says, smiling shyly. His hands fumble, then settle in his pants pockets. "You can put it on a necklace. Or a bracelet."

I nod but can't speak. I don't know what to say. A thank-you seems too simple. I showed up at his door nearly four years ago, a stranger, telling him a story of growing up here and missing the memory-filled family tree. He introduced himself with a trustworthy smile that reached his eyes.

"I'm Joseph. Joseph Bridle—like in horse gear, not weddings—but you can call me Joe."

I asked if I could visit the tree. He said yes. I asked if I could return. He said of course.

I've shown up at his door dozens, maybe even a hundred times over the years and he's always looked past the strangeness of my visits. Despite my initial resentment, I've grown from merely tolerating Joe, to actually liking him. I'm so touched by his gift I do something completely out of character for me. I hug him.

"Oh, glad you like it," he says with flushed cheeks. "Sorry it's a little late, November snuck up on me."

"No, it's fine…but how do you know when my birthday is?" I make it a point to never discuss personal details.

"You told me once." His gaze lowers to the floor. "Last year, don't you remember?"

I didn't, but then again, our visits are usually a blur. Excusing myself, I hand Joe the envelope with the charm tucked back inside and walk out the back door.

The massive oak tree towers above me from the far right corner of the yard. Thick branches dip nearly to the ground, like a giant's hand awaiting a passenger. I reach up to my branch—the one I've used to climb it since I was five—and lift myself into its arms. The urgent energy transforms into soothing waves, twining through my fibers, entrancing me. My breath comes in short gasps, taking in what feels like clearer, sweeter air than before.

I'm lured higher and higher until I get to my chair, a forked branch that makes a perfect seat. I wilt into it, my cells merging with the tree's essence. My arms and legs are the branches: weighted, powerful, rough with thick bark. Warm sap runs through my veins, and vibrations from the earth tremble in my bones. I reach up and feel my bark crackling, the warmth of the sun, and the undeniable, immense connection down deep in the earth. Anchored. Rooted. Part of something bigger.

The vision comes immediately.

I'm with Nodin. We're young. He's chasing me around the tree faster and faster. I'm squealing and laughing. He's wearing long sleeves and a hat to protect his pale skin.

He almost reaches me, but I bolt toward the fence and lose him, sticking my tongue out and taunting him. His face gets red with frustration. He walks to the rock towers we built by the porch and kicks mine over. I start to cry.

Nodin doubles over, my sadness saturating him. He stumbles to my side to console me and I punch him in the shoulder. It starts to rain as he returns to the rock piles and begins to rebuild mine.

I calm into sniffles and give him a tiny smile when he

shows me my tower is now taller than his. He hangs his head in relief, rain dripping from the brim of his hat.

Behind him a young boy and girl stand in tattered, filthy clothes. They are sad for Nodin, and although Nodin and I are soaked, they are bone dry.

My eyes flutter open and I bolt upright, shocked. I've never seen that boy and girl in a vision or otherwise, yet I'm almost certain who they are. I need to talk to Nodin. I start to climb down when thunder rumbles in the distance.

I cherish storms. I collapse back against the branches just as cold rain begins pelting my skin and nature's symphony starts its slow march across the sky.

Remnants of the energy tingle in my fingertips as the connection fades. It's dark. I look at my wrist for the glowing numbers of my watch and realize it's been almost two hours. Fatigue hangs off my bones like weights. I carefully climb down the slick tree.

Joe is waiting, as always, squinting with his head tilted. I follow him through the house without a word, the vision of the boy and girl still haunting me.

Joe is accustomed to my hasty exits. I'm often too spent to speak.

"You need a towel?" he asks, before opening the front door. He hands me my envelope.

I shake my head, whispering a quick thanks as I leave. I walk all the way to the curb before remembering I have no car. I reach in my damp jacket pocket for my cell and call Nodin.

"You ready?" he asks.

"Uh-huh."

"You soaked?"

"Uh-huh."

"Do you still want to come over tonight? I probably have

clothes you can borrow. I guess I could take you home to change—"

"I'll borrow." I can't stand being left out of anything. I've spent my life bound to the unpredictable calling, tethered to this tree, this town. I cling to Nodin's friends and experiences like they are life rafts.

"Be there in a minute," he says.

I hang up and sit with my head on my knees. Fifteen minutes later, he pulls up. I fold the envelope in half and slide it in my jacket pocket, then climb in the passenger seat, which he's covered with a towel. Nodin, my brother, always ten steps ahead.

"You all right?" he asks.

"Better, thanks."

"I brought you water." He motions to a small bottle.

"Thanks." I empty it in six gulps.

"You sure you're up for hanging out tonight? You can come over tomorrow—"

"I'm fine. Did they get in okay?"

"Yeah, about an hour ago."

"Cool." I glance at him, his face going light then dark as we pass under streetlights. "I meant to tell you earlier, I'm diggin' the scruff."

Nodin runs his fingers through his goatee. "Do you? I wasn't sure."

"Definitely. It suits you." I pause. "Are you gonna ask the redhead out? She seems to like you."

"No," he says, his jaw stiff. "We don't really have much in common."

Nodin has never had a girlfriend. Hell, he's never even been on a date. He's painfully shy, but more than that, I think he's ashamed of his pale skin. When we were little, people used to ask if we were twins, but as I got older my hair turned more yellow and, although fair, I'm not nearly as pale. Poor Nodin with his near-white hair and papery skin. Years of teasing and torment chipped away at him, leaving a grown man who, even in the hottest summers, wears clothes that cover his arms and legs. He may hide behind feigned indifference, but I see the sadness behind his eyes.

I'm all too familiar with the toll loneliness takes. For this reason, I don't resent him. I envy things about his life, but never resent.

"Nodin...I saw something tonight I need to talk to you about." I pause and decide to go for it. "I think I saw Train and Emilet." I peek over, gauging his reaction.

We never discuss his spirit guides. In fact, he hasn't talked about them since he was little. For a while Mom and Dad thought Nodin's *friends* were imaginary. Not uncommon for a child. In fact, they thought it was adorable Nodin always pulled a chair out for "Train" and pushed the swing for "Emilet." Adorable until his one-sided conversations began to get suspiciously sophisticated for a five-year-old, and items out of his reach mysteriously ended up in his hands.

The proverbial last straw was when Mom witnessed Nodin sitting by himself on the kitchen floor, pushing a ball across the tile. The ball repeatedly stopped on the other side of the room and then rolled back to him. This is another reason it was so easy to keep my secret from Mom and Dad. They were so busy with Nodin, nothing I did even blipped their radars.

His jaw drops. "What do you mean you saw them?"

"In my vision. We were young, playing in the backyard together. A boy and girl stand just behind you. Both scrawny. Pale. Kind of sickly looking. Wore really bad clothes, all torn up and stuff."

"Yeah, that's them." He stares straight ahead.

I remember hearing my parents whisper about how his guides must have been alive in the 1920s. A six-year-old Nodin had recounted details about the time period they lived in, details he couldn't know. Shouldn't know.

But Nodin had made it clear there was one subject therapists could not ask about: why and how Train and Emilet died so young.

"Why do they look like that?" I ask.

"Because they were orphans," he whispers, so quiet I can barely hear him, "taken in when they were young by a train station manager. He let them stay in the station at night, fed them enough to keep them alive in exchange for work. The manager's wife kept an eye on Emilet until she was old enough to also work. They were basically homeless."

"Oh," I say. "Is that why he's called Train?"

"Train was five when the manager took them in. He wouldn't speak, wouldn't tell anyone his name, but he was fascinated with the trains, so that's what they called him. Train told them his younger sister was named Emilet."

"What happened to their parents?"

Nodin's fingers grip the steering wheel. I know I'm forcing him to talk about things he doesn't even like to think about. "Dr. Beckman thinks maybe their parents were too poor to feed them, not uncommon during the Depression. They probably thought their children had a better chance being rescued by people with more money, someone who would see them at the train station and take them in."

I shudder at the horror of having to abandon my children to save them. "Are they with you always?"

"Pretty much." He stares at the red light.

"Do you love them?" I ask. The light turns green, we accelerate.

"They're a part of me," he says, his voice hollow. Wooden.

I remember Nodin telling our parents Train and Emilet were related to us, although he couldn't or wouldn't articulate how. I want to ask him. I want to know how they died, and how they're related to us, but I feel like I shouldn't push him further. "Why do you think I saw them tonight?"

"I have a pretty good idea," he says.

"You do? Why?"

"I need to talk to you about something. I should've brought it up before, but I wasn't sure how. I'm sorry I have to dump this on you all at once." He pulls into the parking lot of the grocery store right behind his apartment complex and parks.

I brace myself. "Dump what on me? What's going on?"

Nodin hesitates and then it all comes out in single a burst. "Baron. I need to talk to you about him. The reason he's never come here before. It's because you two have deliberately been kept apart until now, beca—"

"What? Me and Baron?" I'm dumbstruck. "What the fu—"

"Just let me finish." He holds his palms out toward me. "Baron is an extremely powerful energy worker, arguably the *most* powerful. You're a rune with access to infinite energy. That's why you couldn't be around each other until you were older. Stronger. It would be like giving kids explosives to play with."

A mixture of anger and excitement boil in my belly. I've never had a name for what I am. "What did you call me?"

"What do you mean?" He shifts in his seat.

"You know exactly what I mean. You called me something. A ra—"

"A rune," he says. The glow of an overhead light illuminates his face, highlighting the sweat gleaming on his brow.

Hot tears blur my vision. "And what is the definition of a rune, Nodin?" *How long has he known?*

"Someone who channels energy. You're like a satellite dish. It comes to you, or you can summon it yourself. That's really all I know."

I think about my experiences with the tree and decide this is a disgustingly simplistic definition. "You're saying what happens with the tree, that's channeling? Like I'm getting energy from it?"

He looks me in the eyes. "No. Not from it. Through it. And not just any energy. All life energy."

"Life energy? What does that mean?"

"It means the energy that makes you, Devi, and me, Nodin. The spark that makes life in all living things."

"You mean…souls?" I grimace.

"No, not individual spirits. The energy that creates them. Like the spark that creates fire."

My brain scrambles to make sense of this. "What else do

you know? Why can I do that? What's it for?" I'm hungry, no, *starving*, to understand my ability.

He looks down at his hands. "I don't know anything else. I'm sorry."

"That's it? That's all you can tell me?" I'm gritting my teeth so hard, I fear I will chip one. "Who? Who kept Baron and I separate all these years? You? Who knows what I am and what I do?" I try to keep a lid on the emotions surging underneath. I can't overwhelm the *delicate empath*.

"Well…I…uh…I mean, that's…"

"Just answer the question," I say. "Who's calling the shots?"

"Train and Emilet." He sighs and looks down to his lap.

I put my head in my hands and try not to burst out in hysterical laughter. "Train and Emilet. That's just perfect. Your ghost buddies tell you things about me, which you decide to keep to yourself, making my whole life a cave of darkness and secrecy." Rage takes over and I dig my fingers into my scalp to keep from lunging at him.

All this time, all the isolation, the endless, pointless research and he could have told me. I could have met others like me. I could have a life. A purpose. I slam my fists on my knees. "Why do they care what I'm doing anyway? Tell them to mind their own goddam business. They're guides to you, not me."

His voice booms in our confined space, "Wrong."

I snap my head up, shocked by his anger. Nodin deals with a veritable sea of emotions, and he's an expert at keeping the waters calm.

"Train and Emilet aren't here for me." His pale skin flushes. "They never were. They're here for you. I was just following orders. This hasn't been pleasant for me, either. My whole life, I feel your anger, your sadness—do you know how easy it would've been to just tell you and end it?" He exhales slowly and lowers his voice. "They're with me so I can protect you. I was forbidden to tell you anything, do you understand? *Forbidden*."

I realize my mouth is open and snap it shut. I've been wallowing in my own shithole for so long, it never occurred to me Nodin might be in one. He's probably been pining for days, wondering how to tell me all this. No wonder he looked so stressed. But I'm not ready to pity him just yet. "Protect me from what? Why use you? Why couldn't they have been my guides?"

"Because then you would know what you are, and so would Mom and Dad, and friends, and therapists, and who knows who else." He looks me in the eye. "That would make you vulnerable. Do you realize how many times I covered for you? How many times Mom worried you were depressed, or Dad wondered why you never went out with friends? I fixed that. I made them feel like nothing was out of the ordinary. No one could know anything, including you, until you're old enough to have your knowledge hidden from seers."

I throw my hands in the air and utter a half guffaw, half exasperated sigh. "My *knowledge hidden*? What does that even mean?"

"When you're young, your mind can't be blocked. It's sporadic, unfocused and completely readable. When you're older, someone can block you."

"So I'm being blocked now?" I ask.

"Not yet."

"Who's going to block me? You?"

"I would, but I don't have the ability. Only psychics with highly trained mind-control can block."

"Who will do it then?"

He sighs and puts the Bronco back in drive. "Ben."

"Ben?" I practically shriek. "Does he know about any of this already? Does Baron?"

"Yes. And yes." He winces.

"Mother fuc—wait, do you know anything about the dream? Do you know what happened that night?"

"No," he says. "I swear I don't know anything about the dream. But I think we're all about to learn a lot more." He pulls into his apartment complex.

"Why do you say that?"

"Because Train and Emilet deliberately showed themselves to you today." He glances my way, his face hard, eyes so intense that I freeze. "And they orchestrated this meeting tonight."

Ice incases my spine. "Why now? What's going on?"

He circles the parking lot of his apartment for a spot. "Because it's time," he says at last.

"For what?" I whisper.

"I wish I knew." He parks the Bronco and looks at me. "You up for this?"

"Absofuckinglutely."

No way will I miss out on meeting Baron, not after spirits have spent two-thirds of my life keeping us apart. This is just getting interesting. And finally, *finally*, I might get some answers. I follow Nodin upstairs, shivering as the fall breeze blows against my cold, wet clothes.

4
The Arc

I'm barely breathing when I enter the apartment, but I only see Ben sitting on the couch.

"Hey, Benstein." I haven't seen him in about six months, when he was here to celebrate his seventeenth birthday.

He stands to greet me and seems taller. A Pearl Jam T-shirt hugs his fit physique, shaped by years of karate. Short, sandy blond hair frames his face. How do guys do that? Perfect hair and long eyelashes with zero effort? He even has gorgeous olive skin. I had a crush on him in eighth grade for about ten minutes, but it felt icky to crush on a guy who was like a brother.

"Hey, Devi-licious." He opens his arms for a hug, but stops short when he realizes what a wet mess I am. "What the hell happened to you?"

"Got caught in the rain." Until tonight, I didn't think Ben knew many details about what I do.

"Aw, poor Devi." Ben reaches a palm in the air, opting for a high-five, which I have to jump to meet because I'm five-foot-four. "Why don't you make sure she has a more dependable car?" he asks Nodin with a mischievous smirk.

Nodin rolls his eyes.

The two of them are always competing for Brother of the Year. Most of the time it's playful banter, but a few times Ben has come to my rescue in ways Nodin couldn't. Like the time Nodin told him about a guy who'd spread a rumor through our high school that I was screwing my way through the male student population. Ben came in town that weekend and the guy didn't return to school until the following Thursday, looking like he'd gone a few rounds with Tyson. Nodin had no part in it. He's not the physical type.

Ben denied it, but I'm not stupid. Although I appreciated

him wanting to stick up for me, I felt bad. The guy whose ass he kicked wasn't exactly lying.

Well, screwing my way through is a bit of an exaggeration. I did mess around with a few—many—and yes, I slept with two—okay, three—guys. I don't have the luxury of forming lasting relationships. Relationships mean intimacy, and intimacy means no secrets.

The biggest part of me is a secret, how can I ever be completely present in any kind of relationship if I can't be honest? Or during the calling, when I can't explain where I'm running off to in such a hurry, or why. The calling may rule my life, but that doesn't mean I don't crave the fireworks of a first kiss, the adrenaline rush of skin against skin, or the empowerment of feeling wanted—all thrilling enough to actually *feel* despite the eclipse of my ability.

"Where's Baron?" Nodin asks.

"He's out on the balcony on the phone," Ben says.

"Ah," Nodin says. "Devi, I put some clothes in my room for you. They're on the bed."

"Okay." I'm grateful I can change before meeting Baron.

A pair of sweatpants and a UTPB sweatshirt is on the bed. I peel off my wet jeans and light green Boho top—very disappointing since I picked this outfit special for this occasion—and change into the dry clothes. I hang my wet stuff in his bathroom, and take a look at myself in the mirror.

"Crap."

I do my best to towel dry and comb out my long hair. I can't blow dry it; Nodin doesn't own a hairdryer. I scrape smudged mascara from under my eyes in an attempt to look halfway decent. I survey the finished look: baggy oversized sweats, no makeup, and stringy, wet hair. My feet are cold so I slip back on my Mary Jane flats. Nodin makes fun of me for always wearing this same pair of shoes, but I love them. They're cute and look good with everything, with the added benefit of being damn good tree-climbers.

I walk out of Nodin's room and am instantly cognizant of a strange hum in the air. The pressure in the room pushes in on my ear drums like when I dive too deep in the pool. My eyes lock on those of the dark-haired stranger. The energy flows around us, out of control, like an electric current loose in the apartment. From somewhere a million miles away, I hear my brother introduce us.

"Devi, this is Baron. Baron, this is my sister."

"Nice to finally meet you," Baron says, reaching out to shake my hand. When our skin connects, the erratic energy begins coursing through us in a steady thrum. I can't let go.

Thoughts. I can hear what Ben, Nodin and Baron are thinking.

I'm aware of Nodin's panic and confusion. He's over-whelmed by the intensity of the energy. Ben's mind is a flurry of thoughts and images. I see myself through his eyes and he's shocked I'm sensing everyone psychically.

And I hear Baron, who's thinking a singular, clear thought: *It's her.*

Fear and anxiety grip me, although I can no longer dis-cern who it belongs to.

"Separate them!" Ben yells, and slams his arm down on top of our hands, forcing us apart.

The easy thrum becomes spastic again. I wince as it rever-berates through me and whips around the room. Something instinctual makes me back up to the fireplace. Baron follows suit, backing to the couch on the other side of the room.

At this distance the energy wanes. It's less painful, but the air pressure and hum are still present. I should be alarmed. Terrified. But I'm not. I'm exhilarated.

Nodin and Ben meet in a frenzy of hushed discussion. Nodin's eyes pull to his right, as if trying to see without turn-ing his head. He does this when he's communicating with Train and Emilet.

I glance at Baron, whose fiery gaze captures me, holding my eyes to his again. He's sitting on the couch, elbows on his knees, not quite shoulder length hair framing his just-enough-scruff face. He has on a black, long-sleeved T-shirt that clings to his toned arms and chest. Jeans hug long, muscular thighs. Damn, even his hands look strong, and then I remember he's a competitive rock climber, because my brother went to Canada once to see him climb in a big competition.

The urge to move near Baron is monstrous. I want to touch him again.

"Devi," Ben says, his tone full of warning.

I suck in air and dart my eyes to him. I need to be careful around Ben. His psychic senses are highly alert right now. He looks away as Nodin pulls him back into discussion.

Heat burns in my cheeks as I sit down on the hearth. My gaze lifts back to Baron.

His eyes soften. "You alright?"

"I'm fine."

"You have a ton of energy around you. I don't know how you carry it with you all the time. Your aura is…" His eyes seem to follow my energy around the room. "Huge."

"Is it?"

"You didn't know?"

I shrug and shake my head. "Evidently, I know very little about myself."

A low laugh rumbles in his chest. He runs his fingers along his scruffy jaw and looks back at me.

We gaze at each other in silence. It should be awkward, but it's not. We're too distracted by the sensations of the energy. I just stare, pulse pounding in my fingertips, painfully aware I look like hell wearing my brother's clothes. Nodin and Ben finally re-join us.

"Are you gonna explain what just happened? Why could I hear all your thoughts?" I ask Ben.

He inhales deep, like he's about to recite something he's had to say a thousand times. "It's called arcing. Your energy reacts to another strong field and spindles to a peak. When this happens it can umbrella out, or arc, and tap into the other sensitivities in the room. You connect to them and take on their abilities, read their thoughts, feel their feelings."

I'm fascinated. "I can get inside anyone's head if I arc?"

"No. You can't read Normals. Only SAIs," he says. SAI is an acronym for sensitive and intuitive, and is pronounced *sigh*. It's a nickname started at CISC.

"Wait a minute, she just arced?" Baron asks.

Ben nods. "Until now, I thought only alpha energists could arc. No one else has that kind of react-able energy in their aura. I've never witnessed it before today. You probably have," he says to Baron. "Isn't your teacher an alpha?"

Baron, who had been transfixed on me, jerks his eyes away. "Yeah, yeah, he is. But I've never seen Hahn arc."

"What the hell's an alpha energist?" I ask. "And who's Hahn?"

"Baron's healing teacher," Nodin says. "An alpha carries more aura than the average energy worker, and they're so sensitive to energy they can see it."

"That sounds like Baron. What's the difference?"

"You want to take this, man?" Nodin nods at Baron.

"Sure." Baron looks at me. "The difference is the ability to manipulate the energy. I can see it and affect the balance, like energists do, but I can also hold it, grow it, change its properties and propel it."

I'm dizzy with excitement. Talking with other SAIs about our abilities is something I've never done in my life. "But I'm not an energist. Why am I able to arc?"

Baron looks above and around me again. "You have more aura than I've ever seen, way more than even Hahn, and it's reacting to the charge we're creating."

"Yeah, what is this?" I gesture in the air. "Why is it happening?"

"Ever seen a plasma globe?"

"You mean the sphere you touch and little lightning bolts reach for your hand?"

He nods. "That's us, basically. The energy around us becomes a charged field when we're near each other. You're the bolts of light that reach out for the hand on the surface of the globe. I'm the hand. It's the nature of our gifts. You carry the energy. I receive it."

It takes a second to inhale before I can speak. "But why? Is this common between runes and shapers?"

All eyes are on me, followed by awkward shifting.

"Devi, you don't know?" Ben asks at last, his brows crushed together.

"Know what?"

"You're not *a* rune." He hesitates before continuing, "You're *the* rune."

His words settle in my bones like a sickness. "There are no others?" I whisper through a vacuum of sorrow.

"You're the only one."

I look at Nodin, who keeps his mouth shut, but the shame in his eyes tells me he knew. For the second time that day, confusion and rage ignite under my skin. I feel myself start to quake as I stand to unleash my disapproval on him, but the room starts spinning and goes black.

I blink rapidly. Through a clearing haze, I see Ben hovering over me.

"She's awake. Seems all right." Ben is fanning his hand in front of my face.

The rapid movement irritates me. I smack his hand away.

"Yeah, she's definitely back to normal," Nodin says.

I remember what led to my black out and set my jaw. "Nodin, I swear, if one more thing is kept from me I'm gonna lose it." I sit up with a hand to my throbbing head, but it pales in comparison to how stupid I feel.

I resent needing all this explained to me, when I'm just as much a SAI as they are. I didn't have the luxury of therapists and other intuitives to teach me the SAI lexicon. I feel like a fucking foreign exchange student.

Ben sits beside me and hands me a glass of water, which I sip. I can see Baron pacing by the hallway leading to the second bedroom.

"I've never passed out in my life. What the hell is going on?" I rub my hands over my eyes.

"It's probably all the energy. It overwhelmed your system," Nodin says.

"It's probably all the bullshit," I say.

"Look. I know how badly you want to know others like you." He sits down with a sigh. "I just didn't want to upset you."

"Well, you're going about it backward." I glare at him. "It's simple. Tell me everything."

"Devi," he says, so low it's barely audible. "I'm finally able to tell you, but I don't have all the answers. I don't know how to do this without you hating me, but I had no choice in this. You *have* to understand that."

He looks so sincere, so pathetic with his sad eyes, yet resentment lingers. "Then complete disclosure from here on out. Starting now," I say, gentler. "What else is there? What does it mean that I'm the only one?"

Nodin nods at Ben. "You can block her?"

"Yep," he says.

"First I want to clear something up." Nodin looks me in the eye. "I know you've felt like the last person to know anything, but Baron didn't know a thing about you until the ride up here, and even then it was only what's relevant. And Ben, well, he's Ben, he knows what he knows, but I've never once had a conversation with him about you until a few weeks ago. Understand?"

I nod.

"We know you're the only one because there are no records of anything called a rune, or anything like you in the SAI community," Nodin says.

"Then how do you know that's what I am?"

"I've been told."

"By your guides?" My tone has a deliberate bite.

"Yes," he says, exhaling.

"Go on."

"Train and Emilet were positioned with me to protect you

from knowing what you are, and to guide you to the people you need." He pauses. "All I've ever known is to keep your ability a secret. Two weeks ago, they told me it was time for you to meet Baron. They said you're a rune and your ability has a purpose, but we have to figure it out."

"Figure it out? How do we do that?" His words are just sounds carried on wavelengths, yet they hold the meaning of my entire existence. "Why can't Train and Emilet tell me?"

"Because it was supposed to be passed down to you by our biological parents. They're the only ones who know. Train and Emilet were chosen to get us this far. They are children, so it was easy for them to establish a bond with me when I was young and too naïve to know it was strange to see spirits. Devi, we have to find our blood relatives to learn the purpose of your gift. Ben will block what you learn."

I turn to Ben. "You're doing this blocking thing mentally?"

He nods.

"How?"

He shrugs off my question. "Long story."

"Wait, who are we blocking? I still don't understand."

"Other SAIs, but I'm not entirely sure why," Nodin says. "Yet."

"This makes no sense." I push my palms against my eyes. "Why can't Ben just tell me what my purpose is? He's freakin' psychic."

"It doesn't work like that," Ben says, "I rely on information given to me by Spirit, but I don't have control over what I'm given. I can't look into a magic ball and see the future. That's all bullshit. As far as you're concerned, I'm not being told anything."

"Then how did you..." I gesture between his head and mine, wondering how he's so aware of what I'm thinking.

"I have telepathic tendencies," he says.

"What the frick does that mean?"

"It means sometimes I can detect what others are thinking, others who I have a connection with and who *are thinking something clearly*." His brows rise and he tilts his head toward me. Heat rushes up my neck and I look away.

"One more thing," Nodin says, bringing us back on subject. "Whatever the purpose of your gift, the ability for you to work with Baron is integral to its success."

My eyes shift to Baron who has seated himself back on the couch. The way he's looking at me sends a shiver through my body. I want to look away, but can't. Inexorably captivated, I stare back at him. It's not until Ben knocks his knee into mine that I snap out of it.

I turn my attention back to Nodin, who seems to be communicating with his guides. "What are they saying?" I ask.

"Well…the most important thing right now is for you two to begin working together."

"Working *how*?"

"You have to practice with the energy."

"What energy? This craziness?" I motion between Baron and me.

Nodin's eyes settle on mine. "No. The energy you channel."

I have a miniature heart attack. "How exactly is that going to work? I can't take him to my…" I hesitate. I've never spoken of the tree to anyone but Nodin.

He nods. "To start, he can work with the energy you carry. That'll do for now. But eventually we'll have to—"

"No, that's impossible. I can't—"

"What's the problem?" Baron asks.

"The energy you see around her is just hers, her aura," my brother says. "When she channels, she brings in life energy."

"You mean…?" Baron's brows furrow.

"I mean universal chi, prana, bio magnetism or whatever you prefer to call it." Nodin pauses. "All life energy."

Baron's jaw drops. Nodin's not lying; he doesn't know much about me. I bask in not being the last person to know something for a change. "What are your sources?" he says.

I shake my head. "Source, singular. A tree. And it's only accessible to me."

Baron shakes his head. "I don't understand. Then how can I work with the energy she channels?"

"We'll have to improvise until we figure it out," Nodin

says. "For now, you can take from her aura and practice working with it. Can you do that?"

Baron's eyes are scanning me, scanning the room. "Yeah, of course. She has enough for days."

"Working with it how?" I ask.

"Like I said," Baron says. "You channel the energy. I'll harvest it from you, manipulate it and transform it into a kinetic force."

"English, please."

He smiles. "I'll turn your life energy into something that has energy because of movement, like wind or waves."

"And blast it into the sky like a freakin' rocket," Nodin says. "Or so I hear."

"Wait, you've never seen him do it?" I say, surprised.

Nodin shakes his head. "We've talked about it on an educational basis at retreats and I hear stories through the SAI community, but I've never seen it."

"It's not something I whip out at parties," Baron says, and we all laugh.

"Was channeling ever taught?" I say.

"Channeling was discussed," my brother says, "but only as far as psychics are concerned, like channeling spirit energies or, in Baron's case, harnessing energy. As far as I know, a channeler like you is an unknown phenomenon. Channeler simply means conduit. No one is a conduit like you, Devi. No one."

"Then how do you know so much about what I do?" I say.

"I was informed."

"Ah. Of course. So your guides made you aware of what I do, but other than us four, no one knows what I am?" I choke back the devastation bubbling to the surface, the realization I may never fully understand my ability. I will never know others who do what I do.

"That about covers it," Nodin says. "Your aura is impressive enough that you're like a neon sign to seers, but you didn't know anything so you weren't a threat to yourself. Now that you know, Ben can block you."

"But what could someone want from me?" I turn to Ben. "What's the appeal?"

Ben shrugs. "Depends what my motives are. Probably depends on your ability's purpose. Maybe I want to be involved. Maybe I want to partner with you. Maybe I get enamored with your power, your status so to speak. Maybe I want to stop you. Who knows?"

"By the way, how did you know I arced?" I say.

"I didn't at first, until I got a look at your eyes. Psychics can detect each other a lot of the time. You were temporarily one of us. It's like your third eye was open."

"There's something else," Nodin says with some hesitation. "You and him…" He gestures to me and Baron. "You're to avoid being alone together."

Baron shoots me a look that makes me go all Jell-O inside. "What are they afraid of?" he asks Nodin.

"They say the energy is powerful and unpredictable. You should always have someone with you…in case something happens."

"Like a buddy system?" Baron says with an amused grin.

"Yes. Like a buddy system," Nodin says without smiling. "The reaction between you two can be extremely dangerous." He looks at me sternly. "Consider yourselves warned."

I'm not sure how I feel about two ghost kids telling me what I can and cannot do, but I let it slide because I don't plan on being alone with Baron anyway. He's great eye candy, but he's Nodin's friend and seems way older than me.

"Does anyone else need a beer?" Baron interrupts the long silence.

A unified yes rings through the room. Ben goes to the kitchen and brings back three beers for us and a soda for himself. He doesn't drink. I don't drink often either. But tonight I am.

"So we'll coordinate times to practice together," Nodin says. "and Devi and I will start research on our family." He holds up his beer. "Cheers?" A plan born. We lift our bottles for pseudo clinks.

"Let's order a pizza. Anybody else starving?" Nodin says.

"Yeah. Pepperoni and mushroom," Ben says.

Baron and I nod in agreement. Nodin goes to the kitchen to order the pizza, while Ben turns on a football game. I'm grateful for the distraction.

"Did you get ahold of your dad?" Ben asks Baron.

"Yeah, I did. Thanks."

I know they're referring to the phone call Baron took on the balcony earlier. I'm shocked at how relieved I am he hadn't been talking to a girlfriend.

Before long the doorbell rings and our pizza is delivered, but I have trouble eating. I'm a truffle of emotions: fear atop curiosity, atop anxiety, atop a smidge of hope, atop a layer of sadness. I try to keep my eyes averted from Baron, but it's not easy. Our reacting energy surrounds us like a womb of percussions. I can tell by his lack of appetite and clenched jaw he's overwhelmed, too. Despite the colossal urge to stay near him, I need to get away from here.

"I'm exhausted. Do you mind running me home?" I ask Nodin.

He's visibly surprised. "Sure, no problem. Lemme just finish this slice."

I go into his bedroom to get my wet clothes. When I come out Nodin is getting his keys from the mantle. "You ready?"

"Yeah."

Ben stands, and I go on tip-toes to hug him. He turns to Nodin. "We may have to cancel the concert tomorrow night so we can meet here and start working."

"Here? We can't do anything here," Baron says. "We need to be out in the open, in a field or something." He stands, arms crossed, towering over five-foot-eleven Ben.

Lord help me. "Why?" I ask.

"I need room when I pull energy. I have to change the frequency and compress it to get rid of it. During the day, ideally, so no one can see it. When the energy is dense, it's hot and bright."

"Then we'll find an area that'll work," Nodin says.

"Somewhere secluded. You'll need to scout out a location in Oklahoma, too. You can't always come to Odessa."

"How often are we getting together?" I ask.

"As often as we can. The more practice you two get the better."

I shame myself for being so happy about this. This energy reaction between us is painful, yes, but it's also like a pull, and I find myself drawn to him in a way I can't explain. It's strong and intriguing. "What about tomorrow morning?" I say.

"I don't think we'll have time. When's your climb?" Nodin asks Baron.

"Ten," Baron says. "I need to be there a little earlier than that, though."

"What climb?" I say.

"I have a competition tomorrow at the indoor gym," Baron says. "You're all invited."

Nodin and Ben exchange glances. I already know what's about to come out of Nodin's mouth. "Uh, I don't think…"

"You don't think I should go," I say a little more angrily than intended. "I get it. But I think we should set up a time to practice while he's here, don't you?"

Truth be told, I'm grateful to not be going to the climbing competition. I don't know if I could handle seeing him in fewer clothes. Glistening with sweat. Muscles rippling with effort.

"We'll definitely start this weekend," Ben chimes in while throwing me a glance of disapproval. "We're not leaving until Sunday after lunch. How about Sunday morning, early. Eight o'clock. Does that work for everyone?"

We all agree.

"I'll find a location between now and then," Nodin says.

"Happy belated birthday, by the way," Ben says, "Oh, wait, is that a grey hair?"

"Oh, shut up, ass." I punch him in the shoulder, hard.

"Happy birthday," Baron says.

My eyes catch his from across the room. "Thanks."

"She's just eighteen," Ben says.

I roll my eyes at his lack of subtlety and a blush warms my cheeks.

"Oh, wait, I have something for you." Ben reaches for his backpack hanging off a kitchen chair and retrieves a sketch-pad. He pulls out a page and hands it to me. "Here."

It's an intricate, beautiful charcoal drawing of a cherry blossom tree. "I love it. Thank you, Benstein. You're an ass-hole, but I love you." I stand on my toes and hug him again.

"It's important to love your asshole."

I laugh. "Something's fundamentally wrong with you."

"Can we go now?" Nodin asks, jingling his keys.

Baron steps around the coffee table. Just three steps closer and the energy reaction resurges, flooring me. I practically lean forward with the fierce desire to touch him and make the whipping vibrations settle into the thrum we felt earlier. Ben and Nodin's bodies tense as Baron nears me.

He stops only a few feet away and looks straight into my eyes. "It's great to meet you. I'll see you soon."

"It's good to meet you, too," I say, or maybe I just stand there with my mouth hanging open.

As Nodin turns toward the door, Baron nods at me almost imperceptibly, but I see it. He's trying to tell me something. I don't know what it is, but I have a funny feeling he intends to ignore the rule about being alone with each other.

5

REVELATIONS

In the Bronco few words are spoken. Embers of resentment still glow in my bones. I know it isn't Nodin's fault. I understand it's what his guides told him to do to protect me. *But they could do it again.*

No more. I can't—won't—let myself look like a fool again. And I know the means to my empowerment: arcing.

My rental house is only about six miles from Nodin's apartment. We've both positioned ourselves close to the college. As we near the street I live on, he finally speaks. "When's the truck out of the shop?"

"Hopefully tomorrow."

"Do you need a ride anywhere?"

"No, but if I don't get my truck back I'll need a ride to work at one."

Nodin grimaces. "I have no idea how long Baron's competition will take. I don't know if we'll be outta there in time."

"Maybe I should just go along then."

His jaw clenches.

"I'm just messin' with you. I can walk to work if I need to. It's a couple of miles. No big deal," I say.

"You understand the magnitude of this, right? I know how stubborn you can be. You can't pursue him on a personal level. It's too dangerous."

I jerk my head in his direction. "What on Earth makes you think I intend to pursue Baron?" I say.

"Are you kidding me right now? I saw the way you looked at him."

"Oh shut up. So he's nice to look at. That doesn't mean I'm some weak girl who fans herself in the presence of a man. I have no interest in Baron."

He glances at me. "Just because you two are allowed to

meet doesn't mean you can handle the energy yet. One of you could get hurt."

I'm being schooled and it's pissing me off. I squeeze my hands into fists. We pull up in front of my house.

"See you Sunday morning," I say, clipped and angry, and fling the car door open.

"Call me if you need a ride."

"Don't count on it." I slam the door and stomp to my porch. I know I'm acting a bit like a petulant brat, but I loathe being treated like a moron.

The house is pitch black. I'm the first one home. Not uncommon on a Friday night with two bartenders for roommates, so I grab water from the kitchen and go to my room. I get the gift from Joe out of my still-damp jacket pocket, then toss the rest of my wet clothes on my bathroom floor. I've lived here since the end of June—nearly five months.

My dad found it for me and, in a roundabout way, knew my roommates. The bar they work at is a campus staple, and my dad knows the owner, whose son, Jamie, is one of my roommates. He's a junior at UTPB. Finance major, which is ironic because he looks more like the lead singer of a Europunk band. He's a party animal, and hearing his sex-capades through the walls is awkward as hell, but he pays his rent and stays out of my business. I think our dads have an agreement because mine is always asking about Jamie and I have a feeling Mr. Wilkes is interrogating his son about me—both of us participants in a spy program so our parents can keep an eye on us. But we aren't that stupid.

My other roommate is a female also named Jamie. It could be confusing living together, but aside from them both preferring women, the similarities end. Serious student. Driven but sweet. Reminds me of Betty Boop because of her small stature and big eyes. To avoid confusion, I refer to the female as Jamie One and the male as Jamie Two. Why does *she* get to be number one? Because she keeps our house clean, which I appreciate more than anything.

I don't do clutter.

In my bedroom, I get a tack from my desk and hang my newest Ben drawing on the wall next to my window. This one makes fourteen. Each one is a tree. The first time he came to visit Nodin in Odessa, way before my parents sold the house, he gave me my first drawing. I had been shocked to see it was a tree. Of course, I was aware of his psychic abilities. I had to assume that's how he knew the significance, but I buried the notion he knew any details. It was too uncomfortable. Too *naked*. So I accepted his drawings over the years without a word about them.

I take a quick shower to get the tangles out, then put on sweatpants, and an old concert T-shirt that has been downgraded to pajamas because of a rip on the sleeve, compliments of my tree. Or rather, attempting to climb the fence to get to my tree before I knew Joe. I will wear this shirt until it falls apart. It was the first, and only, concert I'd ever been to. Dad took Nodin and me to see one of his favorites play, B.B. King. That's when I fell in love with the Blues. I had never really connected to music before then, but something about the soulful rhythm of the Blues speaks to me.

I put on my favorite Blues CD, John Lee Hooker. While brushing my teeth, I realize I have to do something else before going to bed. Inspiration tugs at me as it often happens on tree days. Words play in my head, repeating, elaborating. I grab a paper and pencil from my desk and scribble them down. Sometimes it is short stories, but most of the time I write poems. I've never shown them to anyone. They're just for me.

I finish the poem to my satisfaction and crawl into bed. As I reach to turn off the lamp on my nightstand I see the tree of life charm I set there. I'm not really a jewelry person, but the gift is so special to me, I'm going to make an exception.

About four years ago, Mom gave me a charm bracelet with a horse dangling from it for Christmas. Although I appreciated the thought that went into it, I never wore it. Horses are her thing, not mine.

I crawl out of bed and root through the small, wooden

jewelry box I've had since I was little. There are only four things in it, so I find the charm bracelet immediately. With my teeth, I pry open the ring holding the horse on and do the same to attach the tree of life charm. I jingle my wrist and smile, happy to have something that's uniquely mine.

Turning off the lamp first, I resume my spot in bed. I'm afraid I'll be up for hours, spinning off of the day's craziness, but soon the heaviness of my lids says otherwise. My muscles ache. Not just from the exertion at the tree, but from the energy with Baron, the tension with Nodin…all of it. Fatigue takes over and in a matter of minutes John Lee's "Boom Boom" lures me to the land of nod.

Shrill beeps pierce my brain. As the heavy fog of sleep lifts, I realize it's my cell phone. I jump out of bed and fumble in the dark for it. The caller ID reads *Unknown*. My first thought is a solicitor, but in the middle of the night? I answer.

"Hello?"

The voice on the other end lights me up like a candle. "Devi," Baron whispers.

Hearing my name come off his lips is like sugar.

"It's Baron."

"I know."

"I'm sorry to call you so late—I had to wait until the guys were asleep. I got your number from your brother's phone, I hope you don't mind. We need to talk. Alone."

Butterflies twirl through my stomach. "When?"

"Now."

"Now? What time is it?"

"Quarter to one. Ben's asleep. He won't know what we're up to if we're careful. I can leave right now."

"Okay. Okay, yeah. Come over."

I give him my address and we hang up. *Holy shit.* I brush my teeth again and change into jeans and a T-shirt. The

Jamies are thankfully not home yet. They close down the bar on weekends and don't get home until nearly three in the morning.

By the time I get myself together and to the front of the house, I can see headlights beaming through the blinds. I peek out and see a silver Jeep. The headlights go out. There's no movement. I start to grab my jacket to go out to him when the driver's door opens. He's halfway across the lawn when the hum surfaces, like an amp left on way too loud.

Baron's wearing a dark corduroy jacket over a different T-shirt, with a logo on the front that says *Climbers Rock*, and his hair is held back by a red headband. Nodin's warning rings in my head and I feel a little leery without the others around. As he gets closer, the energy begins thrashing violently between us.

"Stop," I say just before he walks up the three porch steps. The pressure on my ears hurts.

He backs away. At about ten feet apart we reach a comfortable level.

"It's so strong," I say, looking around at the fireworks I feel should be visible.

"I'm sorry to do this to you. Are you okay?" he asks.

"I'm fine, don't apologize."

"It's affecting you."

"What do you mean?"

"When I first see you, your aura is all creamy yellows, like sunshine. But after about a minute, like right now, your energy is agitated by our reaction. Now you're oranges and reds."

"That would explain why I feel…tense."

He nods. "Definitely."

We stare at each other for a minute before he breaks the silence.

"The reason I'm here is because I wanted to tell you something first." Baron takes a deep breath. "I have visions. I've gotten them most of my life. They start as a symbol I see in a dream every night. When I've figured out the meaning of the symbol, the vision stops. Eventually, another will start. I've re-corded and researched them, never understanding their purpose, never knowing what to do with the information."

He pauses, holding my gaze with his steady one. "Now I know they have to do with this. *With us.*"

It takes a few seconds before I pull my thoughts together and respond. "Do you have the symbols with you?"

"I always do." He unzips his jacket and slides it off his shoulders. The shirt he changed into is short-sleeved. He holds out his arms. They're covered in tattoos.

I gasp. "Those are all the symbols?"

"No, but I'm not going to get half-naked in your front yard." He gives me an irresistible crooked grin that makes my stomach drop.

I beckon him in the house, careful to stay a comfortable distance from him. He shuts the front door and sits on the end of the couch. I sit in a chair on the other side of the room.

"Tell me everything," I say just above a whisper. The energy between us is palpable. I grip the arms of my chair and stare at his tattoos, mesmerized.

"When I see a vision enough times to have a clear image of it, I tattoo it. The first time I did it was just instinct I guess. I'd been seeing this vision for years, since I was about seven. It was a bear. This one." Baron pulls up his right sleeve to reveal his shoulder. It's a bear, his mouth wide open and exposing teeth.

"At seventeen, I inked the bear on my shoulder because it had become such a part of me. Then the vision stopped. Pretty soon a new one began. After I saw it nightly for about a month, I inked it as well. And that vision stopped too." He turns his left forearm up and points to a smaller tattoo just inside his wrist. It is two red dots with a red line over them. "The Mayan symbol for the number seven. Now that I know how to stop the visions, I don't wait as long. As soon as I start seeing one enough to get a clear mental picture of it and an understanding of what it is, I ink it."

"What's the significance of the number seven?"

"I have no idea what its relevance to us is, but it's considered nature's perfect number. You see it in math, science, astronomy, religion, biology—"

"Wait a minute, how come Nodin doesn't know about this?"

"Because I never told him. I mean, he's heard about the visions before, years ago, and he knows I have tattoos, but he doesn't know the tattoos are symbols. It's not something I talk about. Since I began getting the tats, we've only seen each other a handful of times. The last thing we want to talk about when we hang out is anything SAI." His voice, his demeanor, are so calm and confident they lure me to him. He knows who he is, a quality I'd do anything for. I want to take it off him and wear it.

"Why the secrecy?"

He shrugs. "I guess I feel protective of them. They're sacred. I have them tattooed as a symbol – a ritual—to make them a part of me. It was never to advertise them."

I nod, understanding. "So what do you think the visions mean?"

"I wish I could tell you. We'll go through them and see what we can figure out."

"Earlier at Nodin's, when I arced, I heard you think something. I'm sorry if this seems invasive..."

"Go ahead."

"You thought, 'it's her.'"

He leans forward. "That's actually something I wanted to talk to you about. I had a vision a couple years ago." He closes his eyes. "It's a pitch black night except for the full moon. I see the silhouette of a girl with long hair standing in a field with her back to me. There isn't a sound, until a crowd of people I can't see chant something so quietly I have to strain to hear it. They chant it seven times." His eyes open and fix on mine. "You're the girl."

It feels like caterpillars are crawling under my skin. "What were the people chanting?"

To my surprise, he stands and pulls his shirt off. His body

is perfection. Long and lean. Beautiful olive skin stretched over toned muscles. His jeans hang off his hips, accentuating tight abs. A huge yellow sun tattoo sits in the middle of his torso with long, red rays stretching across his chest and down his navel. Words are etched under the length of his collar bone and more ink peeks out from under his arm along the side of his body. My eyes drink him in.

Someone who looks like him should be arrogant, but he's not. Confident, but not cocky. Intense, yet approachable. I'm out of my element. He's not predictable like the guys I've been with. He doesn't look at me like a conquest or as though he expects me to want him. He looks at me like a person.

"This is it," he says, pointing to the script under his collar bone. "It took forever for me to learn what it meant. It's not English. Hahn helped me translate. He knows a lot about ancient tribes from all around the world. We ended up figuring out it's a derivative of an Incan language from Peru. It means, 'She walks shining under the moon.'"

I peer at the script and can make out the first two words. The blood drains from my face. "What did they say in your vision?"

His green eyes lock with mine. "Dakahn manyan—"

"—mah pih tah nili hasi," I finish.

His eyes widen.

Without even thinking about the consequences, I leap up and run to him. As I get closer the air pressure eases and the pull mounts, then releases with a smash as our bodies meet. My hands go to his chest, touching the letters with disbelief, tears stinging my eyes.

"How did you know that?" he demands, squeezing my shoulders.

"This is me. This is my name." I can't even feel the floor under my feet. My fingers sweep over the letters to make sure they're real. "You couldn't have known. Has Nodin seen this?"

"No. I don't think he has." He pauses. "What do you mean it's your name?"

I wipe my damp eyes with the back of my hand. "I have

one memory from before we were adopted. It's stuck with me in a reoccurring dream. I'm in some sort of tribal ceremony with masked people and drummers. One man in particular is the speaker. He stands and says these words to me and everyone goes nuts, cheering and reaching to touch me. I know it's a title or name he's given me. My name."

He pulls me tight against him. "This is unbelievable."

I tremble and lay my head against him. The formerly throttling vibrations are now wrapped around us like a warm blanket. Since we've come in contact, I'm arcing with him. To say it's an odd sensation is an understatement.

Random thoughts intrude mine. Snapshots, sometimes seeing myself from his perspective. Knowing his feelings is the strangest part. It's like a suggestion from somewhere I can't pinpoint. His entire mind is vulnerable, blurring with my own reality, like two video reels meshing.

It dawns on me I'm pressed against his bare chest and I've only known him three hours. I'm not entirely comfortable, yet it doesn't feel as awkward as it should. I feel close to him, though I'm intimidated. Not just by the energy, but by him. I've only been with sloppy-handed boys. This is different. Baron is a man.

In my mind, I watch the vision he told me about. I'm standing under a full moon, breeze blowing my hair. *It's you. You're finally here,* he thinks. I sense his affection for me. I peer into the darkest recesses of his mind and know I can trust him.

The formerly impenetrable wall I've spent years building around myself begins to weaken. *Oh. Shit.*

"The energy, it's less painful." His voice vibrates against my cheek. "Do you notice that?"

"I do," I say. "It's going through us now, rather than at us."

"You okay now?" he says. His hands fall from my shoulders to my hips.

My stomach clenches at his touch. "Yeah, I'm fine." I start to go back to the chair when he takes my hand and pulls me with him to the couch.

I'm still processing the magnitude of what we just discovered, my mind whirling like the spin cycle of a wash machine. Baron releases my hand to retrieve his shirt and put it back on, and when he does the energy thrashes again. We relax against the cushions, my hand folded back in his, when something dawns on me.

"Hey, you said the language is Incan?"

"That's right." His free hand subconsciously touches the tattoo, now concealed again by his shirt.

"Nodin and I always assumed it was Afrikaans or some other African language—no wonder we couldn't get anywhere with it. What else do you know about the people who speak it?"

"Unfortunately, I don't remember a lot. It's been a few years." He looks thoughtful, searching his memory. "I know they lived in the mountains of Peru a long time ago. They were called the Tabari, which, if I remember correctly, means White Spirit or something close to that. The rest I have in my notes back home."

He's talking tribes, but that's not what he's thinking. *She's beautiful,* I hear him say inside my head. Heat burns in my face and I can hardly think straight. I feel a little bad trespassing in his mind without his knowledge, but not bad enough to stop.

"I'll see what I can research about them on my own until then," I say.

"You can research all you want, but you won't find anything online or in books, trust me."

"Why not?"

"Because that's what I tried first. The reason Hahn is able to help me is because of his connections, because of who he is. He's not just my teacher, he's a spiritual guide and a scholar of ancient holistic practices. He's travelled his whole life researching tribes. Campuses book him for conferences all the time; in fact, he knows your dad."

"Seriously?"

"Well, sort of. Hahn spoke at your school two years ago.

Your dad was on the panel. I remember him telling me he had met Nodin's father."

I recall a photo in my dad's office, of himself shaking hands with a short Asian man with glasses, both smiling giant, goofy grins. Before I ask Baron what Hahn looks like, he pictures him and I see it. Same guy.

"The majority of info we got on the Tabari people came from a trip Hahn took to Panama where he visited a colleague who's been studying them." He's rubbing his thumb over my hand. My heart is trying to break out of my ribs like a caged animal. It's unnerving not being the one in control.

"Are you all right?" he says.

"I'm fine."

He gives a little half-smile that kills me. I notice a necklace he's wearing, a milky green stone hanging from a red thread. I reach for it, purposely losing contact with him to roll it around in my fingers. The stone feels cool and heavy. I look at him, prompting explanation.

"That's peridot. Hahn gave it to me. It's supposed to help the wearer balance energies."

"Does it work?"

"I think so, yeah."

I let the stone plop back against his shirt and point to another tattoo just above the red symbol for seven on his left forearm. "What's this story behind this one?"

"It's a Tabono—sometimes called The Paddles. It's African." His eyes don't leave mine. "It represents strength and perseverance."

I see another one on the inside of his right arm, just above his elbow. "That one? Is that a white bear paw?"

"No, it's a Native American symbol for buffalo. In my vision, I see a white calf being born. When I researched it, I found that the birth of a white buffalo is considered sacred and prophetic to the Lakota Indians, symbolizing renewal and hope." He pulls up his shirt, revealing the huge sun I saw on his torso earlier. "I got it done with this one. The Seven Rays sun was in the vision too. I initially just did the white calf hoof, but when the vision didn't stop I looked harder. Next time I had the dream, I realized the whole vision played out under an immense sun with seven red rays."

He lets his shirt drop back down and takes my hand in his again. *Her eyes are the prettiest blue I've ever seen,* he thinks.

It feels like my veins are pumping molasses and I can hardly look at him.

"What about the one on this shoulder?" I indicate a circular one peeking out from his sleeve.

More of his feelings infiltrate my mind. He's also conflicted by the logic that we just met, combined with the intense bond and physical attraction. I swallow hard. He's talking again, but I can't concentrate on his words, enjoying watching his mouth move, until I realize he's no longer speaking.

"Are you okay? Did I lose you?" he asks.

I pull my hand from his, cheeks burning. Although deliciously torturous, I can't bring myself to touch him anymore. "No, no, I'm sorry. I've just…today's been a lot to process." The tension in the air is so thick it's like another person in the room. I fumble with my charm bracelet, thinking of something to say. Finally, "Can I ask you a question?"

"Of course."

"Why didn't you tell me this at Nodin's apartment? With the others?"

"It felt too personal. In a sense, you've been with me for years. And there you were tonight, in the flesh. It felt like I should tell you first."

My protective wall splits in two. Large chunks fall away, leaving giant gaps in the facade.

I hear a tiny beep sound twice, indicating two in the morning. Baron looks at his watch and sighs. "I guess I better go. I do have a competition in the morning." He stands to leave.

I'm both devastated and relieved as he gets his jacket and we walk to the door. "I'll tell the guys about the symbols tomorrow," he says, putting his jacket on as we walk across the lawn.

At his Jeep, he turns to me. A cold breeze brushes past me

and I shiver. He opens his arms and I don't consider hesitating. I wilt against him, warming, the energy thrumming.

His thoughts come trickling in, crumbling the last of my wall into a giant heap of dust. *I don't want to go. I don't want to leave her.* The intimacy between us is completely illogical, but I give zero fucks. These feelings are new to me and thrilling, and I wouldn't dare get off this ride.

He nuzzles his face in my hair. We stay like this for several minutes and I notice something feels weird. My muscles twitch with mounting tension and I don't understand why.

"Something's wrong," I whisper, my hands balled into fists. "I feel…" I struggle to articulate it. "Hot and angry." I step back and look at my hands. They're shaking.

Baron looks around me. "I know. I see it. Your aura looks like a thunderstorm brewing."

I wince. "That's creepy. Why is it happening?"

"I have a hunch. Let's try something. Stand back a minute. No touching."

I do as he says. The energy gets erratic again, whirling around us like fireflies on cocaine and the pressure on my ears returns. I wait while he watches me, or around me, really. After a few minutes, he asks how I feel.

I exhale slowly. "Better, yeah." I look down at my now steady hands. "But the energy between us is strong again."

He nods. "I think I know what's going on." He pauses as if gathering his thoughts. "When we are touching, at first, you're shades of yellow again because you're doing what you're made to do, you're channeling. That's why it feels so much better. Initially. After a few minutes, your energy is getting blocked, and evidently pretty pissed about it." He looks around me.

"Why is it blocked?"

"Because I can only receive so much. There's an interruption. Your body is trying hard to channel into an infinite space, but instead it's flowing into a finite space: me." He leans against his Jeep. "How does it feel when you're with your tree?"

I take a deep breath. "Transcendent."

"Exactly, because you're channeling the energy some-where—most likely back into the atmosphere—and you retain some, which is why your aura is freaking enormous."

"So what does this mean?" I ask.

"Well, it means when we're around each other, the energy will be chaotic and uncomfortable. And when we touch, it'll feel great, but that'll only last until the interruption of energy becomes a problem."

"Can you do anything about it? You can alter energy, can't you?"

Baron considers this for a minute. "I could try. I might be able to take some from you, calm it and return it. It wouldn't work for long, but it could settle things down. Like putting a cup of cold water in a boiling pot. It'll cool at first, but eventually it'll be up to boiling again."

"How do I look now?"

He takes my hands, and the pulses course through us like a river. "Yellow," he says with a little grin.

"So it took at least five, six minutes for my energy to calm back to yellows, yes?"

"Seems about right."

"How long would it take for you to do it?" I ask.

He shrugs. "You're getting orange again, so let's see. Relax. Take slow, easy breaths."

"We're doing it now?"

"Shhhh." His eyes close and his face is serious. His hands hold mine.

I stay steady and calm like he asked, waiting. A warm whoosh of air rushes through me toward him, pushing me up onto my toes. I'm left with a strange feeling, like I'm standing inside an enormous cavern and if I yelled, it would echo. I watch him. The moonlight licks over his face and angled jaw. He looks sexy when he's serious. Cold air blasts through me, from front to back, and I feel like myself again.

Baron opens his eyes and gazes first around me, then at me. "There. You look normal. For you. How do you feel?"

"Good, I think. Yeah. I feel relaxed." Actually, I feel like

I've taken a muscle relaxer. Drowsiness forces my mouth into a yawn.

He grins a little. "You won't be for long if we stay like this." He lets go of my hands. "Today's been overwhelming. We're both exhausted. I'll see you tomorrow, okay?"

"Okay, but I don't think I'm going to see you until Sunday morning. I think you guys are going to some concert tomorrow night."

"We'll see." A little smile curves his lips.

"Good luck at your competition."

"Thanks." He pulls his necklace over his head. "Take this. You need it more than me."

"No, I'm not taking your stone."

"Hahn can give me another. Trust me, take it." He puts it over my head. The peridot plops against my chest, solid and cool. He tugs me close and holds his soft, warm lips to my forehead. I lean in, craving more, but with an abrupt turn he releases me and gets in his Jeep.

It takes a second to recover from the energy lashing at our hasty separation. I gather my wits and walk inside. Baron waits until I get in to pull away. I slump on the couch and hold the stone, rubbing the flat side with my thumb, grateful to have a part of him with me. The events of the evening swirl through my head.

I hear a car door slam, peek outside and see Jamie One and her girlfriend. I'm not in the mood for small talk, so I bolt to my room before they get to the door.

I toss for a while in bed before I'm able to fall asleep— hours where I can't stop thinking about my name on Baron's chest and the symbols, but more than that, how bad I want to kiss him.

6
BONDED

I awake with a start, gasping, crying out for Nami. As the dream fades, I remember Baron told me my name is Peruvian. I wonder if the brown skinned woman with braids could be Peruvian. I look at my alarm clock and realize I have half an hour to get to work, and bolt out of bed.

"Women's lit is on aisle four," I say to the girl at the counter two hours later. She thanks me and walks away.

I'm curious how Baron's climb went, but haven't heard from anyone. I turn my attention to my computer, wanting to make use of my time and see if there are any books at my disposal for research. I know Baron said I wouldn't find anything in books, but it beats just sitting here.

I search ancient Incan tribes and it sends me to several books under archaeology and anthropology. I jot down their titles and, seeing the store is relatively empty, head over to the anthropology section.

I scan the shelves and find one of the books. Flipping to the index I locate the Ts. I find nothing resembling Tabari.

I locate the other two on my list in the archaeology section and take them back to the front counter. One is a large, thick textbook. The other, a smaller paperback with lots of photos. I choose the smaller one first because the entire book is dedicated solely to Incan tribes. I flip to the back and search through the Ts, Baron's stone dangling from my neck as I slump over the pages. There is nothing. I sigh, frustrated.

My cell phone rings. It's Nodin.

"Hey, Devi."

"Hey, what's up?"

"Not much, do you have your truck back?"

"Yeah, I pick it up after work."

"You need a ride?"

"No, it's not that far. I can walk."

"Seriously, when are you going to get more reliable transportation?"

I huff. "Shut up about my truck."

"All right, whatever. What time do you get off?" he asks.

"Five-thirty."

"Good. After you pick up your heap, you need to head over here. Baron called a meeting, says it's important."

"Okay. You don't know what it's about?"

"Nope. He wants to wait for you."

"Oh, okay. By the way, how did his competition go?"

"Awesome. He won two of his three climbs."

"Cool." I'm jealous Nodin and Ben got to attend. It feels like I should've been there, too. "I guess I'll see you a bit later."

"See you then."

Baron managed a way for us to be together after all. I smile and bite my lip.

My coworker arrives to take over until closing. I speed walk to the auto shop, my mind abuzz with anticipation. I pay for the repairs and push my faded red beater of a truck to its limit, racing to Nodin's place, where I park and check my hair and makeup quick in the visor mirror.

When I enter the apartment, the air pressure and pull hit me like a shockwave. Ben is at Nodin's laptop at the kitchen table to the right, and Baron is looking over his shoulder. I see him grip the back of the chair as I walk in.

"Hi," I say, setting my things down by the door. I walk past Baron, suppressing the urge to reach out and touch him, and take a seat in the family room chair. I grab the peridot stone and stroke it with my thumb, hoping it'll calm the energy. It doesn't.

The guys look my way and return my hello. Baron gives me a half-smile, winks, and taps his chest.

He's wearing grey sweat shorts and a faded orange T-shirt. He taps again, and I realize he's indicating the necklace. If the guys see it they'll know we've been together. I quickly tuck it into my shirt.

"So what's this about?" Nodin asks.

"Last night, after you guys crashed, I called Devi." He flashes me a quick, private wink and I know to go along with what he says.

Nodin and Ben glance at me, confused, and back at Baron. He continues with his story about the visions and subsequent tattoos, why he felt the need to talk to me about it first, and ends with matzo ball: my name on his chest. Baron pulls down the neck of his shirt to show them.

Nodin's mouth drops, his eyes huge and rushing from mine to Baron's and back to mine again, fumbling for words. "Whoa," Ben says, awe etched on his face.

"I know. I know," I say. "But the most intriguing part is the language is in Incan, Nodin. Not African."

He shakes his head. "No wonder we couldn't figure it out."

Baron taps a green notebook on the coffee table. "We need to catalogue each symbol. Watch for connections. But first, I need to tell you about a conversation I had with Hahn today."

"You didn't give him any details, did you?" Nodin asks.

"Of course not. I only said what was necessary."

I notice the energy isn't as distracting as when I first arrived. After the first few minutes, I'm able to zone out of it. It's not pleasant, but it becomes background noise, only changing in intensity if our distance from one another alters.

Baron pulls a chair from the kitchen table and sits. "I told Hahn I'd been talking to your dad. He knows I have interest in the tribe because of the tattoo, so I said I asked your dad about them, which is believable since they know each other. I said your dad heard some stuff and I pretended to corroborate the facts with Hahn."

"Perfect. So what did he tell you?" Nodin asks.

"He told me they were originally a large tribe from the mountains of Peru tens of thousands of years ago, but harsh weather conditions forced them north. Over another couple centuries, the tribe suffered and their population decreased. Around the sixteen hundreds, small groups managed to stay together and one in particular eventually migrated into Central America. They ended up in present day Honduras, where they still are today.

"Their name, which means White Spirit People, originated because they were known for a genetic hiccup in their tribe: each generation, an albino child was born and thought to have mystical powers. He was their shaman, their guide, their preacher, their...everything. The tribe would raise the child like a king, readying him to take the place of the one before him. When the child was fourteen years old, he would take the helm."

"Wild," Ben says.

"It gets wilder. Hahn said one of his archaeologist friends has been working with a team in the mountains of Peru for a few years, and they've uncovered new evidence. Because of the artifacts found, they're pretty sure this is the original Tabari land, before they split and moved north."

"So? What's the big deal with that?" I ask.

"They discovered carvings of human figures on pottery, cave walls and tablets in the area. The figures have stars and moons over their heads and squiggly lines thought to be snakes—both symbols of mystics. Star maps and calendars were uncovered too. The maps point to astronomical locations, and when coordinated with certain dates also point to large formations. *Famous formations.*" He eyes Nodin. "Ones that take on recognizable shapes when seen from high above."

Nodin's eyes are huge. "Wait a minute, are you saying what I think you're saying?"

Baron nods. "They think the Tabari were originally a clan of the Nazca and may be partly responsible for the Nazca lines."

"That's unreal," Nodin says.

"Do they have any idea why they made them?" Ben asks.

"At this point, it's believed the Nazca lines are maps."

"Maps for what?" Nodin says.

Baron shrugs. "For water. The Nazca clans left because of severe drought."

"Could someone refresh my memory as to what the Nazca lines are?" I say. I know the name. I've heard my dad use it a hundred times, but can't remember what it is.

"Remember in Dad's office, on the right wall by the light switch, the aerial photo of lines that look like a giant bird-like figure?" asks Nodin. "And next to it the one of the giant spiral?"

I nod. "Okay, yeah, I've seen those. That's in Peru?"

"Yes, and hundreds are in the sand making animal figures and other shapes, all in this one location. It wasn't discovered until planes flew over the area in the mid twentieth century. Scientists have figured out they were made around five hundred to eight hundred AD, and they never really knew how they were made with such accuracy. It's one of those archaeological mysteries."

"Why didn't the lines get covered up over time? How deep are they?" I ask.

"Not deep at all, but you have to realize, it's a dry desert with hardly any wind. They dug down past the red, iodine rich sand to the white sand, which is why the lines are so visible," Nodin says. He turns to Baron. "You said some of the tribe still exists in Central America?"

"Here's the deal. Tabari are still in Honduras. Not a lot, but they are there. Hahn's colleague tracked them down several years ago, but was met with hostility. The Tabari are unwilling to speak to anyone. What's known about them and their history was learned from other tribes."

"Do they still have an albino leader?" I ask.

"That's what I asked, too. Hahn said no one knows. If an albino is living among them, they are hiding him. However, they've been linked to another tribe called the Maz, an *entirely* albino people."

"The whole tribe?" Ben says.

"Aside from a few exceptions, all of them. The Maz have a long Mayan history in Mexico and Guatemala. They go back as early as two thousand AD. Local Hondurans claim the Maz have been meeting with the Tabari for a couple hundred years. Speculation among the archeological community is they're meeting in hopes of having albinos in the tribe again."

"So they breed with the Maz, hoping for an albino?" Nodin muses.

"Exactly."

"Did it work?"

"Another unknown. They're reclusive and private. No one is let inside their community. Only a few venture out for food and goods."

"Wait a minute... Wouldn't this produce a new breed? A half-Maz, half-Tabari?" I say.

"Depends."

"On what?"

"On if they were successful producing any children."

"Let me guess, no one knows."

"Correct," Baron agrees.

"And they speak the language my name is in?"

"Hahn says Amair is their native tongue. It's only spoken by a small sect now and the thousand or so Tabari left."

"A thousand?" Nodin and I say in unison.

Baron nods.

The room is silent. A connection is glaring at me like a neon sign. I look at Nodin.

"You thinking what I'm thinking?" I ask.

He shakes his head, but I think he has an idea what I'm about to say.

"Nodin, my name is in Amair. And you're—"

"I'm *not* albino," he says.

"You're right. You're not, technically, but hear me out," I say, choosing my words carefully. "It doesn't make any more sense for the brown-skinned woman from my dream to be with an indigenous African tribe than it does for us. She could be Peruvian. What if we're the result of these tribes mixing? What if we're both half-albino, but you inherited more of the albino gene than I did?"

He holds a hand up to quiet me and stands, pacing. "It

makes sense on some level, I guess. But if we're somehow originally from Central America, how did we end up in Africa?"

"That's the million dollar qu—" I stop and turn to Baron. "Hey, maybe that word or name or whatever it is I say in my dream, Nami. Maybe it's an Amair word. Do you think you could find out?"

"I could try, yeah."

"Don't do it if it means telling Hahn too much," Nodin says.

"I won't."

"Anything else?" Nodin asks.

"That's it about the Tabari." Baron taps the notebook. "Let's get back to the symbols and see if we can learn anything from them."

My stomach growls loud enough for everyone to hear. "Sorry," I say, a little embarrassed. "I haven't had dinner."

"Oh, I forgot. We had Chinese earlier. Leftovers are in the fridge. Help yourself if you want," Nodin says.

"That's perfect, thanks." I go in the kitchen and begin rummaging through the fridge until I find chicken with broccoli. I scoop some out on a plate and have just put it in the microwave when I hear commotion from the family room.

Nodin has spilled his soda and somehow managed to get it all over Baron's shirt. The guys are laughing and teasing Nodin about his lack of grace. Nodin tells them to fuck off, and comes in the kitchen for a paper towel.

I'm filling a glass with fridge water when I hear Ben asking about Baron's new tattoo. I turn my head so I can see them. Baron has taken his wet shirt off. I'm so distracted, I overfill my glass and water goes all over the floor. I grab a dish towel and wipe it up.

"Holy shit, that's a huge back tat, dude," I hear Ben say.

"Yeah, I got the third part last week," Baron says. "It took forever. There's so much detail."

I fold the dishtowel over the sink. Baron is facing me while Ben inspects his back.

"Turn around," Nodin says as he returns to wipe up the soda. I lift the water glass to my lips as Baron turns.

Glass shatters around my feet. Shock's Novocain runs through my veins. Nodin's eyes are wide with surprise as he looks from the glass at my feet to Baron.

What I see on Baron's back nearly brings me to my knees. I cannot speak. I cannot move. I cannot breathe.

Space and time suspend and a single fact is clear: Baron isn't just a cute friend of my brother's. He isn't merely someone with whom I have a connection. Baron Latrosse, right now, in the past, and long after we're gone, is part of me.

He spun around when I dropped the glass, but I need to see his back again. I have to know it's real. I will my legs to walk over to him, take Baron by the shoulders, energy spiking and reverberating without regard, and turn him back around. I gasp and reach out to touch it so it doesn't disappear.

Etched on the entirety of his back is an enormous tattoo of *my tree*. Each bend. Every branch. An exact replica.

Tears fill my eyes. I'm in a daze. I have that eerie feeling again, like I'm standing in a cave. My forehead tips against his back. I hear my name being called, again and again.

Someone grasps my shoulders and pulls me away.

Nodin turns my face to his. "Devi, are you okay?"

I stare past him, unable to focus.

He snaps his fingers next to my face. "Devi."

I blink a few times. "It's my tree," I whisper.

"I know." He's looking at me like I might break. I hear scraping noises. My eyes focus behind Nodin where Ben is cleaning up the glass.

Baron pleads for someone to tell him what's going on and Nodin explains his tattoo is *the tree* I source energy from. Baron runs his fingers through his hair.

I shrug off Nodin's grip and turn to Baron. "How? When?"

"I started seeing the tree about seven or eight months ago. I waited longer than usual to make it permanent because of all the detail. I wanted to get it right."

"Let me see it again."

He turns his back to me. "It's perfect," I say.

He turns again, facing me. I lift my gaze to his beautiful green eyes. He gives me a little half-smile. It's a smile I've known for a thousand years and for just a day. One that makes my heart pound and my body ache with desire. And I know that look in his eyes because I feel it in my own. The one you have when you care about something so much it hurts, and your soul is shattering into a million pieces because you've just been made so vulnerable you're now *scared to death*.

Awkward shuffles sound behind me as Ben enters from the kitchen. Nodin takes the notebook and taps it with his pen. "This. This is why we need to stay in constant contact. This is why we need to pay attention to detail. We're not in control here. Something else is orchestrating every move, every clue. We—"

"For what?" I ask. "What are we doing here?" My voice gets louder as the enormity sinks in. "Why are we being spoon-fed information? Who are we being protected from?" I look around at their faces. "Don't you all want to know what the hell's happening?"

I turn to Nodin and glare. "What do Train and Emilet have to say?"

He stares at me long and hard but doesn't answer.

"What? They have so much to say yesterday, but nothing today?"

Ben walks in from the kitchen. "Devi, lay off him."

I whip my head around. "He's my brother. I can say whatever the fuck I please."

"Jesus, you can be such a bitch sometimes," Ben says, glaring at me.

"What did you say to me?" *Bring it*, I think. I'm a mass of riled energy, anxiety and fear. A good argument would feel fantastic right now.

"Apologize, Ben," Nodin says.

Ben's eyes widen. "Why should I apologize to her? I was sticking up for you, dude."

"She's just scared. We all are." He plops on the couch. "She doesn't mean anything by it."

Ben stands still as a statue. "Sorry," he says at last.

"I'm sorry, too," I say, sitting before my legs give way. "I feel like I'm outta my mind."

I'm not mad at Ben, or any of them for that matter. In my peripheral vision, I see Baron leave and come back wearing a dry shirt. He and Ben sit on the couch.

Nodin holds up the notebook. "I think we should all have copies of this. We need to make notes of any connections we notice, no matter how small they seem. We have to stay in communication about any new information, visions. Even the tiniest thought should be shared with the whole team either by group email or a phone call, text, whatever."

We nod in agreement.

"Ready?" Nodin asks. "Let's start with the obvious." He lays the notebook on the table and flips to a blank page.

Baron tells us about the entire tree vision as Nodin writes. He's standing in tall grass near the tree. Nothing else is around and it's eerily still. Rushing water roars loudly, so close it trembles the ground beneath him, yet he can't see the source. He stares at the tree as if it has something he needs. He feels a sense of urgency. He's waiting for something. The vision abruptly ends here.

We continue this for the rest of Baron's tattoos. He removes his shirt so Nodin can draw them. I stare at his shoulders and mentally ingest each shredded muscle down to his waist. I swallow hard and decide it might be better for me to look elsewhere.

I glance at Ben and catch him looking right at me, disgusted.

I try to appear captivated by Nodin's drawing of the seven symbols down the side of Baron's torso. Top to bottom, they represent Earth, air, wood, unite, water, metal and fire. We note the word "unite" is the only one not an object of nature and it's in the middle of the other six earth symbols.

Nodin records the meaning and origin for the bear, the symbol for seven on the inside of his left wrist, the African Tabono just above it, the white buffalo hoof and the seven rays sun. The latter represents the giver of day and night. Across the top of his right forearm is a geometric design he explains is Celtic. It's a buck with large antlers, considered a messenger from the spirit world. On his left shoulder is a Buddhist symbol called a Tomoe, which looks like three comets inside a circle chasing their tails. This represents the ever turning, ever replenishing cycle of energy in the universe.

He pulls up one leg of his sweatpants to show us a large serpent striped with the colors of a rainbow, its head high on the front of his thigh. The body curves into an "S" and ends with the tail above his knee; Australia's rainbow serpent, a symbol of the importance of water in human existence. It can be the giver of life but also the destruction of it.

The tattoo exploration finishes with my name under Baron's collar bone and the tree on his back. Counting the seven earth symbols separately, he has seventeen tattoos.

We discuss the repeating theme of seven. It shows up in the Mayan symbol for seven, the seven rays of the sun, and the seven pictographs down his side. Baron also reminds us that during the vision where he sees me in the moonlight, my name is chanted seven times.

Nodin draws a large seven on the inside of the notebook's cover.

When we're done, I collapse against the back of my chair with a sigh. My ears hurt from hours of uncomfortable pressure and I can no longer tolerate the energy bashing. I have to touch Baron or leave. I have no choice but to do the latter or freak out Ben and Nodin.

Nodin's brows furrow as my fatigue drapes over him. "You should head home. It's already eleven. We have to be up early if we're going to meet at eight," he says.

"Where are we meeting?" I say.

"Oh, I forgot to tell you. We found a secluded area just outside of town yesterday after Baron's climb."

I look over at Baron. "Congratulations, by the way. I hear you stole the show."

He waves away my compliment. "They didn't make it easy. The talent there was sick."

"Come on, I'll walk you to your truck," Nodin says as he stands. As I follow him to the door and wave bye to the guys, my eyes linger on Baron's green ones.

He stands and takes two steps forward. "I need to talk to her for just a minute, alone," he says.

Nodin stiffens. "Why?"

Baron doesn't answer. He walks past Nodin, takes my hand and pulls me outside. I'm shocked but don't have time to react as he pulls me against his chest.

Our proximity causes the energy to warp and crash down around us, pulsating through our bones before settling into a more tolerant state. I wrap my arms around him tight.

His breath tickles my ear. "I'm so sorry. I would've shown you the tree last night if I'd known."

"I know." I lift my face to his and resist the urge to close the tiny sliver of space between our mouths.

We can't, he thinks, still wrestling with the shoulds and should-nots of this insane situation. He lifts his chin and kisses me on the forehead.

I nuzzle against his chest, intoxicated by his Baron smell: freshly laundered shirt and man. I want to eat him. Drink him. Inhale him. I want our cells to dissolve into each other. I want all of him.

Nodin announces he's coming out and I hear the doorknob creak. We tear ourselves apart before he opens the door.

Baron walks inside, brushing past my brother as Nodin glares at him. Although I arced with Baron, I couldn't read anything on Ben and Nodin through the door, but it doesn't take arcing to know how they feel. Their faces say it all.

Ben is worried and highly annoyed, and Nodin is furious.

"What are you so worked up about?" I say as we walk through the parking lot.

"I can't believe you'd go against me like this. Against strict orders," he says.

"What have I done? I'm not pursuing anything with him," I say.

"You forget I know your feelings. You're infatuated with him. And Ben *knows*. He can read you like a book—"

"Ben sees what I'm thinking, not doing," I interrupt, my cheeks burning. *Ben knows what I was thinking.* Jeezuz, it was probably like seeing me in a porno. "And you obviously don't know shit about what I'm feeling. He's nice to look at, is all. Do you blame me? Did you see his body?" I'm trying to do two things simultaneously: gross him out and play it down.

Nodin grimaces and he runs his fingers through his disheveled white hair, making it stick up all weird. He sort of looks like a mad scientist. "Devi, that's disgusting."

"It doesn't hurt anything for me to think about him."

"Yeah, but—"

"But nothing. Until I've done something that risks our safety, you have nothing to say to me."

"Why did he want to talk to you alone?" Nodin asks.

I think fast. "To give me this." I pull the peridot necklace out of my shirt and show him. "He's worried about me. It's supposed to help the wearer balance energy."

Nodin glances at it. "If you're lying…if you're doing anything behind my back, I'll find out." He turns and walks off in a huff and I stifle a laugh.

I don't care what Nodin thinks he knows. All I can concentrate on are Baron's thoughts, the ones that flooded my mind before we lost contact. Images that stole my breath. Him kissing me, touching me, ravaging me.

7

WORK BEGINS

I pace the living room from end to end, unable to stop thinking about what I sensed from Baron. All signs point to go, yet we're expected to ignore them.

One word: Torture.

More words: Insane. Impossible.

On one hand, I realize we shouldn't. We've been warned the energy is unpredictable and dangerous. One of us could end up hurt, physically or otherwise. And things would be weird between us, which would be even more of a distraction.

Fuck. This sucks.

What if I only want him because I can't have him?

No. I want him.

I exhaust myself with this thinking and decide to go to bed, but only toss and turn. After what feels like hours but isn't, my phone rings. It's him. My heart is no longer in my chest, but fluttering around the room like a deranged bird.

"Are you okay?" he asks.

"Yeah, but for the record, this sucks balls."

"I know."

Silence.

"Come over," I whisper.

"Don't. We can't."

I exhale, disappointed but not surprised. A few seconds of awkward silence hang before it dawns on me I know little about him. We've never really talked.

"Do you have any brothers or sisters?" I ask, snuggling against my pillow.

"Nope. I'm the oldest and the baby," he says with a chuckle.

I try to picture Baron as a little boy. It's an adorable image. "Are you pretty close with your parents?"

"Yeah, very. They're everything to me. My mom has been teaching middle school math since before I was born. My dad is a sports doctor. I've been working at his clinic for about five years, helping clients who prefer a holistic approach."

"Oh wow. Do you work with any professional athletes?"

"Sometimes, yeah. But mostly it's weekend warrior types who blow out a knee or pull a hip flexor. Lots of bad backs, too. I do restorative energy sessions and they heal faster than they would with physical therapy alone."

I'm impressed. "How do you know how to do all that?"

"Hahn taught me everything I know. My dad met him at a medical conference. Hahn was there speaking on a panel for Reiki healing. My parents already knew I had some sort of sensitivity to energy. I remember always telling them about people's auras, and once, Mom was in a minor fender bender that left her with a bruised left shoulder. I could feel the heat emanating from that area, so I put my palm against her skin and concentrated on moving the heat. When I lifted my hand, the bruise was gone." He laughs softly, reminiscing. "Luckily, they'd been exposed to energy healing and weren't too freaked out. Dad tracked down Hahn and he's been my mentor ever since."

"That's fascinating. I wish I had a talent like that," I say, then remember his other talent. "When did the rock climbing start?"

"I guess around fifth or sixth grade. For a while, I just rambled around on the rocks for fun, but soon I found the effort and focus it requires helps me balance energy more efficiently, so I started taking it serious. I climbed every rock face in Ardmore. In ninth grade, I joined my first competition and won. After about a dozen more wins, companies were lobbying to sponsor me and I had the opportunity to travel for competitions."

Someday I'm going to one of those competitions. "I bet that was so exciting."

"It was, actually. Really exciting." He pauses. "I got lucky. Not everyone snags a sponsor."

He's humble and I adore it. I ask something I've been dying to know. "How old are you?"

"Twenty-three," he says in a sleepy-husky voice.

I'm relieved. I was afraid he was more than twenty-five. Not that I would've been bothered. More like I was afraid *he'd* be bothered if the age gap was more than five years.

He asks about my tree, about channeling, which is quite possibly the most intimate of subjects for me. But it's him, so I step out from behind my protective wall, naked and vulnerable, and tell him about it.

"It wasn't unusual for me to spend entire afternoons climbing it, daring myself to go higher each day. I guess, looking back, I was being lured to it, but was too young to recognize it. I'd wake up and my first thought would be how high I was going to climb that day.

"I was five the first time I channeled. I went higher than ever before and found a little nook to sit. I was peering over the rooftops of our neighborhood and listening to the birds, when vibrations pinned me against the branches. It was like..." I struggle to articulate something I've never spoken of before. "Like the tree was breathing life into my lungs, into my being. My senses were in hyper drive. I could smell the garbage cans in the alley across the street, and the sun was so bright I had to cover my eyes." I'm so caught up in the moment, I realize I've sat up in bed and am wringing the front of my shirt in my fist.

"Then the vision came. I wasn't seeing it like a movie, I was in it: I'm bursting in our backdoor, laughing and squealing because Nodin is chasing me. I stop dead in my tracks. *Cookies.* I smell them. Nodin and I look at each other and grin, then run as fast as we can into the kitchen. Mom is there in her favorite apron, the one with owls on it, and she's smiling, holding out a baking sheet full of chocolate chip cookies. When the vision ended, so did the connection with the tree. But the next day? The entire scenario happened in real life, exactly the way I'd seen it." I held my breath waiting for Baron's response.

"That's intense. Did it scare you?" he asks.

"No," I reply after a few seconds of thought. "It didn't scare me. It entranced me. I had no idea what was actually happening; I only knew it felt like nothing else I'd ever experienced. A few years ago, I watched a show about sky diving. This lady was really nervous before her first ever jump, but afterward, the look on her face…it was a mixture of awe and wonder and exhilaration. She looked *alive* and you just knew she was hooked for life. *That's* how it felt."

"And you still get visions when you channel?"

"Always." I'm relieved. He seems interested and is being respectful. I don't feel judged, like I always feared I would if I ever told anyone. Of course, I never thought I'd be telling a shaper.

I tell him about the reoccurring dream of my naming ceremony, and how it has been revealing new details.

"Update me of any new changes in your dream," Baron urges. "I agree it's trying to tell you something. This could be the key to finding your biological family."

"Why do you think all this is happening?" I ask.

He pauses before answering. "Something important. Something much bigger than us."

I close my eyes. "It's all scary and unknown."

"It's okay. As long as we trust the journey, everything will be okay," he says.

"But how do you know that? How can you be so sure?"

"I believe we're being led by Divine energy."

"Do you believe in God?"

"I believe in a higher power, yes. But if you're asking if I'm Christian, Catholic, or Jewish, my answer is no. I don't believe in labels or sects. I don't believe in religion as an organization. I only know what I can see and touch. I believe in energy." Baron pauses. "I hope I didn't just offend you."

I think about what Joe said when I asked about his nativity scene, that day I realized I didn't have to believe the same thing as the masses. "No. On the contrary."

I yawn, which makes Baron yawn and we volley them back and forth.

"I guess we'd better get some sleep," he says.

We hang up, but sleep doesn't come easy. The last time I see the clock it reads five a.m. My alarm goes off at six-thirty, waking me from a fitful sleep of pounding drums, painted tribal people and fear.

"Nami," I whisper through haggard breath.

They arrive to pick me up in Nodin's Bronco promptly at seven.

Baron rides shotgun. I sit in the back next to Ben, who smiles stiffly, which I take to mean he's disappointed or grossed out or both, about last night.

Hell, if you don't like what's in my head, stay out.

I don't like when there's tension between us. I know it seems I don't care at all when I infuriate Nodin. He's my brother; we're chill. In fact, I sometimes take sincere pleasure in infuriating him, but Ben's different. He's not blood, yet he's family. I need things to be cool between us, but I won't dare admit that to him.

Baron and I at this distance is throttling. Our energy acts with relentless enthusiasm, like two Labrador puppies happy to see one another, bouncing and banging into each other in a mad rush. But it feels more aggressive.

I notice Nodin shifting uncomfortably, no doubt sensing our discomfort. "Are you guys okay? I feel...pain," he says.

"That's an astute observation," I say with an eye roll.

"We're getting used to it," Baron says with a quick glance back at me. "Honestly, if you'd stop being so paranoid about us being near each other, it'd be a lot easier."

"Easier *how*?" he asks.

"Because the energy isn't as reactive if we're touching," Baron says.

"Surrre," he says in a tone that is both sarcastic and droll. This makes Ben smirk, but it quickly fades under my glare.

"It's the truth," Baron says. "Feel it." He glances back at me and taps his shoulder.

I take his cue and place my hand there. The energy slows to a tolerable pulse and I melt into it.

I can actually see the tension roll off Nodin. "Okay," he says with a sigh. "I get it."

I somehow resist the urge to stick my tongue out at Ben. I'm arcing and take this opportunity to snoop around in Nodin and Ben's minds, making sure to keep my eyes averted from Ben so he doesn't bust me. They assume I only arced that first night. I don't want any of them knowing it still happens when we touch. I feel bad concealing this from Baron, but if he knows, Ben could find out. It's not worth the risk. This is the only way I can be sure nothing's being kept from me.

So far, they're clean.

Baron continuously checks my aura for color change. About ten minutes into the drive, right as I'm starting to feel irritated with the silence, he looks at me and says, "Take a break. I'll tell you when you're orange again."

"What the hell does that mean?" Ben says, and Baron explains our energy reaction and how it affects my aura.

"How do you know all this?" Nodin asks.

He shrugs. "It's what I do."

The guys have chosen a fielded area with enough tree coverage for us to go unnoticed, a good ten minute walk off the road. The air is cool and smells of pine. Mist still hangs around the base of the trees. Our shoes pad softly on the thick, green blanket of pine needles beneath.

I'm wearing a long sweater over black tights, but neglected to bring a jacket and the cool breeze it cutting right through the fabric. I clench my jaw to keep my teeth from chattering and put my arms inside my sleeves.

Something heavy and warm lands on my shoulders. I look back and see Ben is coatless, crossing his arms against the chill. "Thank you," I say. He nods and walks ahead of me.

I smile because I know we're good.

We arrive at the spot they had scoped out for us. Ben finds a log to sit and observe. The rest of us stay in the middle of the clearing, looking at each other, unsure how to begin.

Baron stretches his neck and arms. "Okay. Let's do this." He urges Nodin to back up about ten feet away and motions me to come closer, stopping me right in front of him. He finds my hands inside the long sleeves of Ben's coat and takes them in his.

I lift my gaze to his eyes, even greener against the tree landscape. I whisper, "Will this be like the other night?"

He grins. "Yes and no. Just close your eyes and trust me."

I did before he asked.

He squeezes my hands. Seconds later, a sensation roars through me so strong, it feels like my cells are compressed into flat discs. A raging warmth courses through me. I can feel it powering through my arms and out my fingertips into Baron's hands. Abruptly it stops and I gasp.

It was different than the other night, much more intense. I can't help but peek. Baron looks tense, straining to harness what he's taken from me. Mesmerized, I watch as he begins to manipulate it.

Eyes closed, his hands move in graceful circles as if he's holding an invisible ball. Muscles rippling with effort, he moves his top hand in slow circles over the empty space, almost caressing it. The area of the circle gets larger and larger, drawing it up and out. His jaw flexes, but his face remains calm. Stepping back with one leg in a reverse lunge, he pivots his hands, continuing to form the circle even larger. He shapes it, feeling its girth, expanding, and then palming its entirety again. He sweeps the ball to one side and holds it. Beads of sweat appear on his brow. He lunges back on the other leg, repeating the same movements.

The energy is more than half the size of me. He holds it in front of him and with one swift motion slices his hand through the invisible circle, scoops out a small portion and sends it to me with a quick snap of his wrist.

I don't expect this, so the wave nearly knocks me off my

feet. He has grown my energy and given my original amount back.

I stay put, not sure if he needs me anymore. Baron continues shaping the ball, working hard to contain it, running his hands around the orb as he walks a few steps back. His face grows tense as he presses on either side. The ball is getting smaller. He lets out a breath of air, slow and steady. Focusing. Compressing. He's covered in sweat. In fact, I seem to feel it emanating to me, eight or so feet away.

Baron forces it smaller, sweat dripping off his chin. I can feel droplets of the salty stuff running down my own back. I let Ben's coat fall to the ground at my feet.

He turns his back to me and raises the now melon-sized orb over his head. His soaked shirt clings to his toned back. He balances it in one hand, winds his arm back and throws it, falling forward with effort, sweat spewing from his hair like a crown of crystals. Seconds later, the top of a sixty-foot pine tree bends clear over before springing back up with violent force. The sun shines through where leaves and branches have broken off.

My hands cover my mouth in awe.

Baron's chest is heaving. He stands up and pulls his shirt off over his head, using it to wipe sweat from his face and body. "Are you okay?" he asks.

I nod, rendered speechless. Not merely from the display of power, but from the vision before me. His body, shining with sweat, muscles pumped, full veins roping under his skin. The tattoos are *beautiful*. He looks like art.

"So is that comparable to what you do with Hahn?" Nodin asks him.

Baron squints, contemplating his answer. "Sort of. I've thrown that much electromagnetic energy, but never that much bio-energy."

"What's the difference as far as shaping goes?"

"Bio-energy gets hotter. Much hotter. And it has the potential to have more inertia. It's more powerful. I didn't mean to hit the tree. I hate hitting trees," he says, peering up at the damage.

"Is that what you train with?" Ben asks.

"No. I don't usually work with it 'cause I can only get it from Hahn and it's not ideal for me to pull from him. He's not able to help me until I give energy back to him," he says.

"Why can't he help you before you give energy back?" Nodin asks.

"It nearly immobilizes him." He motions to me. "Ask her. It's like a puppet with their strings cut."

I blink, my attention caught. "I don't feel like that."

They all turn their heads in my direction.

"What do you mean? How do you feel?" Baron asks.

I shrug. "Fine, I think."

"You think you could move and talk?" Baron says.

I nod. "Definitely."

He stares at me, awe and disbelief etched on his face.

"Why do you think that is?" Nodin says.

Baron shakes his head. "Probably because she has so much to begin with. What I took had little effect on her."

"So what now? Can you do it again?" I say to Baron.

He flashes a devilish grin. "Don't worry about me. I could do this all day."

8

AFTERNOON DELIGHT

We exchange energy two more times. Baron has me prove I can move in the limbo state, as he calls it, and I do. His eyes are closed, but Nodin is my witness.

After Baron takes my energy, I move my arms in a slow wave and march in place. It does feel strange, like I'm moving through spider webs, but I have no problem.

By noon we're too exhausted and hungry to continue. Nodin digs out an extra shirt for Baron from a workout bag in the back of the Bronco, although I couldn't begin to say why scrawny Nodin has a workout bag.

It fits, but is delightfully snug on him.

We head back to town. I know this means Baron and Ben are leaving soon. My stomach lurches at the thought of being away from him for two weeks. Forty minutes later, we arrive at my house. I hug Ben, give him back his jacket and tell him to have a safe trip.

"See you soon," I say to Baron, unable to look at him. I open my door to get out when a hand grabs my arm. I don't need to look back to know it is Baron reaching over the seat.

"Call me if you get any new information," he says, but *I don't want to leave you* is what he thinks.

It's after two o'clock and the Jamies are eating and watching TV in our family room of hand-me-down furniture. The room is a mess of pizza boxes and beer bottles. If I weren't so distracted I'd lose my shit about it. Jamie One's girlfriend, Chloe, is curled up in the chair covered with a thick brown throw, her long red hair twisted into an impossibly high bun. Everyone says hello when I walk in.

"Where were you?" Jamie Two asks, his tongue ring

clicking against his teeth. He's shirtless, which grosses me out because his nipples are pierced and it hurts to look at them.

"I had breakfast with Nodin and some friends," I say.

"You want some donuts? We have tons," Jamie One offers.

Donuts in the afternoon? Then I realize they've just woken up and this is their morning. She's in Hello Kitty pajama bottoms and a black tank top, and I wonder how her eyeliner is still so perfect in the morning.

"No thanks. I'm stuffed."

Chloe announces she's going to take a shower and relinquishes the chair to me. I sit in a numb daze watching some obnoxious show where cruel pranks are played on people, which Jamie Two thinks is hysterical and makes Jamie One roll her eyes, but all I can think about is Baron leaving and I want to puke.

My cell phone rings. It's him.

"I told Ben I'm putting gas in the Jeep and checking the tire pressure. I have to see you again before we leave. I'll be right there," he promises.

I head for the door.

"Where are you going?" Jamie Two asks.

"Meeting a friend," I say, and then sit on the steps waiting. Ten minutes later when his Jeep rounds the corner, my stomach flips. I get in the passenger seat and his Baron scent fills my senses. I savor it.

"Hey," he says, with a little smile. He's wearing a black beanie hat and looks delicious.

"Hi. Where are we going?"

"I don't have long. Is there a park or something nearby?"

I tell him of one close by, and in moments he's whipping into the parking lot and turns off the ignition. He leans toward me and laces his fingers through mine. I sink into our energy like a warm bath. Although he seems to struggle to find words, I can hear and feel them so he doesn't need to say a thing. His sentiment runs through me, echoing mine.

"I just wanted a chance to…"

"I know." I look up at him, his eyes reach into my soul, and I want to kiss him.

He's thinking the same thing. He's going to do it. "Let's go for a walk," he says instead.

The temperature is perfect now, cool but not cold, and we walk hand-in-hand along a sidewalk adjacent to the park where a few kids are playing. He tells me Nodin plans for us to travel to Oklahoma as soon as next weekend and I suppress a squeal—even though it'll be my first time to leave Odessa, to leave the tree, and that terrifies me.

It dawns on me as we're walking that I know how he feels, but he can only assume how I feel. There's this abyssal bond and physical attraction, and so many other unspoken things hitting at once. I don't want this to get any more complicated.

I turn and face him. "Are we just going to ignore this?"

His eyes are steady on mine. "We don't have a choice. Not right now. There's too much at stake."

"So when?"

He shakes his head slowly and seems to consider my question. "When this is all over."

"When what's over? We don't know what we're doing…or when…or why."

He tangles his fingers in mine, liquefying my bones with a symphony of vibrations. He says in a quiet, controlled voice, "We don't need the distraction or the tension with the other two. It's better if we wait."

I nod because I can't speak. I know he's right, but I hate it so hard it's making me tear up, which I can't let him see. I look down and bite the inside of my cheek to distract the tears with pain. When I steady myself, I look back up at him.

And then I hear my two new favorite words: *Fuck it.*

He runs a hand behind my head and hovers his lips just over mine. The rest of the world vaporizes into a blur. My legs nearly fold under me when he bites my bottom lip, tugging it softly between his teeth. He kisses me slow and he tastes like maple syrup.

I moan when he increases the intensity, his mouth ravaging mine, hard and hungry. I'm pressing against him, wishing there wasn't so much fabric between us when I notice things taking an ugly turn. I break our kiss and look at my shaking hands, the anger and hostility brewing in my bones.

"I'm sorry," he says, taking a step back.

"Don't say that." I want to say a thousand other things but I can't make them come out of my mouth, so I just stare at my feet and try to be funny despite the building fury inside. "So, we're awesome at waiting."

Baron laughs. "Yeah, we should probably try harder." He takes a deep breath and exhales slow. We take our time walking back to the parking lot side by side.

No touching, not even on the drive home.

In front of my house, I'm finding it hard to leave the Jeep. "I guess I'll see you soon," I say, fumbling with my charm bracelet.

He pulls me into a hug, which I navigate so my lips are against his neck. I kiss him there once. Then again. I know I'm killing him, but it works because he tilts my head up and we're kissing again. I want to taste him forever. He stops, his thoughts worried my energy will get riled again.

It's been several minutes—or an hour—or a day. Time has lost all meaning.

He sighs and leans back in the seat. "I should go," he says. "I'll call you."

I get out of the Jeep and watch him drive away. Two days earlier, I didn't even know this man. Now his absence is an earthquake. I'm sad, but also happy because for the first time, I have someone who knows my secret. I have someone who matters, who I'm not just trying to get a meaningless thrill from.

I have someone.

Stand under me and feel humble
Look up and feel embraced
Lean on me, sense my permanence
Hug me and know pure grace

See my leaves dance
See my leaves dance

Come, climb up my able arms
Leaf shadows dance across your face
Your weight gives comfort to this old man
Who grows alone in such a vast place

See my leaves dance
See my leaves dance

So high up but my branches support you
Hear leaves whisper of my sage-like soul
My deep roots tell you of their history
This makes you feel connected and whole

See my leaves dance
See my leaves dance

Wipe a tear as you behold my solemn presence
And my maternal love and pride
Please protect me from being cut down and destroyed
Like so many for whom I have cried

And my leaves still dance
And my leaves still dance

—DEVI

9

DISCOVERIES

School resumes the next day. I'm taking mostly basics: animal behavior and English literature on Mondays and Wednesdays. Tuesday is economics, and Friday is philosophy.

Animal behavior is the only one I chose based on my interests. So far, it's fascinating and the class I look forward to most. My work hours vary based on the bookstore's need, but I usually end up with about fifteen. This doesn't pay rent, but my parents supplement as long as I keep my grades up, which has always been pretty easy for me. No social life—making out with boys in a car after school doesn't count—means plenty of time for studying. My parents have the same arrangement with Nodin.

My animal behavior class ends and I walk outside, digging in my backpack for my phone, which has been buzzing for the last five minutes. It's Nodin.

"What?" I say.

"That's a nice greeting."

"You know you could leave a message. I was in class."

"Sorry, sorry. I couldn't wait to talk to you."

"About what?"

"About the adoption papers. I want to look over them again. You still have them?"

"No, I threw them away."

He huffs. "Your sarcasm isn't appreciated."

"Actually, I appreciate it."

"How's the clunker runnin'?"

"It's running perfect, Nodin. Anything else? I need to get to my next class."

"Yes. Call me as soon as you get home and I'll come over."

"I don't think I'll have time. I have to work toni-"

"I don't care if it's late. Just call me."

I promise I will.

Jamie Two greets me as I walk in after work that night. He has papers spread across the coffee table and a textbook in his lap. He lets me know there's leftover pizza in the kitchen. Dinner hasn't occurred to me, so I take him up on it. I grab two slices and a bottled water and head to my room, turn on my laptop and start to twist my hair into a bun when there's a tap at my door.

"Yes?"

"Your phone's ringing."

"Oh, thanks." I didn't realize I'd left it on the kitchen table. I follow him into the family room and grab my phone, noticing two missed calls from Nodin.

"Your new silver Jeep mystery lover?" Jamie teases.

"Ram it." I walk back in my room, but before I can return Nodin's call, I hear a car door slam.

Panic grabs my gut. I run to the front door and let Nodin in, hoping Jamie doesn't make any comments about a guy I kissed in front of our house, who happens to drive a Jeep.

Fortunately, it appears the only fun in joking about my new lover is with me. They greet each other with boss nods and Nodin follows me in my room.

"Where are the papers?" he says. His face is flushed with excitement, or maybe it's just the bright orange sweatshirt he's wearing.

"Chill out, dude, I've been home two minutes." I get the manila envelope from a box in the top of my closet and hand it to him.

He pulls out the official adoption documents and the three yellow pieces of notebook paper covered in my adoptive mom's handwritten notes, which he hands to me. She kept a log detailing their trip to Johannesburg to adopt us. I hold the papers up to my nose and inhale.

"What on earth are you doing?" Nodin asks.

"They smell like Mom." I hold them out for him to smell. "Cinnamon."

"That's okay. I take your word for it."

We sit side by side on the edge of my bed, just scanning her words since we've read them before. We both smile when we read the part where Mom and Dad gave us our first bubble bath in the Johannesburg hotel. The bubbles "scared Nodin half to death, but delighted Devi."

I run a finger over the faded yellow paper. "It's sweet that she did this and kept it all these years."

"Yeah." Nodin turns the pages over. "Too bad it doesn't tell us anything we need to know."

"Do you remember anything from that weekend?" I ask.

He shakes his head. "Not a thing. Is that weird?"

I shrug. "Not necessarily. You were three. That's pretty young to have memories."

"Yet I remember things from before then. I remember playing a game with a dark-skinned boy, like soccer, but you moved the ball with a long stick."

"It's strange what the mind chooses to remember, isn't it?"

He nods and folds Mom's notes to the back. On top are the official documents, the ones our biological father filled out when putting us up for adoption. In the top left, in bold, are the words *Biological Father: Ashon Mahtembo. Race: White. Age: 21. Province: GR. City: 32.*

"God, twenty-one. He was so young," I say.

"I know." Nodin taps the province and city information, or the lack thereof. "We need to figure out what these numbers mean."

"It could be a code. Can't we just look it up on the Internet?" I say.

"Maybe," he says.

The section for biological mother is empty other than the word *deceased*. It echoes in my head.

I'm sad for her, sad her name wasn't provided. There's nothing under medical, no specific address or phone number, no other names. The second document is the information about us. I hate this one. The missing information is a slap in the face. Only our names, genders and race, listed as Caucasian, are provided.

I sigh. "I don't see much to go on here."

Nodin takes the document and moves to the laptop at my desk. "You want your dinner?" he asks, pointing at my pizza.

I shake my head. "I don't feel like eating anymore."

He opens a search engine and types in *South African city codes*. The links lead nowhere. He sighs and tries a few other combinations of words. Nothing.

"Try just typing in the code with South Africa," I say.

He types in *GR South Africa*. The word Gauteng pops up first in the search. He opens the top link and a page with a map appears. Not far from Johannesburg is a star labeled Gauteng.

"There it is," he says. "GR is for the province Gauteng."

"What about the thirty-two?"

He goes back to the search page and types *GR32 South Africa*. Bronkhorstspruit is the top link, a city in the province of Gauteng.

"Holy shit, we did it," I say.

He reads aloud, "Gauteng, Bronkhorstspruit. A small farming town east of Pretoria, South Africa. It is home to the largest Buddhist temple in the southern hemisphere... was the location for the first Boer War in 1880...is supposedly beautiful and known for great bass fishing by the dam."

"How far is that from Johannesburg?"

Nodin looks it up. "A little over an hour. Not far at all."

"But in my dream, we are with a tribe. Is there tribal land near Bronkhorstspruit?"

Clicks sound as he types a new search. "Wow. There are a bunch."

I lean forward and peer at the links. "Right there." I grab the document. "See?!" I point to the name *Mahtembo* listed on the paper as our father's last name, and then to the same name among the list of tribes.

Nodin takes the paper from me. "You're right. It's the same. But why would his last name be the same as the tribe?"

I shrug. "I don't know, but it can't be a coincidence. Look up the tribe."

He types *Mahtembo tribe, South Africa* into the search bar. A Wikipedia page comes up, and in the top right corner is a photo that sucks the air out of my lungs.

I grab Nodin by the shoulders, speechless. My jaw moves up and down without success until I gasp, "It's them. The people from my dream!"

The caption underneath reads, *Members of Mahtembo Village in front of a traditionally painted dwelling.* The hut is circular and made of clay or mud with a straw roof. The outside walls are decorated with blue, yellow, and white symbols: stars, the moon, two elephants, and a human figure. Two dark men stand in front of the hut wearing a narrow red cloth around their waists. They stare at the camera, stone-faced. The women aren't smiling either, but their faces are less stern, a slightly amused contentment. They sit with their legs straight out in front of them, ankles crossed. Their right eyes are adorned like stained glass windows, and their right breast is exposed.

"I can't believe I'm looking at this," I say. I'm numb and my tongue feels too big for my mouth. "What were we doing with them?"

Neither of us speaks as we read the lone paragraph about the Mahtembo.

> The Mahtembo are a tribe located in
> South Africa, twenty miles southeast of
> Bronkhorstspruit. Locally they are known as
> the Elephant Tribe because, translated, their
> name means Man of Elephant (Mah = man,
> Tembo = Elephant). They are animists and
> believe the spirits of their deceased shaman live in
> elephants.

"What's an animist?" I ask Nodin.

"It's the belief that spirituality exists in living and non-living things, like people have souls, but so do rivers, mountains, thunder, plants, stuff like that," he says.

I sometimes forget how handy it is to have an archaeologist around.

I read the rest of the paragraph out loud, "Their chief income is farming, largely made up of Sorghum production. They also grow a wide variety of herbs, which are taken into town and sold by outside sources. Although a tolerant people, outsiders are not allowed onto tribal land except under rare exceptions."

I look back at the photo and wonder who was allowed on the property to take it.

"Wow, there are a lot of them—I mean, compared to a thousand Tabari," Nodin says.

I scan the page. "How many?"

"Eight thousand according to the two thousand and eight census," he says.

"Whoa."

"They speak a Bantu language spelled, m-b-a-l-a."

"How do you pronounce an M and a B at the same time?"

"I guess one of them is silent. Or you go *mmmbala*."

I smile at his attempt at humor, but it wanes. "Where do we go from here, Nodin? What's next?"

He lets out a lung full of air and turns to me. "I'm not sure yet."

"Well, we've gotta do something. What we have leads us to the tribe from my dream, which has the same last name as our father. We think. Or..." I grab his shoulder. "Do you think he put that name down intentionally, like as a clue?"

He squints. "Hmmm. That seems like a stretch. What makes you think he wants us to find him?"

"Wishful thinking, I guess." I sit on the bed. "We should call the adoption facility. Maybe they could tell us something not in the document."

"Yeah, I was thinking that, too. But there's something else we could do." He looks at me warily.

"What?"

"We could go to Africa."

I freeze. "No. No way, Nodin. I'm already having a panic attack about going to Oklahoma. You know I can't be away from the tree that long. I've never left town before. I'm sure as hell not going to frickin' Africa."

"Relax, relax," he says, his palms in the air. "I'm not suggesting we go tomorrow. I'm just asking you to consider it when you learn to channel wherever you want."

I laugh. "You know that's not possible. If I could do that, I would've long ago."

"I know you can."

"Really. And how do you know? Please enlighten me." I cross my arms.

"I've been thinking. The tree is just a portal for the energy to get to you, but energy has to travel to the tree some way. When we find out how the energy is getting to the tree, we find out how to channel it from other places."

I roll my eyes. "Why couldn't it just travel through the ground?"

He stands and gathers the papers. "It needs a less broad vehicle to travel to a specific spot."

"Like what?" My interest is piqued.

"Like water."

"Water? Odessa is a desert, in case you didn't notice."

"Trust me, I noticed." He looks at me, thinking. "I'm going to do some research on the ground water in the area. If I find anything, I'll let you know."

"Let's say you find something and I can channel at other trees. You expect me to go to Africa?" I huff. "And even if I agreed to go—which I wouldn't—how could we miss school and who would pay for it?"

"Those details would work themselves out." Nodin waves his arms through the air like a magician about to say *voila*.

I grin, amused at his undying enthusiasm. "They would, huh?"

"All right, maybe it's a crazy idea, but it might be the only way to find him."

"Enjoy your flight. I hope you get peanuts."

He looks at me, exasperated, but I can see the smile he's trying to smother. "You're terrible, you know that?"

"Bring me back a souvenir."

"I'm leaving." The papers ruffle in his hand and as he turns on his heel.

"I think you should go, and I'm not lion." I make my fingers like claws and feign a growl.

He walks out of my room, shutting the door behind him. I giggle, but my eyes catch the image still glaring at me from the computer.

Gently I run my finger over the photo. It looks so familiar. I can feel the cool dirt under my bare feet and the sun on my shoulders. I search their faces. "Who are you?" I whisper.

10
CONNECTIONS

I t's Tuesday morning and I'm having a bowl of Cinnamon Grahams in the kitchen, chatting with Jamie One, who's up early for a change. Cinnamon Grahams is not my favorite cereal, nor is cereal my favorite breakfast—that's English muffins with a smidge of butter, and *sometimes* grape jelly if I'm feeling adventurous—but I couldn't help but buy them. They remind me of my mom, not only because Nodin and I ate this cereal as kids, but because cinnamon is her favorite spice. She uses it in her tea, coffee, baked goods; it's even the secret spice in her chili.

I guess I miss home a little.

I take a bite but drop my spoon when energy bolts up my legs and rams me right in the gut. I cough, spewing cereal and milk out in all directions. Jamie is alarmed, but I tell her I just sucked some milk down the wrong pipe.

It's the calling, but the intensity is different. It usually begins with vibrations I feel from afar, accompanied with anxiety, and the intensity increases throughout the day. I've never been assaulted out of the gate like this. Maybe I slept through the beginning of it, but I don't think so.

I wipe my mouth and clean up the mess with paper towels, excusing myself to get ready for work and, later, economics. As soon as I shut my bedroom door, I'm hit again.

This time I feel it coming. It's more subtle, but out of character with strength. Like an earthquake, it rumbles across the room, hits my legs and shoots up my body. My breath hitches and I grab the doorknob to steady myself.

"What the fuck?" I whisper, reaching for the peridot stone.

I put off showering as I get ready for the day, for fear another one will hit. It doesn't. When I have nothing left to do, I take a record-fast shower and throw on yoga pants, a shirt, and a cardigan. It seems like things have calmed down, so I head to work.

About thirty minutes into my shift, the vibrations start again. Anxiety makes a nest in my stomach, ripping and tearing. I can't concentrate on anything. When I begin to shake, I call in another employee to take my place, telling her I'm throwing up. She arrives a half hour later and I rush out the door and drive straight to Joe's.

Panic rips through me as I consider the possibility he won't be home. I will have to jump the fence. I have no choice.

I pull over in front of the house and throw my truck into park. I go to his porch slumped over in pain and bang on the door. No answer. I moan and bang again. Joe opens it and I try to stand up straight and appear normal. I am so *not* normal.

"Devi. What a nice surprise. I almost didn't come to the door. You sure are coming more often lately," he says with a wide grin. He opens the door and beckons me inside. Assface serenades me with snaps and growls.

I walk past him inside the house. "It's the holiday season. Brings back memories, you know?"

"Ah, yes, that happens." He squints at me. "You don't look so good. Are you sick?"

"No, just tired. Finals coming up. I don't have much time today."

His face drops. "Oh, okay."

"But I'll be coming over again soon…when I have more time," I say, attempting to appease him.

"Oh, that'd be nice. I have some new pieces I'd like to show ya."

"Oh good." I reach out for the wall, jolted with another wave.

"Heavens, girl, you can't even stand up. Do you want to lie down?"

"No, I'm fine, really. I'm gonna go out back now so I can get home to bed soon." I don't wait for him to respond, but walk out the back door and veer straight to my tree. I reach up and grab my branch, pulling up, climbing to my sanctuary. As

I collapse into my seat, succumbing to its demand, the hum of the tree's energy webs its way through my fibers.

I'm somewhere I don't recognize. A grassy plane with tall golden reeds blowing in the breeze takes up my entire field of vision. Trees dot the area and something large looms across the horizon. It's hard to make out. I think at first they're clouds, but then I realize they're mountains.

This is a vast place, and I feel an emotion attached to it. Fear? Anxiety?

I keep watching, waiting for something to change in the vision. The only sound is the grass being pushed back and forth by the wind. It's warm here and the wind feels good against my sweaty body. I might be waiting for something or someone. Yes. I'm expecting an arrival.

I hear a noise and cock my head to find its origin, seeing nothing. It sounds like a growl but continues too long. Maybe a distant motorcycle? That's too mechanical. This sounds animal, but too consistent for a growl. Still, it continues. I look around for it again. I still see nothing. My whole body quakes.

I blink back to awareness as the vision fades, still shaking from residual anxiety. This vision didn't have a déjà vu sensation. It felt like something yet to come. I check my watch. It's been forty-five minutes. Shorter than usual. I wait until I feel stable and climb down.

Joe leads me through the house. "Bye, Devi. Come back soon," he says as he holds the front door open for me.

Later, I call Baron and tell him about the new vision.

"Don't you think that's eerily similar to my tree vision?" he asks. "With the tall grass and the feeling I'm waiting for something?"

I get chills. "Wait, do you hear the rumbling sound in your vision?"

"I hear a roar of rushing water. Do you think what you heard is water?"

"No," I say. "The tone is too…something, too guttural. I can't place it, but it's not water." We both pause. "You there?"

"Yeah, I'm here. It's just…well, I'm wondering if I made an assumption the sound was water. You know, when your brain tries to make sense out of things, sometimes misallocating sounds. I wonder if we're hearing the same thing."

"It's possible." Feeling overwhelmed, I sit on the bed with a sigh. "Wait, you're still having the tree vision? I thought the visions stopped when you tattooed them?"

"They do, usually. There must be something I'm missing. Something I haven't noticed before."

I sigh again. "Things are accelerating so fast. I've never had the tree call me like that, and then I have this vision…."

"This is good. We're getting the answers we need."

"I know, but I'm scared."

"Of what?"

"Of whatever it is that we're doing. I mean, am I going to the place in my vision? What if it's Africa or Peru? I can't go, Baron. I can't go that far."

"Stop. You're worrying about something that hasn't even happened. That place could be Arizona for all we know. And you're not alone. I'm with you on this, remember?"

I exhale. "Yeah, I know."

"I've got good news."

"Really?"

"When I asked Hahn questions about the Tabari and told him I wanted to know more about them, he contacted some of his colleagues. He learned about an archaeologist named Jim Mealy who's been studying the Tabari for about three years. They've evidently started tolerating his nosing around. Hahn is in the process of trying to get in touch with this Mealy guy. I'll get back to you as soon as I hear anything. This could be good. Cross your fingers."

My phone chimes, indicating I'm getting another call. It's Nodin. Baron and I say quick good-byes and hang up.

"Wassup?" I say, answering the other line.

"It's water!" Nodin's voice is high and excited.

"What?"

"Water. That's the answer—the conduit for the energy." He's talking so fast I can hardly make out what he's saying. "There's an underground spring going right under the old house."

"But how do you know it's carrying the energy?"

"Water is a natural conduit for energy. That's a no-brainer, but then there's Baron's Australian serpent tattoo that symbolizes the importance of water to mankind. And the Nazca lines, they're maps to water. It makes sense, doesn't it?"

Yes. In some strange, fucked up way it makes total sense. There's only one way to know for sure.

I have to try to channel at another tree by water.

11
THUNDER

On Wednesday, I sit up front in my animal behavior class. We have a guest speaker, an ecologist. She's lecturing on the evolution of communication in certain mammals. My mind wanders, but my attention is caught when she connects her laptop to a TV so we can see her screen.

A title marches across the top in red letters: *Elephant Thunder*. She explains female elephants have the ability to use infrasound communication, which is too low for the human ear to hear. It's typically in the range of fourteen to forty-five hertz. The elephants can send warnings to other herds or communicate their locations.

At the end of her lecture, she pops a CD in her laptop and turns the volume up. It's a recording made of an elephant call, the frequency sped up so humans can hear it, and then slowed down to replicate how an elephant would hear it.

I practically run out when class is over, fumbling for my phone to call Baron.

"The rumbling sound in my vision—I know what it is," I say. "It's elephants." I explain what I heard when the lecturer played the tape.

"And the Mahtembo worship elephants," he muses. "It's another clue to your biological family's whereabouts."

"You think it confirms my father is still in Africa?"

"It could."

"Baron, remember how you said the sound you heard in your vision sounds like continuous, rumbling water?"

"Of course."

"What if you're hearing elephant communication too?"

Silence.

"Baron?"

"Huh." He pauses. "You could be right. That would explain why it sounds so close, yet I don't see any water source."

"How can we know for sure?" I ask.

"We wait."

It's Thursday. I planned on going to the tree tomorrow, the day before we leave for Oklahoma, but as usual the tree dictates my life. I awake, surprised I'm feeling the familiar anxious sensation that marks the start of the calling. The vibrations resound at my feet as I shower. By the time my four-hour shift ends, my muscles quake. The vibrations are strong. Constant.

I drive straight to Joe's from the bookstore and sit on his couch while he shows me new pieces in his skull collections. He has one made of pink quartz he's proud of, explaining it's good for balancing female energy. He also shows me a skull made of hematite, which strengthens connections to the Earth, enhances focus and clarity, and protects the wearer.

"Do you like this one?" he asks, inspecting the pink skull. He holds it up to the light and squints.

My eyes drift to the other one, drawn to it. "I like that one," I say.

"The hematite skull? Well, goes to show ya. I'll never figure women out." He picks it up and puts it in my palm. "Take it. It's yours."

"No." I try to hand it back. "I'm not taking one of your skulls."

He ignores my outstretched hand. "I'm not asking. Consider it a belated graduation gift."

I laugh. "My high school graduation was more than five months ago."

Joe grins. "I said it was belated."

I roll it around in my palm. "Well, thank you. That's sweet." I tense for a round of vibrations I sense coming. They blast

through me, leaving my ears throbbing. I open my eyes to see
Joe with his head tilted and eyes squinting at me.

He pats my hand and stands to walk me to the backdoor.
"Put that skull in your pocket. It'll help you."

Crunching through fallen leaves, I walk across the yard
and reach for my branch. Once in my seat, I stretch like a well-
fed cub and surrender.

I'm in the field. The canopy of darkness so thick, it's
difficult to see ten feet in front of me. Moonlight is my
only beacon. I hear the papery sounds of grass being
swayed by the wind.

The anxiety is strong—so is the fear. I'm afraid. I look
around, waiting. I tremble, but not from the chilly air.
The sound begins. A rumble. It continues, low and long,
seeming to come from everywhere at once. I clench my
fists, tense with anticipation. I feel a different vibration—a
hum—coming from behind me. It's familiar and I'm un-
alarmed. It's Baron.

The rumble turns to a deeper tone, almost a growl,
and then stops. Whatever I—or we—are waiting for has
arrived. I peer into a small group of trees about forty feet
away to our left, but don't see anything.

I take a few shaky steps forward, holding my hair out
of my eyes.

Then I see it, the outline of an elephant's head. I freeze.
It steps forward from the trees without a sound, taking
steps toward me, stopping about twenty feet away. I'm
shaking so hard I fall to my knees. Our eyes meet. Hers
look familiar.

"Mandah," I hear an ambiguous voice say in my head.
I know to stand.

"Nami," I whisper, tears streaming down my face.

On my way home, I call Nodin from the car and tell him about the vision.

"Wait. I don't understand," he says. "The elephant is the brown lady with the braids?"

"I know it sounds crazy, but the eyes were human, and the Mahtembo believe their shaman's souls continue to live in elephants. Like a reincarnation thing. It was her, Nodin."

"But that would imply she was a Mahtembo shaman. She's Tabari, or at least that's our hunch. How does a Tabari woman become a Mahtembo shaman?" he says.

"I don't know." I park my truck in front of my house.

"Are you packed for Ardmore?" he asks.

"Not yet. I'll do it tomorrow. What time are we leaving?"

"Bright and early. I'll pick you up at six on Saturday." He clears his throat. "I wanted to let you know there's no shortage of streams and rivers in Oklahoma. I think you should try channeling at another tree."

I stop before opening my front door. "Okay. Yeah." Anxiety grips my throat. The idea freezes and frees me simultaneously. "I'll tell Baron about my vision. Talk to you later."

We hang up. Both my roomies are home. Jamie Two is sprawled on the couch watching TV in his boxers.

"Wassup, chica?"

"Not much." I point to his crotch. "Can you cover up a bit? I can see."

He grins and folds one leg over the other, amused.

"Where's Jamie One?" I ask.

He points toward her bedroom.

"Ah. Okay. You guys work tonight?"

"I'm bar-backing for a few hours. J-One's off."

I plug my nose. "What's that smell?"

"The eggs J-One made."

"No, it's not eggs."

"Then it's probably the megalithic dump I just let loose."

"Ewww. You're disgusting." Thank God I have my own bathroom because he's a pathological shitter and a total slob.

This arrangement would be out of the question if I had to share a bathroom with him.

"You asked…"

"Whatever. I guess I'll see you later. I've got homework." I turn toward my bedroom.

"Shake that ass for me," he calls.

"You're such a perv."

If anyone else talked to me like that, I'd sic Ben on him, but Jamie is harmless. He's a good guy with a warped sense of humor.

In my bedroom, I shut the door and sit at my desk to call Baron. He answers right away and I tell him about the vision.

"Well, that seals it then," he says.

"Seals what?"

"The part of the tattoo I'm missing. It's an elephant."

I gasp. "You really think so?"

"I'm inking it Saturday night. Will you come with me?" he asks.

I know how sacred a ritual this is for him. To say I'm honored is an understatement. "Of course I will."

"Good, because I'm gonna need your help on this one."

"You are? Why?"

"Because you're the only one who's seen her."

The hair stands up on my arms. "You're tattooing the elephant from my vision?" I begin to pace. "How? I don't know if I can describe her well enough."

"You have nothing to worry about."

"No doubt, I'm not the one getting it tattooed."

He laughs. "Just trust me, okay?"

I sigh and sit on the edge of my bed. "All right. I trust you."

"Good. Now get some sleep. You'll be here in thirty-six hours."

Flurries charge through my stomach.

12
FIRSTS

It's Friday. Baron has been gone five days. Although we've spoken on the phone, I am acutely aware of our time apart.

He calls again Friday night as I'm packing. Just hearing his voice sends a purr of warmth through me. Nodin and I leave tomorrow morning for Ardmore and I don't think I can stand the wait.

"How are you?" I ask, waving hi to Jamie One as I walk into the kitchen.

"I'm good. How are you?" Baron says.

"Surviving." I crave to touch him, to hear his thoughts.

"I thought it might be worth asking Hahn about tribes in Africa. He's studied just about every culture."

"What did you tell him?" I peer into the fridge. There's leftover pizza, a bowl of strawberries, sliced American cheese, milk, and salad dressing.

We need to go shopping. I take the strawberries and bottled water. Surveying the pantry, I see there's a hundred different brands of chips and a bag of almonds. I grab the almonds. I've had way too much fast food lately and I know I should eat healthier.

"Nothing. At this point, I can ask him anything because it all falls under you two looking for your birth father. I don't have to give any information that would be a risk to us."

"Cool. What did he say?" I go in my room and shut the door behind me, setting up my little dinner at my desk.

"A lot, actually. He says in many African regions, the man's last name is the tribe they belong to."

"So it *is* his last name."

"Wait 'til you hear this. Hahn's been there."

"To the tribe?" I almost screech.

"No, no. He's never heard of the tribe. He was in that area of South Africa. The town with the long name, Bronk-something?"

"Bronkhorstspruit, but I'm sure I'm butchering the pronunciation."

"Yes, there's a huge Buddhist temple—"

"Yes, we read about that online. It's one of the biggest in the world or something."

"That's the one. He did an apprenticeship there years ago, before I was even born, but this is what's interesting. He said the Buddhists use herbs locally grown by tribes for healing and medicinal purposes."

"Wait, I swear I read that the Mahtembo farmed herbs and sold them in town."

"They're probably not the only ones, but if the Buddhists are friendly with local tribes, they could know of the Mahtembo."

"Holy shit. This is huge," I say, standing and pacing.

I finish packing for the weekend, careful to pick a cute outfit for Saturday night when we go for Baron's tattoo.

I try to get sleep, but instead have fitful dreams of running through fields, sweaty and panicked, looking for something in the trees. At two in the morning I sit up, frustrated. Something gleams across the room. I squint to see through the darkness.

It's the hematite skull Joe gave me. I walk over and pick it up, surprised by its warmth and weight. I snuggle back in the sheets, the plum-sized skull tucked in my fist, and drift to sleep. A hard, deep sleep that lasts until my alarm goes off at five.

By quarter to six, I'm sitting in the family room with my suitcase, ready to go. Just as I see Nodin's Bronco pull up out front, I realize I've forgotten something. I run back in my room, get the hematite skull and shove it in my suitcase before walking out the door. I no longer doubt its ability to calm my energy.

Nodin drives the first half. I nap a little and then drive the second half, determining this distance is bullshit and suggesting we meet halfway next time. He laughs, but I don't think he disagrees.

"It's a lot to wrap your brain around, isn't it?" Nodin says. "The magnitude of this, everyone who's involved. It's…"

"Fucking mind-blowing," I say.

"Yeah. That."

"Will Ben be meeting us?"

"Maybe late tonight or early tomorrow morning. I booked you and I separate rooms. Mine has two doubles, so if he gets into Ardmore tonight he can crash with me."

"He's still blocking me?"

"Absolutely."

"How does that work?"

"I don't know, but from what I've pieced together, I think it's by combination of telepathy and meditation. He goes into a state of relaxation and envisions a force field of energy around that area of your mind. It acts as a road block for anyone trying to read you."

"And he can do that once and it holds?"

"I asked him that. He said he meditates each morning, and during the day he has to do mind checks to reinforce it."

"Sounds exhausting."

"I'm sure it is."

"So, the block only intercepts information from being seen, but not received, right?" I say.

"Yep. It makes your mind like a two-way mirror, but anyone trying to read you doesn't know it."

"Huh. Pretty cool." It's bizarre to think there's a mental force field around my mind.

As soon as we cross over the Texas-Oklahoma border, the landscape changes. Dense forests flank either side of the highway in vibrant shades of yellow, orange and red. The road hugs curves, rolls over hills, even passes through mountain tunnels.

Oklahoma is the most beautiful place I've ever seen. Then again, it's the only place I've ever seen outside of Odessa.

We aren't meeting Baron until two. It is quarter to one when we arrive in Ardmore and we're starving. We stop for lunch in the historic downtown before checking into our hotel.

"You didn't tell me Oklahoma is so cool," I say.

He smirks. "You should leave home more often."

We leave and check into our hotel. We're on the same floor, but Nodin's room is down the hall and around the corner from mine. I freshen up and meet Nodin downstairs ten minutes later to head to Baron's apartment.

I'm so excited, nervous, and anxious to see Baron I can't sit still. "How long of a drive is it?"

"Just a few miles." He glances at me. "You seem awfully giddy."

I pause before speaking. "Remember when you told me Train and Emilet were a part of you?"

He nods.

"Baron is a part of me."

Nodin remains silent on the drive to Baron's apartment.

As we approach Baron's apartment on the second floor of a complex, the hum resonates and the air pressure closes in on my ears.

Baron opens the door before Nodin knocks.

I want to run to him but can't. The energy field is charged and whipping around us. He backs up to let us in, staying a comfortable distance from me until the energy settles.

I scan his efficiency apartment, a family room and bedroom separated by a half-wall. In the family room, there's a small reddish couch, a chest for a coffee table, a TV on a small cabinet across from the couch and a funky, gold wingchair.

"How was the drive?" Baron asks. His hair is held back with a black headband. He looks delectable.

I ache to touch him.

"Good. Long, but good," Nodin says. "Don't forget to bring water and a towel."

Baron points to a backpack on the floor by the door. "I've got us covered," he says. Next to the backpack is a tall, wooden coat rack with at least four rock climbing harnesses, several coils of different colored rope, and other climbing equipment I don't know the first thing about.

"Let's get going then," Baron says as he slings his backpack over his shoulder.

Behind him, I notice along the top of the half-wall there are rocks and crystals of all colors and sizes. I see the foot of his bed peeking out and lose myself thinking about how good it would feel to curl up in sheets that smell like him.

"How far away is it?" Nodin asks.

"It's where I practice with Hahn. Not far, but secluded." He glances at me. "There's a stream nearby, too."

"Oh." It's all I can muster. I'm nervous it won't work. I would almost rather try this alone for fear I will fail in front of them. If it does work, I don't know how I will feel channeling in front of an audience.

"It's okay. Only try if you feel up to it," Nodin says. I can tell by the look in his eyes that he feels my apprehension.

Baron and I follow Nodin out the door. While we walk through the parking lot, Baron takes my hand in his. The resounding throb encases us. I'm so drunk with it, I nearly stumble.

We ride together in Baron's Jeep. I sit in the back behind Baron, reaching around the side of his seat to intermittently rest my hand on his arm. After what seems like a hundred turns, asphalt turned to gravel turned to dirt roads, what looks like a bear Baron swears isn't, and a short hike that crosses a stream, we arrive at a clearing in the woods.

Baron stretches his shoulders, neck and back, and Nodin takes his place near the edge of the tree line.

A chilly breeze blows my hair. I button my cardigan and pull the collar up around my neck. My mouth falls open as Baron takes his shirt off. "Baron, it's cold," I protest, incredulous.

"Not for long. Remember last time?"

"Yeah, I know, but—"

"Don't worry, I heat up quick." He grins and steps closer to me, so close our bodies almost touch. I want to run my hands over his chest so bad that my fingers twitch. "I can't wait to be alone with you later," he whispers.

Every part of my body clenches with delicious desire. "What time are we going?" I ask.

To avoid the possibility of Nodin asking to join us for the tattoo, Baron had made a point on the drive over to freak him out with talk of needles and blood. Nodin doesn't do needles and blood.

"Eight o'clock." His gaze drifts to my lips. "You still cold?"

"Not even a little." I'm swooning.

"What's the hold-up over there?" Nodin calls.

Baron grins and takes a step back. He closes his eyes, and within fifteen seconds I feel my energy coursing through my body toward him. He takes a lot, enough that I feel weak in the limbo state.

I'm mesmerized by the fluidity as he grows it, and stumble backward when he returns energy to me. This time, I'm grateful for it. He works hard to compress the orb, straining, sweat pouring off his face and body. When it's the size of a cantaloupe, he holds it above him and throws it hard and high.

"Where'd it go?" Nodin asks, jogging to Baron with water and a towel.

"Up." He takes the towel and wipes sweat off his face and body. "I don't let it hit trees. I'm here all the time, so it would look like a war zone."

"Where does it end up?" I ask.

"It eventually dissipates and is absorbed into the atmosphere."

"You took a lot. I felt it that time," I say.

He looks up at me. "You did? How?"

"I felt weak. I still could've moved, but I definitely felt more vulnerable."

"Did you feel like you're near the limit of how much energy you can take?" Nodin asks Baron.

"No," Baron says, then gestures to me. "But she is."

102

"Devi," Nodin pleads, "You're going to have to try to channel. He needs more to work with."

It doesn't take long for me to decide. Letting them see me afraid is worse than letting them see me channel. "Okay. I'll try it."

Nodin smiles. "Atta girl."

"Right now?"

They both nod. I look around. I have no idea where to start. "Should I just pick any tree?"

"I don't know," Nodin says. "You tell me."

Baron steps toward me and takes my hand in his. "I think this will help," he says. Our energy purrs and I feel more focused. "Just let it all go. Use your gut."

I relax my shoulders and empty my mind. The first thing that enters my head is the sound of bubbling water from the nearby stream. I feel the urge to go nearer. "We need to go closer to the water."

We walk to the bank of the stream. I stare into the water, hypnotized by its movement. Hundreds of tiny swirls and eddies are happening independently, but at the same time they are a part of this giant movement downstream. It reminds me of models of our solar system—each planet a spinning world unto itself, but also orbiting the sun, part of something bigger.

"Trust your instincts," Baron says and squeezes my hand.

I close my eyes and concentrate, picturing myself in the tree. I can feel its energy whir through me and its bark rough against my skin. My eyes open and rest on a large tree just off the bank with a huge V split in its trunk; half of its branches reach toward the sky, while the others are gnarled and bent, hanging over the water.

"That one," I say, releasing Baron's hand and rushing toward it.

The leaves and twigs crunch as Baron and Nodin race after me. I stop and kneel at the base of the tree and study it, admiring its height, my breath coming fast and shallow. With half-fear and half-exhilaration, I lay my left palm on its trunk and whimper as the energy drives through my body, taking me, becoming me.

I'm a small child, sitting in the brown woman's lap near a fire. Men are pounding drums while women move rhythmically to the beat. I stare nervously at the man sitting to our left—there's something strange about the color of his skin. It's black, but not like the others. His eyes don't look right. He stares at me, and I shudder.

The woman hugs me, trying to comfort me. The people watch the man across the circle from us, the man with the bear mask. I feel like I know him. I trust him. He stares at the sky, moving his lips. He has a long decorated stick with an elephant head carved on the end of it. He holds his stick out toward me, quieting the crowd.

The woman pushes me to stand.

I won't.

The bear man points his stick at me and bellows, "Mandah."

I stand.

"Dakahn manyahn mah pi tah nili hasi," he booms.

Gasps break the silence and everyone repeats the name in unison seven times, reaching out to touch me. The creepy man to my left smiles. I feel uneasy.

There's a commotion, scurrying, shrieks. Pride turns to panic. I'm shoved into the arms of someone new. The brown woman and the scary man fade from my view while I scream.

I blink back into awareness. Nodin is crouching nearby and I stare at him, dazed.

"Are you okay?"

"I saw the dream. The memory from the night of my naming ceremony. That's never happened before with the tree. But this time, it's different. The brown woman. She wasn't taken that night."

"What do you mean?"

"There was no struggle. He wasn't dragging her away." I pause. "Nodin, she was clinging to him."

His mouth drops open. "Are you sure?"

I nod. "And the speaking man's stick—it had an elephant's head carved in it. I've never seen that before in the dream."

He stands. "You're being given new information."

"That's not all."

He crouches back down. "What?"

Chills fight for property on my arms. "After I'm given the name, the tribe chants it. Seven times. Just like in Baron's vision."

He stares at me.

"Where's Baron?" I ask.

"Over there." He motions up the trail, where I see Baron working with an enormous orb of energy.

"He pulled it from me just now?"

"Oh, yeah."

"A lot?"

"Oh, yeah."

"Has he given any back to me yet?"

"No, but I don't think he intends to."

"Why do you say that?"

He gestures to Baron. He has the energy in front of him, compressing it, this ball the biggest I've seen. I don't know how he's withstanding the heat; Nodin and I can feel it from where we sit. Baron works on compounding the energy, slow and steady, until it's where he wants it. He winds the ball back in one arm and hurls it upstream with a growl.

Nodin and I jump up and run to him. I look in the direction he threw it and notice a rippling effect in the air like one sees on a hot day over asphalt.

Baron leans over, palms on his knees, chest heaving. "Keep watching," he says.

We keep our eyes on the water. After about a minute, I can hear a roaring sound and grab Nodin's wrist. It gets louder.

A white-capped surge appears from around the bend, raising the water level at least three inches. It rushes past us like a runaway train, ripping roots and branches out of its way. The roar wanes as the surge travels on downstream.

"What the hell?" I gasp.

Baron straightens. "When the energy scatters, the water absorbs it. It has inertia going upstream at first, but the downstream momentum eventually turns it around." He looks at me. "You just saw your energy in wave form."

"Cool," Nodin says.

It dawns on me what just happened. "I can't believe I just channeled at another tree."

Nodin nudges my arm. "See? I told you water is the key."

"Why didn't you give energy back to me?" I ask Baron.

"I didn't have to. I could've pulled for a month and never run out. I wasn't taking from you. I was taking from what comes through you." He shakes his head. "It's unreal."

"This is how it needs to happen from now on," Nodin says.

"How much longer are we doing this?" The enormity of it all crushes my chest, threatening to squeeze the air from my lungs. "This is a shit-ton of energy we're working with. What on Earth could we be preparing for?"

Baron and I look at Nodin for an answer.

"I don't know more than I did two weeks ago," he says. "I swear."

"I don't understand why we can't know anything yet. Aren't your guides telling you anything else?"

Nodin looks at the ground and shakes his head. "No. They're not." He pauses. "They're gone."

"They're *gone*?" I say, loud enough to echo.

"They vanished after the night you two met. I guess their job is done." He straightens and sets his jaw. "I don't want to talk about it anymore. They told us we have to find our biological roots to know the purpose of all this."

His gaze settles on me. "Devi, get a drink of water. We're going for round two in five minutes." He brushes past me.

I sit on the ground, my gut twisting in knots. Train and Emilet are gone. No longer in Nodin's life...or mine. I can't help but feel a little lost. Abandoned. If I feel that way, I know Nodin is crushed.

I take a sip of water and watch Baron towel himself dry.

Despite the overwhelming events of the day, I've never felt so alive. I just channeled at a different tree. I'm no longer a prisoner in my town and I'm about to spend the entire evening with Baron. Alone.

13
CHERRIES

"So what is the plan?" I ask as we near Baron's apartment.

He glances at me in the rearview mirror. "It's six-fifteen. Let's eat and then you and I will go."

"Sounds good. How about burgers? I can't eat any more pizza," I say.

"I'll eat anything. I'm starving," Nodin chimes in.

"Burgers it is," Baron says, whipping the car into a drive thru.

Back at the apartment, we eat our burgers and fries without speaking. When Baron is done eating, he takes a quick shower and changes into fresh clothes while Nodin and I relax and flip through TV channels.

"We should get going. We're meeting my guy in twenty minutes," Baron says as he walks out from his bathroom. He's changed into jeans and a black shirt. His hair is still wet.

"Your guy?" I say.

"The guy that's been doing my tattoos since I was seventeen. Ethan."

"Oh. Is the tattoo shop pretty close by?"

"He doesn't do mine out of his studio. We're meeting him at his house."

"You said you think you'll have her back by eleven?" Nodin says. I try not to roll my eyes.

"Oh yeah, it shouldn't take longer than that. I'll call you when I drop her off at the hotel. I'd come up and show it to you, but it'll be freshly wrapped. You'll see it later."

"All right. Let's go." Nodin stands. I follow suit.

"Wait," Baron says, walking into the kitchen. "Over here, both of you. I have a pre-tattoo tradition. You have to partake since you're here." He pulls down a bottle of Silver Patron.

"Oh hell," I laugh.

"Oh hell is right," Baron agrees, getting three shot glasses from a cabinet, which he fills with tequila. We clink glasses and shoot them back. The alcohol burns its way down my throat and I cough.

So does Nodin.

"All right, now we can go, ladies," Baron says, heading toward the door.

"Oh shut up," Nodin snaps. "I only coughed 'cause I didn't have a lime."

"Whatever you need to tell yourself, ma'am," Baron teases. "Don't forget your purse."

"You're so annoying."

"Are you two always this dorky together?" I ask.

"Just him." Nodin walks ahead of us to the parking lot. Arriving at his Bronco, he extends a hand to Baron and they shake. "Be careful," he says with a look of warning in his eyes.

"Will do. I'll have her back as soon as possible, and thanks," Baron says.

Nodin gets in his Bronco and Baron and I get in the Jeep. Alone at last. I lay my head back on the seat and exhale as Baron drives out of the parking lot.

"Why does Ethan do your tattoos at his house?"

"The salon is too public. I feel better doing them in a private setting, and Ethan's cool enough to accommodate me."

"I see."

Fifteen minutes later, he parks in front of a little yellow house. We're in an older neighborhood.

Baron's hand rests on my thigh. "You made it hard to concentrate this afternoon," he says in a low voice.

I lean toward him, my whole body a fit of tingles. "Why's that?"

"When you channeled, you were so powerful," he says and then kisses my forehead. "But so vulnerable." He kisses the tip of my nose. "It was so damn sexy." He kisses my mouth and my insides liquefy in a heap of flesh and nerve endings. The kiss ends way too soon. "Thanks for being here for this."

"I wouldn't miss it."

"I guess we should get in there." He meets me on the other side of the jeep, takes my hand and leads me around the side of the house to a detached garage and knocks on the door. "It's me."

The door opens, revealing a symphony of sights.

Ethan is tall, with a nice body and light brown skin. He wears a red and gray striped beanie over a head of dreadlocks. He flashes a great smile with dimples, and the outdoor light glints off a nose piercing, a ring through his bottom lip, another through his eyebrow, and diamond studs in his ears. He is, of course, covered in tattoos.

Ethan reaches out and shakes Baron's hand as they exchange hellos and boss nods. Baron introduces me, and Ethan greets me with a warm smile.

I like him already.

Inside I recognize a faint smell as weed. Not freshly smoked, but baked into the walls and furniture. I've never partaken. SAIs rarely do because quite frankly, we don't need to enhance our experiences, but the Jamies are frequent fliers.

Ethan's garage is set up like a studio – part lounge, part tattoo parlor. It has a retro vibe with funky colors and furniture, but the best thing is the music. He has Billie Holiday playing. Ethan and I make small talk about our love of Blues music. He's also a fan of John Lee Hooker and shows me his collection of his CDs, some of which I've never heard of.

"Can we get started? We're on a time crunch," Baron interjects.

"Yeah, yeah, yeah. We're doin' an elephant, right?" Ethan says.

"Yes, but a specific one."

"You got a picture for me?"

"Yes and no. I need you to draw it from a description."

"Oh, it's like that?" Ethan gets a sketch pad and pencil. He sits at a glass top desk and snaps on a bright lamp. "Go ahead."

"Devi's going to describe it to you."

"I'm going to try," I correct him.

Baron looks at me. "You've envisioned it. I know you have. Tell him what you see. Don't judge it or rethink it, just tell him."

He's right. I close my eyes. "It's the elephant's head—"

"Full front or profile?" Ethan says.

"She's looking at me."

I can hear his pencil scraping the paper. "Ears out to sides or flat against head?"

"Out."

"Tusks or no tusks?"

"Tusks."

"How is the trunk positioned?"

"Hanging, but about halfway down it's turned up, crossing in front of its left tusk."

"What else?"

"Eyes with emotion. Almost human-like. Showing compassion."

"Where?" he asks.

"Where?"

"On Baron, where do you see it?"

"Oh, uh...on his back. Next to the tree trunk, under the big branch—almost on his side."

He draws for a couple more minutes. "Okay, open your eyes. How's this?"

I inspect his artwork. Baron chose this guy well. "Oh, wow. It's perfect." I look at Baron. "Is it okay with you?"

"If you say it's perfect, then it's the one."

"How's the size?" Ethan asks me.

"Too big. Make it about the size of my palm." I hold my hand out. "Is that okay, Baron?"

"Whatever you say."

"Let me transfer this." Ethan turns on a light under the table, illuminating the glass. He gets clear paper, waxy paper and a marker of some sort. We watch as he turns a dial underneath the table and it shrinks his original picture so he can trace it. He finishes about ten minutes later.

"Get naked, pretty boy," he says.

Baron takes off his shirt and leans over a table.

"Damn, man, you been liftin' since you been here last? You're making me look bad."

"I doubt that's possible," Baron says.

Ethan asks me to direct the transfer paper where the elephant should go. He places it where I indicate, then pulls off the paper. A purplish-black outline of the elephant stays on Baron's skin.

"How does that look?"

"I love it," I say.

Baron walks over to a full-length mirror, then nods his approval. "Let's do it." He lies on his stomach across a table covered in white paper.

Ethan puts on funky, black-rimmed glasses and then washes his hands before sitting on a stool next to Baron. He pulls a metal stand with the tattoo gun and ink closer to him. Pulling latex gloves on his hands, he says, "Ready, B?"

"Yep."

I hover near Baron, not sure where to stand.

"Devi, you can pull up a chair if you want," Ethan says.

"Okay." I grab a zebra print stool and set it next to Baron's table, not sure how much I want to see.

"Do you have any tattoos, Devi?" Ethan asks.

"No."

"We might need to remedy that." He points the ink gun at me.

I laugh and lean away. "Not tonight you're not."

"Just promise you'll bust your tattoo cherry with me."

I roll my eyes. "Okay, I promise if I ever get a tattoo you can do it."

"Can we start please?" Baron says.

"Sorry, sorry. So demanding, this one." Ethan turns the needle gun on. It's a god-awful noise that reminds me of a dentist's drill. I watch with a hand over my mouth, wincing as it pierces Baron's skin. It takes several minutes to become accustomed to the noise and sight, but I didn't expect the blood.

Ethan and I talk while he works. I'm amazed he can be so casual and relaxed about drawing something so permanent. Nodin would've been a goner, watching this.

"Doesn't it hurt really bad?" I ask Ethan.

"For sure, but you gotta go to your Zen place."

I glance at Baron. He looks asleep. "Are you in your Zen place, Baron?"

"Mmhmm," he says, but he sounds like he's humming. Ethan and I trade grins.

About two and a half hours later, it's done and looking amazing.

"Damn, that's bad to the bone," Baron says, looking at it in the mirror.

"Thanks, man. Let's get it wrapped up." Ethan covers a square of gauze in antibiotic cream and then tapes it over the tattoo. "You know the routine."

"I do." Baron replaces his shirt and hands Ethan a wad of cash, thanking him again.

"No worries, man."

"Nice to meet you, Ethan." I reach out a hand.

He pushes my hand away and hugs me. "Remember, I get your cherry."

"How could I forget?" I laugh.

We walk to the Jeep, and it hits me I have Baron alone again, and I'm pretty sure I'm levitating with excitement.

14
LIMITS

When Baron starts the Jeep, the time illuminates: ten-forty. Sadness uncoils in my chest. We only have twenty more minutes together. I lace my fingers through his.

"I wish we could hang out longer," I say.

"Me too."

We drive in mostly silence and arrive at the hotel just before eleven. Baron parks. "Do you want me to walk you to your room?" he asks.

I shake my head. "That's okay."

He brings my hand to his mouth and kisses it. "Thank you again for your help." We lean toward each other and kiss, soft and sensual. My insides evaporate.

I flinch when my cell rings with the ridiculous tune I assigned to Nodin. "Dammit," I say before answering, "Yes?"

"Where are you?" Nodin asks.

"We just pulled up, psycho. Relax," I say with a little more irritation in my voice than I intended. "I'll be up in a sec." I hang up on him and grab Baron's hand. "I don't want to leave you yet."

He hesitates, staring at me with dark emerald eyes. "Trust me. I don't want you to go either."

"Come up then. Come to my room."

He shakes his head. "We can't."

"We won't. Just lay with me for a little while. Please. This can't be all the time we have together for who knows how long."

"What about Nodin?"

"I'll take care of Nodin. Just give me a few minutes. I'll call you when it's safe to come up."

"Okay," he says with a little smile as I leave the Jeep.

I hurry back to my room and call Nodin with the hotel phone so he believes I'm in my room. "I'm back," I say when he answers.

"How did it go?"

"Great. The tattoo is amazing. It turned out perfect."

He yawns. "Good. Good."

"I'm beyond exhausted. I'll talk to you tomorrow."

"Okay, yeah. I'll meet you in the lobby at eight. Packed and ready. We have to check out before we pick up Baron."

"Gotcha. See you then." I hang up with Nodin, switch my boho top and jeans to yoga pants and a T-shirt and call Baron. "All clear."

Four minutes later, a soft knock sounds at my door. I open it.

Baron's eyes never leave mine as he steps inside and softly shuts the door with his heel. He takes my hand and we walk a few steps closer to the bed. "We're going to be careful," he says. His hands fall to my hips and pull me against him.

"Just lay with me," I say, but I can barely convince myself. His lips look so edible and his scent is dizzyingly masculine. *We're here. Alone. With a bed.*

Like a magnetic certainty, our lips come together in a kiss so hot, my yoga pants ignite. I dig my fingertips into his back, hungry for more. He kisses his way to my neck, his rough scruff scratching my skin, ending with a soft bite above my collar bone that sends chills down my spine.

His every sensation and thought permeates my mind, raw and wild. I'm drunk with it.

I pull at fabric and buttons, anxious to explore him, yet he halts my roaming hands more than once. He wants to take his time. While we kiss, his hands move slow and deliberate over my curves, heating my flesh. This is new terrain for me. Nothing like my past experiences, rushed and selfish.

This is intimate.

His thoughts reveal the extent of his feelings for me. It melts my heart, but I can't help thinking I've robbed him of the opportunity to tell me how he feels on *his* terms. I'm weighted with guilt for not being truthful about arcing. I will tell him. But not tonight.

Baron stops and looks at me, brows crushed together with concern. "Are you okay?"

"Fine," I lie. I know I'm shaking. I felt the storm brewing in my aura, but I hoped I could fly under the radar and be okay.

"We should chill." He glances above me. "Those aren't good colors, Devi."

I'm so damn sick of energy being in control. "No. I'm good, I promise." I lace a hand behind his head and pull his face to mine in another ravenous kiss. He doesn't resist, but his doubts trickle into my thoughts. He feels responsible for me and is trying to be careful. I feel protected. Cherished, even.

But I don't want to be careful.

The thundering energy entwined with arousal and sentiment makes it difficult to think straight. Every nerve ending is frayed and humming like a live wire. I burrow my hand under his shirt and feel his hard chest and six-pack. *Lord help me.*

He breaks our kiss and checks my aura. "You're red." His arms drop to his sides. With reluctance, I do the same. We stand inches apart, eyes locked, breath heavy with want. My heart hammers in my chest and throat. The air between us is alive. Electric.

At last, my energy calms. He cups my face and kisses me again, slow, sensual. I don't fight the pace this time. *Slow is good*, I remind myself. We have all night.

Bending slightly, he wraps his arms around me and then straightens, lifting me with him. I pull my legs up and around his waist, snug. His simmering eyes bore into mine, pinning me to this moment. He turns to the bed, his hand supporting my back as he lowers me to the sheets.

PAIN.

Shocking, excruciating pain explodes across my chest as I'm hit with a force so titanic, I'm knocked backward onto the bed, taking Baron with me. I clutch my stomach, gasping for the air that's been slugged right out of my lungs.

Slowly the pressure eases and I realize Baron is next to me, brushing my hair from my face, panicking.

That was beyond anything I've ever experienced, beyond cosmic energy. That was pure kinetic force.

"Devi, are you okay?" he asks, more urgent this time.

"I think so." I inhale deep and touch my chest. It hurts *bad*.

His head collapses forward with relief.

Tears fill my eyes. "What the fuck?"

"You're okay. You're okay," he soothes.

I wipe my eyes with the back of my hand, exhaling slowly. "My energy didn't do this. What just happened?"

Baron shakes his head. "I think we just saw your limit."

"What?"

"The energy. It gets blocked and starts to back up, distressing your aura. Clearly, there's a limit to how much you can tolerate before you blow. That arc of energy could've just as easily hit me."

"That's just fucking great," I say.

Baron puts his hand over my chest where I've been hit. "Whatever came at you, I heard it."

"You did?"

"It sounded like a fastball whistling past me and smacking into a glove. Are you sure you don't have a cracked rib?"

"I don't know. I've never had one."

"Can you take a deep breath?"

I try. "It hurts, but I can do it."

"Good, then I don't think anything's cracked. Let me see where you were hit."

I sit up and pull down the neck of my T-shirt, revealing an explosion of black, blue and red covering my entire chest, from the top of my breasts to my collar bone.

"Jesus," I say, awed. "I look like I've been tie-dyed."

He runs his fingers softly over the bruising and then leans in, leaving a trail of feathery kisses across my angry skin.

"Is this how you run your practice?"

"Most definitely," he says in a near-whisper.

"If you don't stop that, I'm gonna get hit with another fastball," I moan.

He lifts his head, eyes serious, and lays his hand flat over my bruised skin again, pushing slightly, urging me to lie back down. "Stay still for a minute. Take slow breaths."

"What are you doing?"

"Shhhh." Concentration relaxes his face as he closes his eyes. His palm feels cool. He holds it there another ten seconds or so and then lifts it, hovering just over my skin.

Warmth spreads over my chest like melted wax. What feels like a full minute goes by before he presses his palm against my skin again, holding it there another minute. I wait, taking slow breaths as instructed. He lifts his hand and opens his eyes. I inspect his work. My skin looks less irritated and the edges of the bruising have begun to yellow, the black nearly gone.

"Damn, that's insane," I say, and grin a little despite the severity of the situation.

"Better?" he asks.

I nod.

"Good." He kisses the top of my head and sits up.

"Are you leaving?"

"No. I don't want to leave you alone." He reaches for the hotel alarm clock. "We should try to sleep. I'll set the alarm."

"You better set four alarms. If Nodin catches you here, we're screwed."

Baron smiles while fidgeting with the buttons, then announces he has set it for five. He turns out the light and crawls into bed.

"Think you can keep your hands off me?" I joke as he lies next to me.

"If it means keeping you safe, yes."

I snuggle next to him, my head on that perfect nook, just under the shoulder where his arm meets his chest. "How do you do that? The healing thing?"

"Well," he says, "you have seven energy areas of your body, called chakras. You've heard of those, right?"

"Yeah, but I don't know exactly what they are."

He strokes my shoulder while he talks. "They're the seven energy centers starting at the base of your spine and ending at the top of the head, the crown. They're responsible for everything. All organ functions, your mental abilities, emotions and intuitions." The rumbles of his voice against my cheek soothe me.

"Anyway, it gets complicated and probably boring," he says, "but essentially, when the energy wheels are harmoniously working, so are you. When they're blocked or disrupted, you'll start to see breakdowns in your system, depending on which center is most affected." He pauses. "Are you sure you want to hear this?"

"Yes, I promise. It's interesting," I say, and mean it. "So, how do you help people whose chakras aren't in balance?"

"I manipulate the frequency, altering the flow of energy, speeding it, heating it or whatever, depending on the outcome I want. When there's a physical injury, a minor one like yours, I can do the same thing to get blood flow to the area which speeds the healing process. Does that make any sense?"

"That's some crazy shit, dude."

He chuckles. "This coming from someone who channels life energy through trees. Yeah."

We lie there in silence a few minutes. "Baron?"

"Mmm?"

"What are we gonna do? Seriously." I reach for his hand, twining my fingers with his. "There was no warning. No way to know that was coming at me."

"Next time could be worse than bruising." His chest rises with a deep inhale. "No more playing around."

I squeeze my eyes shut. "For how long?"

"I don't know," he says, in a way I take as indefinitely.

I wince from head to toe.

"Remember what I told you before?" he asks. "About how we're being led by something bigger than us?"

I nod.

"You have to trust that." He tilts my chin up and looks into my eyes. "You *have* to."

I decide to believe him. It's the only way to keep my sanity.

What feels like a blink later, the alarm buzzes. We stretch like sleepy cubs, winding into each other.

"I don't want you to go," I whisper against Baron's neck.

He squeezes me tight. "I don't either. But if we fall back asleep, we're toast."

"You're right." I sit up and stretch my arms over my head. "Ouch!" I flinch, pulling my hands down over my chest. "I forgot."

"You okay?" he asks, inspecting the bruise.

"Yeah, it's just sore." And then something occurs to me. "Hey, can't you do your healing thing with tattoos?"

"I can, but I won't. I feel like the pain and healing process are part of the ritual. I know it probably sounds weird—"

"No. I get it."

He does one more healing session on my bruise before leaving. We embrace at the door like we'll never see each other again, even though it'll only be a few hours.

After he leaves, I inspect my chest in the bathroom mirror and my mouth falls open when I see nothing but a little red skin.

I yawn and my eyes water. I'm exhausted. It wasn't easy to sleep while in bed next to Baron.

I try to go back to sleep, but I can't stop thinking about what happened. I reflect on my old tree in Odessa, then slip out of bed, dig the hematite skull from my suitcase and crawl back in the sheets. I'm asleep in minutes.

15
SIBLING RIVALRY

Nodin calls at seven to make sure I'm awake. My body sags with fatigue. I could sleep another eight hours.

I meet him in the lobby with all my things at ten past eight. He tells me I look like hell. I tell him to piss off.

We decide to eat breakfast at the nearest IHOP before picking up Baron for a final round of practice.

Nodin orders coffee, eggs and pancakes. I order orange juice and an English muffin. The waitress brings his coffee, steam rising off the surface. He takes a sip. "Ben called me this morning."

Terror grips me. *How strong is Ben's connection with me?* "What did he have to say?"

"He won't be able to meet us today."

Relief loosens its death grip on my spine. "How come?"

"It's just bad timing for him. He's got karate tournaments all weekend."

I nod. The waitress brings my orange juice and English muffin.

"But…"

I glance up at him. He's had his eyes on me way too long. My whole body is mummified in dread.

"He'll be able to make it to Odessa next week with Baron."

I exhale. "Good. I'm glad." I sip my orange juice. "Anything else?"

Nodin shakes his head and inspects the food the waitress just delivered. "Nope. Nothing." He takes a bite of pancakes and stares at me with an indifference that's unsettling as hell.

Fuck. They know.

We arrive at Baron's for practice. My stomach is in knots, not only because it's my last day with Baron, but because of Nodin's behavior. I don't know what's worse, the fact that I'm pretty sure he knows I got hurt last night by doing exactly what we were told not to, or the fact that he's not bitching me out.

We switch to the Jeep so Baron can drive. As usual, I reach from the backseat and place my hand on Baron to ease the energy, but this time there's more to that agenda. I have to try and read Nodin. I need to see what he knows.

I arc when our skin meets. Images and feelings flood my mind, but they're all Baron's. I mentally reach for Nodin but all I'm sensing is an overwhelming calm and strange visuals. I glance at him; he appears asleep. "Nodin," I say softly.

He doesn't respond.

I give up and decide to dip back into the luxurious warmth of Baron's thoughts. Nodin sleeps until Baron parks at the trailhead. This isn't like Nodin. I'm unnerved.

We pass the stream and go to the tree I used the day before. I lay my hand against the bark.

I'm at the naming ceremony again, sending the scary man uneasy glances. The woman squeezes me and tousles my hair, whispers something in my ear. This time, I hear it.

"Tanda ny, mi sita, Tanda ny."

I know this is supposed to comfort me, but I don't relax.

The speaking man stands and silence sweeps over the group. He looks at me. The woman nudges me to stand. I don't.

The speaking man bellows, "Manda."

I stand.

He points his stick at me and says my name.

I look at the scary man. He's staring at me, nodding, smiling.

Commotion. Shouting. Panic. The scary man moves

toward us. I scream. I'm shoved in the dark arms of an-
other woman.

The scary man reaches for the brown woman. She
clutches him as they scramble away. I'm pulled backward
toward shelter. The brown woman and I stare at each oth-
er as we get pulled further and further apart. I scream to
her, "Nami!"

The woman I'm now with is screeching Nodin's name.
I look up at her. She's just a girl, dark like the others. The
paint around her eye is bright orange and yellow. She
reaches her hand out to her left. I look.

It's a little boy covered in a hooded robe, white hair
peeking out. A young Nodin. The skin on his hands and
face are black as night.

I blink back to awareness and Nodin's face is above mine.

"I can't believe it," I say.

"What is it? What did you see?"

I lift my head to check on Baron and see him up the trail,
working with my energy. Nodin helps me sit up while I tell
him about the vision.

"Black skin?" he confirms.

I nod.

"What on Earth..."

"I don't know."

"I must have been painted. But you weren't, right?"

"I see my own skin in the vision. There's no paint."

"And you saw me covered except my hands and face, just
like the creepy dude, right?"

"Yes."

"Devi." Nodin grabs my wrists, eyes wide. "Remember
your theory we could be Maz-Tabari half-breeds?"

The hair on my neck stands on end. I know what he's about
to say.

"What if the scary guy is albino and he and I were
painted? They could've been hiding us for some reason."
He jumps up and starts pacing. "This has to be it. We were

being concealed. Why? You said his eyes were scary. Be more specific."

"They glowed. They were white, in a weird way."

He snaps his fingers. "Of course. You were practically a baby then. Nothing looked right. You didn't recognize him so he scared you. His eyes, they probably looked white next to the black paint."

A wave of heat washes over us. We look over at Baron. He's shrinking the energy. We watch him as he presses it to the size of a melon and launches it toward the sky. He leans over, hands on knees. Sweat drips off his nose and lands on pine needles.

We practice three more times. The same exact vision repeats for all three. The last time I channel, Baron takes more energy than ever before. Not just with me. More than ever in his life.

When I come back into awareness, he's shaping it. He swings his outreached arms around a ball of energy as tall as him, wrapping his arms over it and pressing down before doing the same to the sides. Over and over, he works it until it's the right size to hold in his hands. When it's condensed enough to throw, he pummels it into the air with a roar. Then he collapses on his back in the dirt, chest heaving.

Nodin brings him water. I wet a towel in the stream and give it to him. He lays the wet towel over his face, sneaking sips of water underneath until he's emptied the bottle. Only then does he sit up. His back is covered in dirt, leaves and pine needles. I use a dry towel to clean him off. His cheekbones look sunken in, tired.

"That's it for today," Nodin says.

I can barely keep my eyes open on the way back to Baron's apartment. He and Nodin discuss the new details of my vision while the even drones of their conversation lull me in and out of sleep. I keep my hand on Baron, but my intermittent dreams crosshatch with their thoughts, making a stew of strange and indiscernible images. Again, I'm left unsure what Nodin knows.

In Baron's parking lot, Nodin and I say our goodbyes. I hug Baron hard and tight, anxious to sense his thoughts as we touch…but there's nothing. No sentiments. No warmth. He seems completely unaffected.

It dawns on me then he had been acting removed all day. A burn swells in my gut, churning like an angry sea. I worry he is deliberately detaching from me to make it easier to stay apart until this is all over. I try and get a look in his eyes, but they never meet mine.

Nodin and I depart. He squirms as my anguished emotions saturate him, but I don't have a shred left of me to care. For two hours, I stew in anxiety, repeatedly checking my phone for a text from him.

"Are you hungry?" Nodin asks, nudging me awake.

I realize I had fallen asleep at some point. "Sort of."

"Let's eat."

I close my eyes. "Mmkay."

He nudges me again. "Baron called while you slept. He finally heard from Hahn."

I bolt upright. "What?"

"I thought that might get your attention," he says in the tone that often accompanies an eye roll. "Come on. I'll tell you inside."

We walk in the diner and get seated right away by an older lady with a high bun of dyed red hair. She smacks her gum and says, "Ya'll have a nice lunch."

I slide into my side of the booth. "How much farther until we're home?"

"About two hours."

"Jesus. This road trip never ends."

"I can't imagine how tough it must be for you to get so much sleep."

This time I see the accompanying eye roll.

"Sorry," I apologize. "I guess it was all the channeling we did earlier. Must have wiped me out."

"Yes. All the channeling."

We trade glares.

Nodin's sarcasm isn't lost on me, but I ignore it. "Are you gonna tell me what Baron said?"

"Hahn heard from the archaeologist, Jim Mealy, the one studying the Tabari. Turns out he befriended a young Tabari boy by trading trinkets and candy for tribe knowledge."

"That's amazing. Can we talk to him? We have to find out what he knows."

"The only thing Hahn told Mealy is Baron had a vision in which Amair is spoken. Mealy wants to talk to Baron badly, but not over the phone. He wants to meet with him."

"Meet with Baron?" I almost shout.

He puts his finger to his lips and shushes me. "He'll be in Mexico for an archaeology conference in Oaxaca soon. The conference lasts three days and then he'll be in New Mexico for two days. He wants to meet with Baron then."

"Why does he need to meet him in person?"

"He says he has information for him."

"Mealy knows something. This is huge. When exactly is this meeting supposed to take place?"

"In December. Saturday, the seventeenth."

"That's right around the corner. Baron will go, won't he?"

"Of course."

"Then so am I."

He scowls. "No you're not."

"I have to go. There are things we need to find out for ourselves that only one of us will understand. I can't pass up what might be our only chance to talk to this guy."

"If you ask questions, you'll reveal too much. Remember, Mealy only knows about Baron's vision. We don't know anything about this guy or his motives."

"Okay, then I won't say a word. Baron can say he's bringing me because I'm his..." I hesitate.

"Girlfriend?" Nodin says coldly.

I match his tone. "Someone should be there with Baron. We don't know what this guy wants."

"Then I'll go." His face is hard with determination.

"Oh, that's brilliant. Send the albino."

I've hit below the belt. His icy glare cuts me in half, but I stare back. The waitress brings our food. Neither of us looks away. We're at a stand-off in the middle of a burger joint in the middle of nowhere.

My internal debate reaches the conclusion I need to face him head on. I lean in, eyes squinted. "I know you know," I say, just above a whisper.

His brows twitch. "Do you?"

"If I told you we learned our lesson and plan to obey the rules from here on out, will you drop it?"

He looks away first, brows furrowed. "I can't believe you'd risk everything like that. Do you realize how bad you could've been hurt?" He leans forward, almost growling. "Do you understand the gravity of this?"

"Yes. Do you? Do you know how difficult this must be for us? If you'd ever get a girlfriend, you'd understand."

Anger flashes in his eyes, but then I see hurt, and I feel bad for being so vicious. "Nodin, you really shouldn't be so self-conscious. It's not near as noticeable as you think," I say, and I mean it.

His face hardens for a second, but long enough for me to detect sadness. "It's more complicated than that." He clears his throat and his eyes meet mine again, the sadness replaced with resolve. "Besides, we're not talking about me. This is about you and your colossal screw up."

"It won't happen again," I say with sincerity.

He picks up his burger and adds in a snotty tone, "You're right. It won't."

"I said I'm sorry."

"Did you? I think I missed that part."

"Don't be such a dick."

He smirks and winks at me, and I somehow restrain myself from lunging across the table and scratching his eyeballs out. We finish our food in silence, pay the tab and leave.

The remaining two hours feel like ten. Nodin drops me off at home. We don't speak. He's not done punishing me.

Baron doesn't call tonight. He *always* calls.

I'm crushed.

As the sun set one day and threw pink across the sky
I saw an old oak tree standing alone in a field.
It looked so bold and ominous as the
Sunset's colors lit it from behind.

I couldn't help but stare and I listened,
I felt it was trying to tell me something.
It drew me to it and I wanted to connect
Something was so familiar about my new friend.

An image suddenly struck me:
An old Blues singer in a bar.
He sings of his past, woes and lost loves
With such stories he could share.

The way he sits in the corner playing his guitar,
Eyes closed, lost in his lyrics.
He rocks to the beat of the music
Lights cast a blue veil over his weathered face.

He is a presence in this bar that is necessary,
Without him it would feel incomplete.
Yet he's noticed only in passing…
Except for a few die-hard fans.

His old fingers bent to the shape of his guitar
Veins roping under aged skin.
Wrinkles reveal his many years
And add character to his face.

To me the old oak is like the Blues singer:
Barely noticed by anyone.
A presence both subtle and profound,
Content in its anonymity.

The tree rocks with the flow of wind
And reaches to soak up the sun
Poignant and sad at the same time
With such stories it could tell.

Just like the singer, without the tree
Things would feel incomplete,
Although it's hardly ever given a second glance…
Except for a few die-hard fans.

—DEVI

16
TREE OF LIFE

Tuesday morning, I awake to my cell ringing. I see it's Baron and angels sing. I haven't spoken to him since we were in Oklahoma two days ago, and I've barely slept or eaten a thing since the diner on Sunday.

"Hello?"

"I had a new one."

"A new what?"

"A new vision. Last night."

"Oh wow, that's right. The elephant completed the tree. What is it?" It's so good to hear his voice I could cry.

"A jaguar. I watch it run through the forest at night. It has these yellowish, glowing eyes. It runs for a while and then just stops, panting in the moonlight."

"Then what?"

"Nothing."

"Weird."

"My thoughts exactly."

"Do you know anything about it yet?" I ask.

"Just off a quick Internet search, I found the Mayans regarded jaguars as sacred animals, specifically their connection to the spirit world."

"Wow. Cool. Does Nodin know any of this yet?"

"No. I called you first. Can you call Nodin?" he asks. "I'm about to go climbing. I'll be gone all morning."

He's so impersonal. So...not Baron. "Sure. I'll call him right now."

He thanks me and hangs up.

Why does he think it's necessary to disconnect to this extreme? It's not helping us. I stand and pace, getting increasingly upset as I try to pinpoint when I first noticed it. He was fine Sunday morning when we met at his apartment, but by the time we got—

Realization stabs me in the heart and twists it. How could I be so fucking blind?

Nodin.

He wasn't sleeping in the car yesterday. He was meditating. He was influencing Baron's feelings.

How could he? How *dare* he.

I grab my phone and dial his number, but there's no answer. Feeling murderous, I throw on clothes, brush my teeth and march out the door. I'm fuming and headed straight to Nodin's, but as soon as I get in the truck, my phone rings. It's Ben.

Goddamn psychics. I answer and snarl expletives into the phone, lashing out at him for tattling to Nodin.

"I made him do it," he yells, interrupting my rant.

"What?"

"Nodin didn't want to mess with Baron's feelings. I had to talk him into it. If you're going to attack someone, it should be the right person."

"Why do you know every move I make? And why are you watching me with Baron? What are you, some kind of perv?"

"It's not voluntary, trust me. I don't like it any more than you," he says.

"Have you always been privy to my entire life?"

Ben sighs. "No. Not like this. But I've never had to get all up in your biz and block you either."

I sigh. "If you know what happened Saturday night, then you know it scared the crap out of us. This is cruel and unnecessary, Ben." I fight hard to conceal the fact that I'm about to angry-cry.

"I believe you two have the intention to stop, but I don't think for a second you're capable. Not unless I make sure of it."

I grit my teeth. "Tell him to undo it. Now."

"The most important thing should be the research and the work. Nothing else matters."

"What the hell do you care? You're not even a part of this," I say.

Ben's voice goes up two octaves. "I'm not a part of it? I'm killing myself every day to keep you blocked. No one else can do that for you. But by all means, if you'd prefer to be vulnerable, I'll leave you be."

I exhale, feeling defeated. "No. I wouldn't prefer that. I need you. But you can't take Baron from me, Ben. You can't. It's killing me. It's like a part of me is missing and not in a cheesy Lifetime movie way, but like there's actually a part of me not functioning because you've blocked something integral to the energy. I can't feel him anymore and I'm going to fucking—"

"Promise me you'll focus on what's important," he says, cutting me off.

"I promise. I swear to you nothing like this will happen again. But I need him back. Please talk to Nodin."

"I'll talk to him," he says. "Now please eat something."

"Jesus, do you even know when I shit and shower?"

"Uh, no. Thank God."

"Finally some good news," I say with a sarcastic bite. I notice my green notebook on the passenger seat of the truck and remember what Nodin heard from Baron. "Hey, did you know about Hahn's friend getting info from the Tabari kid?"

"Yeah, Nodin told me. Pretty crazy that he wants to talk to Baron in person. When is that happening?"

"The seventeenth, after some conference in Oaxaca, Mealy is travelling to New Mexico. He wants to meet Baron there."

"Oaxaca? Isn't that where your dad was that year I visited during Thanksgiving?"

"You're right. No wonder it sounded familiar to me." *Maybe Dad knows Mealy.* "I need you to do one more thing, Ben."

"What is it?"

"I'm too irritated with Nodin to hear his voice right now. I need you to call him and tell him something important. Baron had a new vision. Tell him it's a jaguar." I hang up and lean against the truck. Nodin can't influence people's feelings unless he is with them, but the alteration sticks until Nodin changes it back. Baron won't be back in Odessa until the weekend. It's going to be a long week.

Sometimes it really sucks to have protective brothers.

The only way to make this week go faster is by distracting myself. I look up my dad in my phone and give him a call as I walk back into the house.

"Hello?"

"Hey, Dad."

"Hi, Devi. Is everything okay?"

"Yeah, I just have a question. You have a minute?" I grab my books for class.

"Of course. What's up?"

"You've been to Oaxaca before, right?" I can tell he's in his car. As usual, NPR is on in the background.

"Yes, several times. Why?"

"Is there an archaeological conference going on there in the next couple weeks?"

"Uh...not in Oaxaca. It hasn't been there in a few years. Why on earth are you asking?"

"It's a long story. It has to do with this guy I'm sorta seeing." I knew this would run him off. It's one of those moves I don't use often. "I don't want to get into the details—"

"I don't need to know anything. Do I know him?"

"It doesn't matter."

"You're right. Let's just move on."

"Can I ask you something else?"

"Of course." He's flustered and distracted—just where I wanted him.

"What do you know about the Maz tribe?"

"The Maz? Devi, how do you know about the Maz?"

"I told you, it—"

"A boy, okay." He sighs and then clears his throat. "What do you want to know? Is this boyfriend of yours studying them or something?"

"Sort of."

"Why don't you just tell him to come by my office?"

I huff. "I thought it would be cool if I could tell him some stuff." There's a long silence. "Please, Dad?" I picture him throwing out comments about his nonexistent gun collection or his nonexistent black belt in karate during all his classes, in hopes of scaring the bejesus out of any guy who could potentially be my new boyfriend.

His sigh is heavy and exaggerated. "All right. What do you want to know?"

"Tell me about them."

"Let's see. They're a tribe in the mountain region of southern Mexico several hours outside of Oaxaca. Probably the most interesting thing about them is that they're all albino."

"How is that even possible?"

"Well, according to Maz legend, the albinism started when a priest named Pechocha was asked by the gods to plant a seed that grew to be what is now the largest tree in the world, El Arbol del Tule. When Pechocha returned from planting the seed, his hair and skin were white as snow because the gods had blessed him. The Maz consider him the father of their tribe. Buuuuut, if you're asking me biologically how that happens, well, you'll have to ask a geneticist because I can't begin to explain it." He pauses. "Did I lose you, Dev?"

"No, no, this is great. Is the giant tree really there?"

"Oh yeah. It's more than a thousand years old and massive. I have photos of it."

"So you've been?"

"Sure I have. It's in Santa Maria del Tule just outside of Oaxaca. Been twice actually. Next time you come to the house remind me to show you the photos."

"Why was he asked to plant the seed? What's so special about the tree?"

"It's known as the tree of life. You can see images of animals in its trunk and branches." I can tell by the rhythm in his voice he's walking now.

Tree of life. I touch the charm from Joe on my bracelet. "Can you really see them?"

"Absolutely. It's kind of like seeing images in clouds, you know, but it's in the twisted branches and bark in this case. I'll show you in the photos. Dev, I'm at my office and class starts in fifteen minutes. Gotta run."

"Wait, Dad, one more quick thing. Do you know of the Tabari tribe?"

"Oh my. The Tabari. I haven't seen anything in the database about them in ages. They're completely misanthropic."

"English please."

"Oh, uh, they're aggressive toward outsiders. Unapproachable. I think we gave up on them years ago."

"Are they friends with the Maz tribe?" I ask.

"Oh, gosh no. They're not friends with anyone. Dev, I have class in a few minutes. I'm so–"

"No it's okay. That's all I wanted. Thanks, Dad. Bye."

For some reason Jim Mealy lied about going to a conference in Oaxaca. Dad doesn't know much about the Tabari, not even that they're connected with the Maz. But Hahn knew, which means the information Hahn's getting from his colleagues isn't being shared on the archeological database.

I know from my dad's work that all research is meticulously detailed on this database daily. It's an international open line of communication. So why does my dad know nothing about the Tabari, but everything about the Maz?

17
ROOTS

I walk to economics after finishing my five-hour shift at the book store. I'm early for class, so I take a seat and flip to the back of my notebook and take out a folded piece of paper.

At work, I looked up El Arbor Del Tule and printed some information. I skim the first page, then turn to the second, stopping to study the animals visible in its bark: jaguar, bear, buck, serpent, buffalo and elephant.

Baron's animal visions.

After an eye-gougingly long class, I walk to my car and my phone buzzes. It's a text from Baron, six words that change everything.

I gasp and almost stumble while trying to process what I'm reading. *Oh my God.*

I have to find Nodin. He is in the arch labs on Tuesdays and Thursdays.

Nodin looks up from a microscope as I burst through the swinging doors.

"What are you doing here?" he asks.

"I need to talk to you, it's important," I whisper.

He looks around then motions for me to follow him. We go out the back door to an outdoor atrium. He turns to me abruptly. "I don't want to argue here. Ben already spo—"

"I'm not here about that. I have information. Big information." I hand him my phone, the text already memorized.

Heard from Hahn. Nami means mother.

Nodin's hand goes to his mouth and he sits down hard on a bench. "So if she's our mother," he says, "then she died after—or on—the night of your naming ceremony. But before we were put up for adoption."

I nod. "And I don't think much time elapsed between those two events, based on our age at adoption and how old we seem in my dream."

"I agree. But what now? What does it mean?"

"Well, for starters, it looks like our hunch is correct. We're a Maz-Tabari mix. I'm thinking I know who our father is."

"The painted man," he says with a nod. "It must be him because he's sitting next to you and…our mother. But still, why were we in Africa?"

"And why was a dead Tabari woman able to carry the status of a Mahtembo shaman?"

Nodin rubbed his eyes and exhaled. "You'd think getting information would enlighten us, but it just gets more confusing."

"Wait," I say, as something occurs to me. "I talked to Dad earlier, and—"

"Yeah, he's been snooping around asking who you're dating."

I shake my head. "I had to tell him something to justify why I was asking about tribes and stuff. Anyway, Dad said there is no conference in Oaxaca this year, so Jim Mealy is lying about that. But he also told me the Maz are just outside of Oaxaca. Do you think he could really be going there?"

He runs his fingers through his goatee. "I guess, but why lie about it?"

I consider this. Something's nagging me. "Well, we can presume he knows a lot about them since the Maz and Tabari have several hundred years of history attempting to breed together."

"So…"

"So, why lie about the conference unless you're hiding something? What if he secretly meets with the Maz? Nodin, Dad didn't know anything about the Tabari. Not even their link to the Maz. Whatever Mealy is learning, he's keeping it a secret from the whole archaeology community. He hasn't told anyone except Hahn, and that's only when Hahn told him about Baron's vision in Amair. Don't you think that's suspicious?"

He nods. "Absolutely."

"Mealy knows something big." I tell him what I learned from Dad about the Maz tribe, Pechocha and the tree of life, and then I tell him about the animals in the tree being the same as Baron's tattoos.

"You can't be serious," he says.

I hand him the printed pages. "See for yourself."

Nodin takes it all in and stares at me.

"What?" I ask.

"I changed my mind. I think you should go with Baron to meet Mealy. We can't take any chances. He shouldn't be alone."

I exhale, relieved. "Okay. Good."

"I assume you're coming over Friday night when Baron and Ben arrive?"

"Of course."

"Good. I'm going to try something that'll help us and keep all this information straight."

I hesitate a second, peering up at him. "Are you going to do something else when they get in town, too?"

His brows rise. "Oh that. Yeah. I'll take care of that." He squints at me. "You're going to avoid getting your chest bashed in from now on?"

I put up two fingers. "Scout's honor."

"I think that's supposed to be three fingers."

I change it to one finger and flip him the bird.

Friday evening I turn the doorknob to Nodin's apartment and the hum encapsulates me. I enter, wincing against the pounding energy. I say hi to the three of them, who are standing with their backs to me, facing the family room wall. They return my greeting, but their eyes don't leave the wall. I follow their gaze and see what Nodin's been up to since we last spoke on Tuesday.

"The Wall of Knowledge," he says with pride. "Like they do on detective shows."

I set my backpack down and walk over. "Wow."

He cleared an entire wall space and filled it with all we know so far. A printed photo from the Mahtembo Wiki site, as well as a bullet-point list of what we know about them. A huge map of South Africa hangs to the left of that, marking the locations of both the adoption agency in Johannesburg and the Buddhist temple in Bronkhorstspruit.

The right side of the wall displays sketches of each of Baron's symbols, along with any information he told us about them. I glance at Baron. On the top of his left forearm is a tell-tale bandage.

I also notice he hasn't looked at me, so Nodin hasn't reversed the coercion yet. The energy whipping around us is violent. I ache to touch him and ease it, but I'm hesitant. It feels awkward now.

"When did you get the jaguar tatted?" I ask him.

His eyes never leave the wall. "Two days ago."

To the left of the section with Baron's tattoos are bullet points of my visions, specifying the most important details of each. In the middle of the wall is a map of Mexico and Central America, marking Honduras, and a spot near Oaxaca where we guessed the Maz tribe lives. Another list has everything we know about each tribe. Right in front of our faces are three enormous print outs of El Arbor Del Tule. The tree of life, from three different vantage points, with red circles indicating the areas where animals can be seen.

On the adjacent wall, Nodin has hung a large whiteboard, complete with dry eraser markers on its ledge.

"What's this for?" I ask Nodin.

"Connections, which we'll start here in a minute."

"You look like hell," Ben says, eyeballing me.

Baron glances at me and I feel myself blush. "What? Shut up. I do not."

"Yes, you do," Nodin says. "You look like you've just returned from the show *Survivor*. Aren't you eating?"

I give a big exhale and glare at Nodin. "It's been a rough week, which you were supposed to *already have fixed.*"

He crosses his arms and darts his eyes at Baron to make sure he's not looking, and then mouths to me, "They just got here."

"Look here," Baron says, interrupting us. He glances at Nodin. "You might want to write this down."

Nodin goes to the white board and readies himself with a marker. We end up with:

> *Number 7: EVERYWHERE. Tattoos, visions*
> *Elephants: tattoo, visions, tree of life, Mahtembo*
> *Tree/life animals same as Baron's tattoos*
> *Trees: Devi's tree, Tree/Life, tree tattoo*

We sit and stare at the wall, taking in the enormity, having absolutely no idea what it all means. We're close, though. We know it and we're just waiting for the puzzle pieces to fall into place.

I glance at Nodin. He looks asleep. I grin because I know he's not.

18
Saturday, December 17

It's cold out. Not chilly. Cold. The sun is just rising.

Baron and I exit the Bronco where Nodin and Ben are slumped in the backseat, hiding. Mist still hangs in the surrounding trees. Since we couldn't have left any earlier due to finals, and we had to wait for the Okie boys to meet us in Odessa, we travelled all night to get here: El Santuario de Chamayo, an old church in the mountains of New Mexico, at precisely the place and time Dr. Mealy requested.

Why here? At a church in the middle of Nowhere, New Mexico? I have no idea. We only know what we learned about this place online: it's an old, sacred church thought to have healing powers in its soil. People come here in droves from all over to be cured of diseases and crippling injuries.

The simple, rustic mission sits behind courtyards of bountiful gardens. Its terracotta walls glow earthy orange in the sun's morning rays. Paths wind around sitting areas for meditation and prayer. Fragrant scents of innumerable blooms dance under my nose. But the most present thing is the solitude. It's strange how silence can sometimes be the most striking thing about a place.

We've been told to enter the church and wait for Mealy. I keep stifling yawns—not just because I spent all night being one of four drivers to another state. I yawn when I'm nervous.

And right now, I couldn't be more nervous.

"Let's go inside," Baron says. The heavy wooden doors groan as he pulls them open and we enter. They shut behind us with a thud.

The sanctuary is small, the only light coming from its candlelit altar. A large statue of Jesus stands in the entrance to our right, his wrists wrapped in rope, painted blood dripping down his hands and fingers.

Once at the altar, we notice a doorway to our left. We walk through it and enter another room with walls covered in religious art and crosses, so luminous with colors and textures it feels like the inside of a treasure chest. Crutches and canes are scattered along the walls, presumably abandoned, no longer needed after their owners were healed. Located at the front of this room is a low doorway that leads to another tiny, bare room with nothing on the dirt floor aside from a hole.

A sign hangs on the wall. I read aloud: "If you are a stranger, if you are weary from the struggles in life, whether you have a handicap, whether you have a broken heart, follow the long mountain road, find a home in Chimayó."

"This must be the soil believed to have healing powers," Baron says, reaching down to grab a handful. He lets it sift slowly through his fingertips back into the hole.

"It's a magical place, isn't it?" says a voice from behind me.

I gasp and leap to Baron, a scream catching in my throat.

The man puts his palms out. "Oh, I'm sorry. I didn't mean to startle you." He extends a hand. "I'm Jim Mealy."

We shake and I introduce myself as Mandi, as we had planned. Mealy's hair is a fit of dark, unruly waves that frame a round, bearded face and kind brown eyes. I estimate him in his mid-forties, although I'm notoriously bad at guessing.

An Indiana Jones style satchel hangs off his shoulder. He's wearing mustard yellow corduroys, a New York Yankees T-shirt and tennis shoes. Although his eyes dart back and forth between us, he's specifically interested in Baron, staring with a reverence like he's just met Al Pacino or something.

Mealy snaps out of it and gestures for us to follow him back to the sanctuary, but not before he takes a small bag from his pocket and fills it with soil, saying with a wink, "Powerful bartering tool."

We follow him back through the rooms and down the hall, our footsteps echoing throughout the chambers. Once back in the sanctuary, we sit on the first wooden pew, with Baron between Mealy and me.

Mealy places the satchel in his lap, candles flickering

shadows across his face. "Do you know why you're here?" he asks Baron.

"Hahn said you have information for me regarding the vision I had in the Tabari language."

Mealy smiles and nods, running his hands over the satchel. "Yes. Yes, I do." He pauses, gazing at Baron with intensity. "I presume it's safe to say you've had more than this one vision?"

Baron hesitates, then confirms with a nod.

Mealy seems satisfied with this, almost giddy. His eyes are bugging a little as he takes in Baron anew. "I thought as much. Yes." He clears his throat. "And you're sure you want your friend present?"

"Like I explained, I wouldn't have come without her. I trust her implicitly."

"And I trust you, my friend. I trust you." Mealy takes a deep inhale and lets it out slow. "I've been able to befriend a Tabari *Reywas*, or errand runner, who the tribe periodically sends to nearby towns for goods. It's taken me years to earn this boy's trust. They would surely kill him if he's caught. He has shared things I could never know otherwise about their culture and history, and there's a large part of their history I believe pertains to you."

His palm caresses the satchel in small circles. "The details of the Tabari history are in here, which I'll be handing over to you. But first I must tell you a story. A Mesoamerican legend. One as deeply rooted in their history as any story in the Bible is to Christians. It's called the Order of Seven."

Baron nods.

"Hundreds of thousands of years ago, the Earth's population was already a substantial presence and growing exponentially. The gods saw this as a time to choose stewards of the planet. These stewards would lead by example and teach others how to take care of Earth, all its creatures, and each other. They would each possess a higher consciousness, thereby being man's direct line to the spirit world. A council of the gods was held and it was decided seven of these stewards would be chosen from around the world. They would be called runes."

I try not to react, but I'm pretty sure my mouth is hanging open. I lean back, concealing myself behind Baron with a death grip on his arm. *I'm not the only one.* The room is spinning. I'm trying to keep myself steady, but inside I'm hyperventilating.

"To commemorate the choosing of the runes, the gods put seven stars in the sky in the shape of a powerful warrior to symbolize their leadership and protection of Earth." He leans slightly forward, as if telling us a secret. "You might be familiar with this cluster of stars; we call it Orion."

Mealy relaxes against the pew and continues. "In exchange for protecting the land, the gods would warn them of impending natural disaster. The runes, who each possessed abilities like no other human, would determine which and how many runes would be needed to decelerate or stop the natural disaster. This plan is called the Order. If it's a super virus, it might take two runes. If it's a volcano, it might take six." He holds up a finger. "But there's a caveat: if humans were not taking care of the Earth and its inhabitants, the gods would cease to warn the runes of natural disasters, which would result in tragedy and mass loss of life." He pauses. "With me still?"

"Let me get this straight," Baron says. "If humans are acting like a cancer to Earth, the gods let natural disaster wreak havoc, decreasing population. But if humans are in harmony with Earth and all its inhabitants, the gods protect us?"

Mealy nods and Baron's inner struggle whispers amongst my thoughts. He's always thought of the concept of god as energy, an energy that doesn't have intelligence. Maybe it moves like a river in that there are ways it naturally behaves, but it's not making decisions. But the Order implies thinking, reasoning energy with intent, which contradicts everything Baron believes.

"Shall I continue?" Mealy asks, seeing Baron lost in thought.

I think we nod back to him. Or maybe Baron does, and I just stare straight ahead like a zombie.

"Upon the death of a rune, the responsibility would be

handed down to his eldest child. If the rune was childless, the gods would choose the replacement. Which is exactly what happened about two thousand years ago, when a Mesoamerican priest of the God of Wind volunteered to replace a deceased, childless rune. This priest's name was Pechocha and to test his faithfulness, the God of Wind asked him to journey far and plant a seed of a tree in a specific valley in Mexico. Pechocha did and the God of Wind blessed him for his deed, which turned him white from head to toe, as well as all his children and their children for generations to come. As the tree grew, its mighty branches formed the likeness of each rune's spirit animal." He leans forward. "The tree still stands and can be seen today."

He's talking about the Maz. I release my death grip from Baron's arm. My body is stiff with shock. Candles cast ominous oblong shadows on the walls. The room seems cavernous and eerie.

Mealy leans forward again. "If the relevance of this legend doesn't make much sense to you now—" he pauses and gives Baron a knowing look while patting the satchel, "don't worry. It will." He glances at his watch. "There'll be a service here in an hour. People will be arriving soon."

Mealy stands and so do we. His hand glides inside his satchel and retrieves a leather-bound journal which he hands to Baron. "This was my life's work, but it is clearly yours now."

Baron takes it, and I see it's difficult for Mealy to release, but he does. Baron thanks him.

Mealy puts a hand on Baron's shoulder, still awestruck. "Be safe in your journeys, sir," he says, and watches as we leave.

About halfway down the aisle, Baron turns back to him. "One question."

Mealy's brows rise.

"Why have me come all the way here? You could've easily told me the legend on the phone and shipped the journal to me."

A smile plumps his cheeks. "I would never trust any shipping service with *that*. I'd have sooner shipped my first born."

He pauses, his face growing dead serious. "Plus, bringing you here had the added bonus of meeting one in person."

"One what?" Baron almost whispers.

I'm holding his hand so tight, I can feel sweat trickling between our palms.

"A rune," Mealy says with the slightest bow. "The one who unites the rest of them."

The air seems to suck out of the room, leaving a silence so loud it's screaming.

We burst through the heavy wooden doors, squinting against the bright sunshine.

Baron shoves the journal at my stomach and I take it. He's walking briskly, and I struggle to keep up. I settle on a jog to keep pace, stealing glances at his grave face. "Baron," I whisper-shout. "Slow down. What's going on? Do you think he's right? Do you think you're a rune? Talk to me."

He whirls around, runs a hand through his hair, his eyes darting, desperate, before settling on me. "The vision I started having after the jaguar, the one Hahn had to help me with..."

"The one you saw and heard at the same time, with the weird symbols for letters? What about it?"

"It's a Sanskrit language that originated a long time ago, like B.C. long ago. Hahn had to make some calls and research ancient texts, but he's pretty sure he got an accurate translation." He pulls up his shirt and reveals symbols inked vertically along the right side of his torso, still fresh with scabbing and redness.

Baron recites the translation: "The Seer Of Seven Will Come To Know And Bring Them Together To Save Our Souls."

I shudder. "Holy fuckballs, Baron. That's..."

"Ominous," he says, which is the exact word I'm thinking but don't want to say out loud. He lets his shirt drop and puts his hands on my shoulders. "Devi, Mealy said I'm the rune that unites the rest of them, and look." He pulls his shirt up again, this time showing the seven Mayan pictographs on his other side. "In the middle of the other six earth symbols, the symbol for unite."

My hand goes over my mouth.

Baron continues. "How much do you want to bet the earth symbols correlate in some way with each of the runes. And my visions—all the animals on the tree of life—they're the rune's spirit animals. He's right, Devi. Mealy is right." His arms fall to his sides. "I'm the seer of seven."

I feel like I can't get enough air in my lungs and I need to sit, now. Baron puts his arm around my shoulders and holds me tight while we power-walk to the Bronco.

Nodin and Ben are waiting, wide-eyed and eager to find out how the meeting went. Baron opens the back passenger door next to Ben and says, "You drive."

Nodin shuffles up to shotgun and Baron and I climb in the back. A common sense of urgency seems to be among us, although in reality we've nowhere to be. We don't say a word, but drive as fast as we can back down the winding mountain road in silence, our ears popping with the descent.

Then Nodin and Ben are talking at the same time, asking about the journal I'm still clutching to my chest and what happened inside with Mealy. When Baron is done filling them in, Ben is so overwhelmed he has to pull over.

We're silent, eyes darting around the car at each other. Nodin and Ben's mouths are gaping. Nodin throws open the car door and begins to pace outside. I know he's absorbing too much from us and is trying to get his emotions under control. I can't imagine what it must be like, feeling what I'm feeling times four. I would die.

It takes about five minutes for Nodin to return to the car. He looks sickly pale, which I take as a good sign because that's how he always looks.

"Let's go," he says to Ben, then looks back at me clutching the journal and says, "Read."

19
The Power of Lore

I slowly turn the journal over in my hands. Thin, leather strips bind it closed. I unravel the strips and open it to see the entire journal is in Mealy's handwriting. It appears generally easy to read, although filled with scribbly side notes and addendums, one of which is on the inside cover:

The following information was collected from both the Tabari and Maz tribes of South and Central Mexico between the years of 2004–2010. I use their words as much as possible, but explanations are provided in some instances. -J.M.

I turn to the beginning, titled in Mealy's blocky handwriting: *THE WAR.* I clear my throat and begin to read aloud.

"More than five hundred years ago, the Tabari tribe was forced north from Peru in search of water. Severe drought had turned their once lush, forested homeland into an arid desert littered with dead trees. Combined with Spaniard invasion, this caused much stress on the leaders of the tribe, which in turn caused panic and dissent among its members. The tribe subsequently split and mostly immersed among other populations in Columbia, Venezuela and Central America, except for one large group that stayed united and still exists in a remote jungle region of Honduras, where they've lived for more than two hundred years."

I turn the page and see he's pasted a map of South and Central America with red circles on the tribe's beginning and ending locations in both Peru and Honduras, respectively. I pass the journal around for the others to see and then continue reading.

"Since the beginning of their existence, the Tabari have relied on spiritual leaders known as runes—"

As soon as I get to that word, my mouth is sucked dry of all its saliva. The journal falls in my lap and I watch as Baron takes it from me.

"Spiritual leaders known as runes," he says, "are born each generation kissed by the gods, white head to toe. However, after the earlier dissipation of the tribe, the birth of runes ceased. This is a devastating blow to the Tabari, whose entire existence is defined by being one of seven rune tribes, as outlined in the Order of Seven. The Tabari believe the white skin is inherent to runes.

"In a desperate effort to reestablish a rune, the Tabari sought the aid of an entirely albino tribe, the Maz of southern Mexico, who are renowned for the ancient priest, Pechocha, who planted the rune Tree in Tule, Mexico, known as El Arbor Del Tule, or commonly, the tree of life. In this tree, the likenesses of the rune's spirit animals are depicted amongst its branches.

"The two tribes met periodically for nearly a century, producing countless children who weren't runes, which the Tabari consider useless half-breeds and abandoned until about fifty years ago, when the Maz chief put a stop to it. He ordered all half-breeds to be released to the Maz after that. See attachment." Baron flips through pages, locating the attachment.

"Oh, wow. This is a population graph for Honduras, ranging from the years eighteen-forty-eight to nineteen-fifty-two. The population goes up by point two percent during this time, but not from native citizens. It says they're orphans living in foster care or being contracted to adoption agencies in neighboring countries."

Nodin looks at me like he's trying to tell me something, but I don't understand.

"Train and Emilet." He looks out the window.

I suck in air, eyes bulging. "What?"

"I always knew they were related to us, but I never fully understood how." He pauses. "Now I do."

"But they lived in America."

149

"It says the orphans were sometimes contracted to neighboring countries' adoption markets," Baron says.

"We ended up here, didn't we?" Nodin points out. "Their biological parents are our ancestors. Train and Emilet were a Maz and Tabari mix, just like us." He rubs his temples. "They were lucky, to start. They got an American family. If only it'd been a decade later..."

I shake my head. "I can't even..."

"Me neither," Nodin says and resumes staring out the window.

"Do you want me to keep reading?" Baron asks quietly.

"Yes," we answer in unison.

"In approximately nineteen-eighty-nine, a Maz male is sent to Tabari land to breed with a Tabari woman. They fall in love, which was forbidden, but probably not the first occurrence. To escape persecution from her tribe the woman flees to the Maz tribe, where they discover the mating attempt worked and she's pregnant. She gives birth nine months later to not one, but two infants. A boy and a girl, who they realize quickly are both runes.

"The Tabari find out about the rune births and want what they believe is rightfully theirs. They're desperate to maintain their status as a rune tribe. But the Maz see it differently. It is not a disagreement or a struggle or conflict. It's straight up war. The Tabari attempt to hunt the runes down and take them. Battles ensue, lives are lost. The tribes' animosity toward each other grows more vicious by the day. When the Maz realize the Tabari will never stop, they move their runes—" Baron hesitates. "Guys? What year did you say you were born?"

A current in the Bronco is electrifying my nerve endings. Or maybe it's just me completely, totally, unequivocally Freaking My Shit.

"Ninety-one and ninety-two," Nodin says. "But it's not for sure. It's an estimate because..."

The magnitude sits heavy in the air on us, on my lungs screaming for air. *Where's the oxygen in this fucking truck?*

Nodin is a rune and we're twins. I'm not eighteen. I'm nineteen, at least.

My eyes catch his and all we can do is stare at each other, reeling, processing, and grappling this new reality. Nodin slumps over and a noise comes from him that sounds like an injured animal. "Pull over," he says in a strangled voice.

Ben does and Nodin piles out onto the side of the road and vomits, our cumulative emotions overcoming him.

Baron's hand is on my arm and he's asking if I'm okay. He looks blurry to me, and then I realize my eyes are wet with tears. I tell him I'm okay in a voice I barely recognize, but I'm lying. I don't know what I am, but it's not okay. It's stunned and confused and overwhelmed all at once.

Nodin gets back in the Bronco. We resume the drive in an eerie silence only utter shock can produce.

20
ANSWERS

We watch the sun get higher as we trade the mountain's narrow roads for the wide highways back to Odessa. We've been up all night and should be collapsing, but adrenaline and shock work like speed in our systems.

"There's more," Baron says, opening the journal and looking at me.

I nod for him to read.

"There's a side note from Mealy that says the following info comes from the Maz chief, Danook." He gets water from the cooler we packed, takes a sip and reads.

"The runes and their parents are moved to another rune tribe far away. A guide is chosen by the Maz to protect the runes and lead them on their journey; however, he is less of an escort and more of a sentinel whose life calling is to be a Lyriad. Lyriads have experience with travel and culture that other tribe members don't. Danook refuses to reveal where the runes were moved, but he does tell me they're with the only tribe equipped with a mystic, which will aid in their desire to stay apprised of Tabari movement."

"Africa," I say. "We were moved to the Mahtembo tribe because of their shaman." The others nod, slow and robotic.

Baron continues reading in a quiet voice, as if afraid we might shatter.

"The Tabari are fierce in their resolve and continue to hunt the runes across oceans and continents to this day. They have hired bounty hunters and used mystics and have located them once, but were unsuccessful in retrieving the runes."

"That's it," I say. "That's why I couldn't know anything about my ability. Their mystic would have detected me. It's me. Don't you see? Nodin and I, we're half-breeds, which means we're runes to both tribes. He's more Maz, which makes sense since he got more of the albino gene than I did. Their mystic can't find him, or at least not as easily. I'm more Tabari. I'm their rune. They're looking for me because they can detect me."

"She's right," Nodin says.

There's a few beats of silence before Baron continues reading where he left off.

"The Tabari wait for a sign that the seer of seven has received a warning and the runes are being summoned for the Order, which takes place in one of seven preordained sites. I have determined those locations based on Danook's detailed descriptions and his knowledge of approximate geographical locations, although he does point out that the locations are not static and have changed many times over the centuries. Pictured below."

Baron stops reading and I glance at him. He's looking at whatever's pictured on the following pages and murmuring indiscernibly. He hands the journal to me and says, "Get a load of the locations."

I flip through the pages. Each has a title and accompanying photo. What I see floors me to my seat with the force of a wrecking ball:

Stonehenge, Southern England
Nazca Lines, Southern Peru
Wurdi Youang, Australia
Wonderboom, South Africa
Chaco Canyon, United States
Sanchi Stupa, India
Arkaim, Russia

I hand the journal to Nodin who studies it then chuckles, then bursts into giggles, and then comes completely unglued in a fit of hysterical-tears-down-cheeks laughter.

These sites are archaeological mysteries that have left thousands of baffled scientists in their wake, scientists who spent their careers trying to figure out how humans could have possibly built these incredible monuments. And that's just the thing. Regular humans didn't build them. Runes did, for the Order of Seven.

"When do we know what the warning is?" I ask. "How do we know how many of us it'll take to stop it, or which site we need to go to?"

Baron's expression changes, a mixture of realization and terror. Nodin's laughter fades when we all realize the same thing at the same time. The answer has been right under our noses all along.

Seven.

Whatever the impending threat is, it's so catastrophic it will take all seven of us to stop it.

"This is it. It's beginning," Baron says.

"How do we know where to find the other runes? How will they know what the threat is or where to go?" Nodin asks.

"The answers are all over me," Baron says, his voice low. "The other symbols. All of them coincide with the same regions as the rune sites for the Order." He looks out the window, lost for a moment in deep thought. "It all connects. The jaguar is Mesoamerican, which we now know connects with our Maz rune, Nodin, plus I had two Mayan visions. The Tomoe symbol I have is Buddhist in origin, specifically India. The Tobono and elephant are African."

"What about the bear?" I ask.

"Russia. My ancestors on my father's side are Russian and the bear is steeped in their culture and history," he says. "The serpent correlates with the Australian site." He looks at me. "Your name, I mean, hell, if that's not a connection to Peru, I don't know what is. And when I researched the buck, I found English and Welsh connections."

His palm pats his chest. "The sun and white buffalo hoof, those are Native American. It's all right here. Always was."

"So what now? What's the next step?" Ben asks.

"We need to search the unknown runes' geographical locations," Baron says. "We look for the symbols or animals rep-

154

resented in a specific civilization or tribe. We narrow it down. We find them. And we wait for the Order."

As we drive back, I realize we need a shit-ton more room for The Wall of Knowledge.

21
THE SUMMONS

I awake on Nodin's couch Sunday morning, the remnants of a strange, vivid dream still clouding my mind. Sunlight streams through the shades, throwing horizontal stripes across the room.

I hear heavy, sleepy breathing. On the floor just below me, Ben is asleep. It was nice of him to let me have the couch. I watch him for a couple minutes. His tan, bare shoulders peek out above the thin cover, his hair a sleepy mess. He looks so sweet. I sort of want to kiss him on the cheek and mess up his hair some more, but I don't.

As I return from the restroom, I notice the door to the second bedroom is open. My parents had high hopes Nodin would get a roommate, clearly underestimating his aversion to people.

I peer inside. The sheets are rumpled on Baron's bed, but it's empty. I check the living room floor, thinking I must have walked right past him, but then I see him through the window. He's outside, leaning against the half-wall that frames the entranceway.

I watch him through the window, watch the way his shirt falls into that valley between his shoulder blades, the way he stands, the way his eyes watch the sunrise, and the swell of love in my chest turns me inside-out.

I open the door quietly and join him, snuggling close. It's cold and he puts his arm around me and I lay my head against his shoulder. With the energy humming through us, we watch the sunrise together without a word.

After two minutes, or two hours, or twenty minutes, or a day, the sun is above the horizon and spilling pink clouds across the sky.

My voice breaks the silence. "I had the strangest dream

last night," I say, remembering. "There was a bear high on a hilltop calling for me, but I didn't know how to get to him. I kept trying different trails but they all led to dead ends and I'd have to start again. Then I heard the elephant thunder rumbling all around me and I knew where to go. It was so vivid. And so random. You think it-"

"It wasn't random," Baron says.

"Huh?"

"The summoning has begun." Baron's voice is monotone and his eyes don't leave the sky. "Last night while I slept, I dreamed I was on top of a mountain. I paced and growled and saw my massive paws on the rocky outcrop."

He runs a hand across his bear tattoo. "I call out to the white buffalo and the buck and the elephant and the jaguar and the snake. There are seven of us but only six spirit animals on the tree. Where's the seventh?" he muses, then continues, "I pace and pant until they are all with me on the mountain. The six of us walk to an enormous, towering tree and right then an incredible feeling washes over me I can only describe as power." He looks at me. "I woke up so covered in sweat, I had to rinse off in the shower."

I ponder the visions and the Tabari's trek north using the Nazca maps. North toward water and lush forests. I think of my tree and El Arbor del Tule and realization slams me in the throat.

"The seventh spirit animal isn't an animal at all," I say, running my hand over Baron's back and the tattoo covered there. "It's the tree itself. The tree is the seventh. The tree is me."

He nods and exhales, slow and deliberate. "Do you think Ben's one of us?" he asks.

I shrug. "There's only one way to find out."

We go back inside and Baron shuts the door hard, waking up Ben. He sits up, yawns and stretches.

"What are you guys doing?" he asks, rubbing his eyes.

"Did you have a strange dream last night?" I ask.

He shakes his head. "Nope. Slept like a baby."

Baron and I have our answer.

The door to Nodin's room creaks open and he walks into the living room, running his hand through his hair. "What's up?" he says. "I had the craziest dream last night."

"Will you grab another banana for me?" I ask Nodin as he refills his orange juice in the kitchen.

Now that the four of us are rested and fed, we plan to spend the morning adding the information from Mealy's journal to the Wall of Knowledge, and do some follow-up research. Baron and Ben are on the couch, hovering over the coffee table where the laptop sits.

"Let's look up the earth element symbols and see how they connect with runes," Baron says to Ben." Earth, air, wood, water, metal, and fire."

Nodin joins us, and I scoot across the floor so I can see the computer screen.

Ben types into the search bar and studies the images for earth elements. "Well, the only thing I can find is a link between the elements and astrological signs. We could try that."

"No, we can't," Nodin says. "Devi and I don't know our actual birthdates, remember?"

Ben rubs his chin, thinking. "Oh yeah. Hmm." His brows rise. "Let's try this." His fingers move fast over the keyboard. "Let's try name meanings. Your names are unusual." He glances at me and Nodin. "I'm curious where they come from."

"Good idea," I say.

"That's why we keep him around," Nodin jokes.

"Oh wow," Baron says. "Nodin is Mesoamerican in origin and means wind."

"That could coordinate with the air element," I say, and then remember. "Not only that, but wasn't it the God of Wind who had Pechocha plant the seed for El Arbor del Tule?"

"Yeah, that's right," Nodin says. "Look up Devi."

Ben does, and I read aloud, "Devi is Hindu in origin and means Goddess of Earth and life." I look at Baron. "Earth. Two down, four to go. We need the other rune's names to find a match for fire, metal, wood and water. That's the only way we'll know for sure."

Ben leans back against the couch. "What now?"

"The rune sites listed in the journal," Baron suggests.

Nodin walks to the dry erase board. "Start with Stonehenge."

We systematically go through each of the seven sites, recording their location, design, and archaeological speculation of why they were built onto the Wall of Knowledge, when I notice a reoccurring symbol.

"Look here," I point to the image on the screen of a stone carving in Chaco Canyon, New Mexico. "This spiral shape. I keep seeing that. It's at every site."

"Is it?" Ben asks, while pulling up the minimized pages for the other sites, one by one.

I sit up taller and reach for the screen. "See? Stonehenge is shaped like the spiral, and so is Arkaim."

"You're right," Baron confirms.

Nodin walks to us and peers at the laptop. "What about the others?"

"Wurdi Youang is shaped like a spiral," Ben reports. "And there are spiral carvings at the India site..." He searches another. "Wonderboom in Africa...." His fingers click across the keys. "Yep, even the Nazca Lines."

The screen reveals an enormous spiral carved into a mountain top in Peru, the same picture framed in my dad's office.

Nodin sits next to Baron. "Search spiral symbol."

Ben types "spiral symbol in archaeology" into the search bar.

We learn the spiral symbol is one of the oldest in history, with several meanings, including the cycle of life, growth and evolution, and the awareness of one's self within the whole, but the most compelling is the representation of the path of the heavenly bodies: the sun, moon, stars and planets. Because this symbol is inherent to archaeological sites, and all the sites were built to measure and map the heavenly bodies, it has become the parent symbol to represent ancient ruins, the structures built by runes for the gods to communicate the Order.

A variation of which is the Tomoe tattooed on Baron's left shoulder.

The spiral is the rune symbol.

On the Tuesday after our meeting with Mealy, I awake in my bed to tremors driving through the floor to my legs. It's the calling.

Twenty-five minutes later, I'm driving to Joe's house with an extra layer of clothes under my coat because it's going to be cold in the tree.

After Sunday and Monday's marathon training days, the Okie boys returned to their homes for Christmas with their families. After the holidays Nodin and I will make that god-awful drive again to Baron and reconvene practice.

Baron is getting stronger. He says he's taking four times the energy and throwing it ten times as far. But for what reason, we still don't know.

I park in front of the house. The tree's calling is gripping me in a vice.

Joe answers the door with a growling, snapping Assface tucked under his arm. He smiles wide and beckons me inside. We sit in his family room and I listen to him tell me about an ancient Pre-Clovis tool found in Colorado. He explains why this is significant with great excitement, his grey eyes gleaming.

I'm overwhelmed with gratitude for this man. If he hadn't bought this house and been the precise eccentric, odd, sweet man he is, I'm certain I'd be up shit creek. So despite the calling clamoring through my bones, I listen to him talk for nearly an hour and that, I find, is my limit today.

I go to my tree. The vision comes fast, urgent.

I'm in a field. It's night and the wind sashays the grass back and forth. The moon is full, illuminating the sky with soft light. Mountains stain the horizon with mounds of purple. Trees dapple our view. We wait. I tremble. I'm anxious, no—afraid. So afraid. I hear rumbling, but also feel it at the same time. It's in the air, in the ground, -in my head all at once. My eyes dart around, looking for a source. It's guttural. An animal. It's the elephant.

I peer toward the trees where I saw her before and she is there. I see her outline. She steps out and walks toward me. Her stature is so overwhelming, I fall to my knees.

"Nami," I whisper.

In my mind I hear her answer, "It is time. Come to me. It is time. Come to me. It is time. Come to me."

My eyes flutter open, my breathing erratic, and there is sweat on my brow despite the cold. I check the time: quarter past noon. I've been up here nearly two hours.

I stretch my stiff muscles and slowly climb down. Joe leads me through the house, wishing me a merry Christmas.

In my truck, I dial Nodin. "You got your wish. We're going to Africa."

That night, I'm lying in bed on the phone with Baron telling him about the vision, and generally freaking out about travelling to Africa.

"But what about the cost?" I ask. "And how do we know *when* to go? Are we talking two weeks from now... six months...a year? I mean, 'it is time' isn't specific enough."

"Devi. Breathe. Haven't we received everything else we need to know when we need to know it? We'll know that too. When it's time."

"What about vaccines? Holy shit. And passports. Do you have a passport?"

"Yeah, I had to get one when I went to Canada for a competition. And don't worry about vaccines. We're runes." He switches to a gravelly, Hispanic accent, "Vaccines? We don't need no stinking vaccines."

I laugh at his movie reference. "*Blazing Saddles*?"

"Nice. Not many people get my movie references."

"Are you kidding? Our parents are huge movie buffs. Nodin and I grew up watching movies with them."

We recite more lines and then we switch to *Three Amigos* references. We're laughing and then, out of nowhere, he says, "I miss you."

"Aw, you do?"

"Mmhmm. I miss your smile. I miss your scowl."

I laugh.

"I miss how your brows furrow when you're serious." He pauses and lowers his voice. "I miss how your hair always smells like cherries and vanilla. I miss your soft skin. I miss your kiss."

I'm straight up blushing now.

"I miss how delicious your lips are."

I'm squirming.

"I miss the little noises you make when I bite your neck."

Stomach clench. His words get sexier, dirtier, and then staggeringly naughty, and I'm so turned on, I'm writhing in the sheets.

I *need* to be with him.

But in the meantime, phone sex doesn't suck.

22

The Bringer of Dark and Light

It's two days before Christmas, which I guess makes it Christmas Eve Eve. My phone rings at exactly six-eighteen in the morning. The caller ID says unknown.

I hesitate but then answer. A man on the other line asks if I'm Devi Bennett.

"Who's asking?"

"My name is Levin and I'm calling on behalf of my sister, Mapiya."

I detect an accent but can't place it. "Okay. How can I help you?" I ask as I sit up and turn on a lamp.

He tells me to hold on, and then I hear the phone being handed to someone else. "Hello?" a girl's voice says.

"Yes?"

Like a faucet on high, she bursts. "Hello, my name is Mapiya and my grandfather said I need to find you because we're going somewhere and I need you to take me." She fills her lungs with air again and I'm waiting for her to elaborate, or tell me she's got the wrong number, when she adds, "I am Seven Rays."

That got my attention. "What did you say?"

"My name, it is Lakota for Seven Rays. I am the bringer of light and dark and I am to go with you, but I need you to come get me because I am eleven."

I stand. *Baron's sun tattoo.* "How did you...? Who told you? How do...?"

She giggles. "I have the owl eye and I saw a vision. You walk with Bear? Yes?" I assume she means Baron, so I tell her yes. "My grandfather, he tell me to find *Nah hi lita* and he tell me your English name, and my brother look you up. You are *Nah hi lita?*"

"I...uh... I don't know what that means," I confess.

"It means she walks shining under moon."

I sit down hard. That's what Baron said my name in Amair translated to in English. I can't talk or swallow, or form a thought.

"Devi Bennett?" she says.

"Yes. That's me. I'm *Nah hi lita*." I swallow hard. "Where are you?"

"My home is Kansas. My grandfather say it is time for you to come get me."

"Is your grandfather there? Can I talk to him?"

She giggles again. "My grandfather pass away many years ago. He walks with spirit now."

"Then how do...?"

Never mind, I think. I don't know why this stuff even surprises me anymore. Of course she talks to her dead grandfather.

"Mapiya, I don't know when we're leaving, but I don't think you can come with us. We're going somewhere far away. It'll be dangerous. I thi-"

"We go where they walk with elephants. I know. My grandfather tell me. It is okay, Devi Bennett. I am ready for this trip, but my father is afraid. He does not understand. I cannot tell him where we are going. But you can help."

"How? Do you want me to talk to him or something?"

"Grandfather says the answer is the wind. You will know what to do." She lowers her voice. "I have to go now. I will talk to you soon."

"Wait," I say, but it's too late.

That might be the most bizarre conversation I've ever been a part of, and that's saying a lot given recent events.

The answer is the wind.

I scroll through my contact list and am about to press *Nodin* when I remember his name means wind. Nodin is the answer. He must influence the feelings of Mapiya's father so she can be allowed to travel with us for the Order.

The day after Christmas I am awoken early again by my phone. At this hour I assume it's Mapiya, but the caller ID says Baron. I answer quickly.

"Good morning." He sounds sleepy, husky, and it warms me all over.

"Morning. To what do I owe the pleasure of such an early call?"

"A new vision. Have you noticed we're getting information faster?"

I freeze. "What is it?"

"It's weird is what it is. Mostly letters and numbers. Like a long license plate number...sort of."

"Have you had a chance to research it yet?"

"No." He yawns. "Just woke up and wrote it down so I wouldn't forget it."

I go to my computer and turn it on, grab a pencil and ask him to tell me.

"Okay, it's in three rows. The top row has the numbers zero-one-zero-seven-one-one. The second row has this little loopy symbol that I don't recognize, followed by capital C, capital M, little A. The third row has the number two-zero-zero-four, capital M, capital N and the number four."

"That's it?"

"That's it."

I do an Internet search for the first row of numbers and get a slew of random hits. The beginning of an overseas phone number, a gun registration number, a docket number from a legal defense case. None of them seem like sensible connections. I try the second row, but "loopy symbol" means nothing, so it's another fail. Then I enter the third row, *2004MN4*.

"Oh God, no," I cry.

"What is it?"

Horror fills me. "No, no, no. This can't be right. Please don't tell me this is right."

"*What?*"

With a shaky voice, I summarize the page. "Near-Earth Asteroid, Apophis, which indicates a possible collision with

Earth in two-thousand-nineteen. Its eight-year orbit around Earth travels on an arc that moves closer with each revolution. The next pass is expected in two-thousand-eleven. It's currently holding the record for the highest level on the Torino Impact Hazard Scale with a Level four. You have to be fucking kidding me." I have a sudden urge to upchuck all over my bed. "Baron?"

"I'm here," he says. "I'm here."

"Tell me we're not stopping a fucking asteroid, Baron."

"Hang on. I'm getting my laptop. I should be able to find that symbol in a word document."

I wait for him to turn on his computer. I hear keys clicking and intermittent sounds, then an audible, "Oh. My. God."

"What is it?"

"It's Alpha Canis Majoris."

"What is that?"

"That would be Sirius. The brightest star in the sky. And guess where it's located?"

I don't guess because I'm currently mute, so he just tells me.

"In perfect alignment with Orion. In fact, it's sometimes called Orion's dog." He pauses, reading. "Yeah, okay, this is starting to make sense. Orion's stars are used as navigational tools. They point to other locations in the sky."

"Which means what for us?"

"It means we just received our coordinates. This tells us exactly where Apophis will be in the sky. Now we just need to know when."

I stare at the first set of numbers and my bones go cold. "What if the first numbers are a date? What if it's January seventh, two thousand eleven?"

He pauses a beat. "The asteroid's orbit *is* closest to us again in two thousand eleven..."

"Less than two weeks away," I say, or maybe I just think it because there's a panic closing around my throat so tight I can't breathe. I hear a chime indicating another call. I check the number.

"Here we go," I murmur. "Baron, I'll call you back. It's Mapiya." I switch lines. "Hello?"

"Hello Devi. My father is here. You talk to him."

"Wait…what?" But it's too late. I hear shuffling and movement and then a man's voice.

"You need to speak to me?" His tone is gruff and impatient.

"Yes sir. I…um…I assume she told you we need her for a short time. It's very important."

"She told me, but I don't understand why she has to leave with you. She's only eleven. She's never been out of Kansas."

"I know, I know. It sounds crazy, but if we could just meet and talk it over I'm sure you'd understand. I'll come to you. Would you be willing to do that?"

There's a pause and I'm afraid I've lost him when he speaks. "If you can get here, you can say anything you want to me, but I'm not letting my little girl travel with you for any reason."

I hear a loud metal against metal plunk and then Mapiya is back on the phone.

"Devi?" she whispers.

"Mapiya, we'll need to leave very soon. Maybe even a few days."

"I know. You come here, three days. I will be ready." She rattles off an address which I scribble down. Before I can say anything else the phone goes dead.

One day God made the butterflies
To send a message our way
He sent them to whisper softly
That everything will be okay

Next He made streams, rivers and brooks
To coo comfort in our ears
And with that came affirmation
That He is with us through the years

Then God made the flowers
To send encouragement our way
He sent them to quietly tell us
That He believes in us every day

Using these things in nature
He sends a message to us all
With tiny whispers, subtle hints,
And barely audible calls.

With all these secret encouragements
God made to send love our way
Why did he still need to make the trees?
Because He wanted to shout it that day.

—DEVI

23

FRIGHT AND FLIGHT

*T*wo days after Christmas, the Okie boys are back. Ben drove this time, but he's going home tomorrow by himself. Baron is staying indefinitely.

"All right," Ben says, taking a credit card out of his wallet. "I think the best flight is Emirates Airlines on December thirtieth. Only two stops—a plane change in Dallas and a two-hour layover in Dubai—and it lands the next day in Johannesburg. Twenty-seven hours total. After fees and taxes, it'll be sixteen hundred and forty dollars per person, round trip."

"Thanks again for loaning us the money," Nodin says. "We'll pay you back ASAP."

"No worries. That's what an inheritance is for, right?" Ben grins, his eyes flitting up and down at Nodin's jeans and blue hoodie. "Hey, the Smurfs called. They want Papa back."

Nodin looks down. "What's wrong with this?"

Ben strokes a phantom beard on his chin and says, "It's just a lot of white cranium hair going on with a lot of blue."

Nodin stomps to his room and returns wearing a black, long-sleeved shirt while the rest of us suppress laughter.

"You're sure you're not coming with us?" I ask Ben. "I can't imagine you not a part of this anymore."

He shakes his head. "You're not doing anything without me. I'm still a part of it. I'm just not supposed to go."

"Book it," Nodin says," but on two separate flights. Put Mapiya and Devi on one, Baron and I on the other."

"What? Why?" I'm terrified of my first plane trip. I'd been counting on having Baron with me as support.

"I'm sorry, but the fact is we can't put you and Baron on a plane together," Nodin says. "We don't know what affect your energy reaction could have on the electrical system or the Doppler radar."

"He has a point," Baron agrees.

"Fuck," I say, putting my head in my hands. "So I'm flying to freakin' *Africa* with an eleven-year-old who's a stranger to me, who's probably never flown before either, by myself." A lump is forming in my throat. "Nodin," I plead.

"The only alternative is for Baron to fly alone," Nodin says.

"That's fine," Baron says. "I don't need the company. Nodin can go with you guys."

Nodin sighs. "Fine. Book it that way. As long as all four of us get there, that's all that matters."

My shoulders relax now that I know I've got someone with me who knows what they're doing. I look at Baron, mouthing my thanks.

"Are you guys ready to go through this?" Nodin asks, holding up his notebook. Using what we know about Baron's symbols, and the wonder that is the Internet, Ben and Baron have narrowed down the locations of the remaining rune tribes.

Ben plops on the couch with his notes and summarizes. "We started with Baron's thigh tat, the rainbow serpent of Australia. It varies a little throughout the country, but basically the serpent was believed by ancient Aborigines to be enormous. It lived in permanent water holes and created all the land features and protects the land, but also punished if people disrespected the land."

"That's a familiar theme," Nodin says.

We all nod.

Ben continues, "We found one particular clan, the Nhanda Balug, whose totem was a great serpent. I contacted the Australian Historical Society for information about clan ancestors. I'm hoping to hear back soon." He flips his paper over. "As far as the elephant rune tribe, which we all agree is the Mahtembo, we plan to call the Buddhist temple in hopes they have a way to communicate with them."

Nodin and I don't know if our father is still there, or if he's even in Africa, but the fact there's a remote possibility of re-uniting with him is so surreal and overwhelming, it's difficult for us to even discuss.

"Good job, Benstein," I say, smiling.

Ben tips an imaginary hat. "Thank you, Devs." He gestures to Baron. "Why don't you take the Brits."

Baron takes the notes from Ben. "Okay. For the white buck, we have the Drade tribe in Southern England and let me tell you, the Drades have their shit together. There's evidently a Neo-Dradonion movement among the Celts. They continue to gather for ceremonies and foster education of the tribe's beliefs, which date back to eleven hundred AD. They even have a website." He holds out his arm, showing his buck tattoo. "A white stag with enormous antlers is their tribal emblem, thought to link them with the spiritual realm."

"It should be easy to get in contact with them, yes?" Nodin says.

Baron nods, setting the notes on the coffee table. "There's an email and contact name on the website. Some guy named Aren. I sent an email this morning. We'll see what comes of it."

He heads for the kitchen and returns with a glass of water, standing behind me for a moment and resting his hand on my shoulder.

I arc and, as I've made a habit of doing, I take the opportunity to spy on the others, careful to keep my eyes averted from Ben.

A barrage of images and feelings reveal themselves, but what I see in Ben's mind startles me: a shadowy figure is watching me. I can't see facial features, but the person feels distinctly male. Ben senses him and is trying to find out who he is. The image is so unsettling, I disconnect with Baron and walk into the kitchen.

I want to ask Ben about it, but I assume he has a reason for not telling us. Maybe it's as simple as not wanting to alarm us.

Or maybe there's more.

My gut says to trust his judgment, so I keep my mouth shut. I try to imagine who could be watching me, think of the Tabari, and shudder.

24
Owls See All

It's December twenty-ninth. The plan is to meet Mapiya and her father at the address she gave me, which turns out to be an Exxon station not far from her home in Kansas.

It's early when Baron, Nodin and I leave for the long drive to pick her up. I'm nervous. I've never been responsible for a child before, never even babysat, and now I'm in charge of one throughout an epic undertaking. And yet, on some level, I know she will be equally in charge of me.

Through several phone conversations the past few days, we've learned how much she's aware of, which is a hell of a lot more than us. She knows the other runes also shared the dream of following the bear on the mountain, as well as another one that occurred two nights ago, when we dreamed of Africa. The seven runes walk up a hill, flanked by elephants, grit from the dusty air crunching in our teeth and the sun hot on our shoulders. At the top we saw two gargantuan boulders. The elephants trumpeted, trunks high in the air.

When Nodin, Baron and I researched the Wonderboom preserve, we learned of the Twin Altas, two ancient boulders believed to align with Sirius during certain times of the year.

I awoke from the latest dream just a couple hours ago. We dreamed of the skies. Low on the southern horizon, Orion and Sirius glowed bright against the dark backdrop of night. The moon was full and high, slightly to our left, its light pouring from above in a glowy haze. We know, up there, a terrible threat looms. And we know we're the ones who will stop it.

Once we're together in the car, we discuss the shared dream. Baron uses his cell phone to look up astronomical positions expected in the skies above Africa on January seventh. It doesn't surprise us to learn Orion and Sirius will be low in the south, and the moon will be full and high in the west. These last two dreams conveyed the where and when to all seven runes.

We arrive at the Exxon station around one in the afternoon. Mapiya and her father are already there, waiting in a bronze, four-door Buick LeSabre under the shade of a large tree, where they said they'd be.

We park next to them and get out of the Bronco. Her father gets out of the car and comes directly to me. He's wearing jeans, cowboy boots and a long-sleeve button-up shirt that's untucked. He has long, straight black hair that frames his tan, leathery face. He is not smiling.

"Devi?" he asks, his black, steely eyes boring into mine.

I swallow hard. "Yes." I shoot a nervous glance at Nodin that screams *hurry.*

"You have three minutes." He crosses his arms over his chest, mouth clamped shut.

I glance at Nodin again. His eyes are closed in deep concentration.

"I appreciate you meeting with me, sir," I say. "What I need to tell you is that this is of utmost importance. Mapiya is very special and we need her for an important job." I notice his features relax and eyes soften. "Her safety will be our top concern."

Before I can say anything else, his entire demeanor shifts from aggressive to friendly. He reaches over and puts a hand on my shoulder. "Her mother and I have known for a long time this is bigger than us. We can only trust what the gods have in store for her." He pauses, his voice cracking with emotion. "We know you will watch over her."

He seems like a completely different person. All the fear for his daughter, the protective aggression, the stiffness... gone.

"I promise you," I say, nodding. "We all will." I gesture to the guys.

His eyes flit to them briefly but come straight back to mine. Nodding once, he turns, dust kicking up under his boots as he walks to his car and opens Mapiya's door. At first it doesn't strike me as odd that he's leading her by the elbow.

Then I see her eyes void of color, white as milk. My mouth falls open. I know my reaction isn't appropriate, but I'm shocked. She looks past me, smiling.

"Mapiya, this is Devi," her father says, coaxing her hand out toward me.

I take her little pudgy hand in mine and shake. "Hi Mapiya. I'm so happy to finally meet you."

She's wearing jeans, purple converse shoes and a long-sleeve pink top with a silvery-maned unicorn on the front. Her long black hair is pulled back into a single braid. Precious, round cheeks frame her perpetual smile. She jerks her attention in Nodin's general direction, cocking her head. She faces her father and points.

"Sure," he says, leading her to Nodin and Baron, where introductions are made. Upon shaking hands with Baron, she smiles and says, "Bear."

Her father walks back to me while she animatedly talks with the guys. "She didn't tell you?" he asks.

I shake my head.

"She wasn't born that way," he says. "She lost her sight the day the white calf was born. Her mother says she gained sight in many other ways. Says she sees things others can't see. Things from the spirit world." He stares at her, lost in thought for a few seconds before his brows rise.

I watch him walk back to the car and return with a little blue suitcase, which he sets at my feet. He walks to Mapiya and hugs her hard, kissing her on both cheeks. As he departs, he glances back at me with tears in his eyes and says, "Return her safely."

We watch him drive away while exchanging relieved glances.

Nodin places a hand on Mapiya's shoulder. "Did you bring it?" he asks.

She grins and pulls a folded envelope out of her back pocket.

It's permission for her to travel out of the country without her parents, written and signed by her mother.

The drive back feels quicker, filled with excited conversation and a lot of laughter. Mapiya is full of life, completely uninhibited and joyous. I've never met anyone quite like her. Her enthusiasm is infectious—she has me laughing like I haven't since I was a kid.

She and Baron are fast friends, joking and exchanging good-natured banter, though she never once refers to him as Baron, only Bear. We talk about the flight and both Nodin and Baron answer her questions about flying. Soon the discussion turns to Africa.

"When we land," I say to Mapiya, "do we go straight to the rune site?" The site listed for the Order in Africa is Wonderboom, a preserve in Pretoria, which protects several ancient archaeological sites dating back to the Stone Age, as well as an enormous, two-thousand year old tree.

"No. First we go to Nan Hua Temple," she says.

Baron reminds me that it is the Buddhist temple in Bronkhorstspruit.

"Oh, okay. But why there?" I say.

"To meet the others," Mapiya says.

"But how do they know to be there?" Nodin says.

"They see the dreams. They know what we know," she says. "Keb made the plan."

"Keb?" Baron asks.

"The Mahtembo rune," she says.

"So we never needed to do all that research on their tribe ancestry to find them?" Baron says.

Mapiya's brow crinkles. "It is good. It will help you understand who they are."

I'm struck by her maturity. One minute, she's like a typical eleven-year-old, chomping gum and bubbling with giggles. The next, she's like a wise, old sage. "All the other runes will be at the temple?" I ask.

She grins wide. "All but one. We ask for Master Tran. He will take us to Keb."

My stomach churns. "*To?* We're going to the Mahtembo tribe?" My eyes meet Nodin's in the rearview mirror. Images of the Mahtembo women with their painted eyes and exposed breasts swirl through my mind, the drumbeat echoing in my bones. I think of our father, painted jet black, the only way I remember him.

"Yes. We stay with Keb until it is time," she says.

"But who is Master Tran and how does he know to expect us?"

She smiles so big, her eyes squish into crescents. "Master Tran is the head monk. Keb talked to him."

That is when it really sinks in: we were the only ones who didn't know we were runes. Like Mapiya, the rest had a parent or ancestor explaining who and what they were since childhood.

When Baron receives a warning vision, the others receive it, too. Without the seer of seven, there would be no sharing of information.

Baron looks up the meaning of the name Keb. It means earth.

If the name Devi isn't linked to the earth symbol, which of Baron's symbols is me?

We arrive in Odessa and it's late. Nodin and Baron drop Mapiya and me off at my house, where I help her get used to the blueprint of my room. I don't see any signs of Jamie Two, but I saw Chloe's car out front so I know Jamie One is home. Her bedroom door is shut.

Mapiya and I speak in whispers. She brushes her teeth and gets into pajamas. We call her father to let her know we arrived safe. They talk for a few minutes and the next time I check on her, she's sound asleep in my bed.

I check my luggage once more, making sure I haven't forgotten anything important. I packed mostly shorts, tanks, and T-shirts because it's going to be hot, but I also threw in two pair of jeans and a cardigan for cool nights. I pack two cinnamon tea bags which I have no intention of consuming. They will make everything in my bag smell like home. Like safety.

I scribble a note for the Jamies, telling them I'll be out of town for ten days. Nodin took care of our parents already. He went to their house for a little visit and told them we were going on a trip together, although he didn't tell them it was out of the country. While they asked questions, he influenced them. He made them indifferent to our whereabouts, and gave them an overall sense of contentment. They'll never be the wiser.

We leave in the morning for a nine-forty flight out of the Midland airport. Other than the quick change of planes in Dallas, we don't get off again until our layover in Dubai. Baron's flight leaves a little later than ours, so we won't see him until we're in Johannesburg. The anxiety I feel about the trip is so encompassing, I'm surprised it's not rattling the bed. I need a shot of tequila, or ten. Or better yet, Baron.

I feel the sensation of someone looming over me and warm fingertips press into my arm.

"Nah hi lita," Mapiya whispers. "You can rest. We will be okay." She puts her thumb against my forehead, just above the crease of my brows, and begins to whisper foreign words in a little song or prayer.

When she's done, I ask her what it means.

"It's a song my grandfather taught me. It asks the Universe for protection and guidance when you're old and young, through battle and bounty, and in return you will take care of the sacred ground."

I'm touched. "It's sweet. Thank you."

She lays her head back on the pillow next to mine. I close my eyes and sleep.

25
SOUTH AFRICA

"Do you want to know how they died?" Mapiya whispers after the stewardess gives us blankets.

"Who?" I ask.

She leans in closer, evading prying ears, although the least of her worries is Nodin, rows away at the back of the plane. Her white eyes settle just past me and she whispers, "Train and Emilet."

My tongue feels paralyzed and I can't wrap my brain around her words, yet I feel myself nodding. Even in the quiet of the plane, I have to strain to hear her.

"They called him Sir. He was strict. Yelled a lot. Not like the lady, who was nice to them, but he gave them food and a place to sleep. Sir told Emilet to come into his office. Said he had candy for her. So she went in." Mapiya is gripping my wrists, her face curled in a grimace. "He shut the door behind her. He tried to touch her in a bad way. She fought him and he got rough. She screamed."

Mapiya swallows hard, her eyes wandering and desperate. "Train heard her scream and went into the office. He saw Sir over her with his hand under her skirt. Train attacked him. They struggled, but Sir hit him so hard, Train flew backward and hit his head on the corner of the desk. He fell on the floor, limp like a doll. Blood came out of his nose. Emilet tried to run to Train, but Sir wouldn't let her go." Her face is red, tears welling in her eyes.

"I know, I know." I'm stroking both her hands, trying to console the horror she sees.

"Sir demanded she stop screaming, but she wouldn't. She couldn't. He wrapped his hands around her neck and choked her," she says. "He killed them both."

I squeeze my eyes shut and hold Mapiya's head to my shoulder.

No wonder Nodin never told anyone.

What feels like a gazillion hours later, we land in Johannesburg. I stand despite the protest of my stiff muscles and exit the plane with Mapiya behind me, holding my arm.

After reuniting with Nodin, the three of us get our luggage, secure our rental car and settle at an airport restaurant for our near two-hour wait for Baron. We realize it is New Year's Eve when TVs in the restaurant tune to countdown celebrations. It's ten p.m. Johannesburg time, two hours from the New Year.

At quarter to twelve, Baron's plane lands. I don't think I've ever been more relieved and elated than the moment he walked off that plane. He gets his luggage and while walking to get him something to eat, we hear cheering and clapping. Happy New Year.

We pass around celebratory fist bumps and keep moving, anxious to leave for Bronkhorstspruit. After roaming an ocean of rentals, we find ours, a Subaru Outback, and are greeted with a surprise. The steering wheel is on the right.

"Oh shit, I mean, shoot. Sorry, Mapiya," Nodin says. "They drive on the left side of the road here."

"We're all going to die," I say, setting my bag down to take my jacket off. It was chilly on the plane, but it's balmy and warm here in South Africa's summer.

Baron rolls his eyes and takes the keys from Nodin. "I'll drive," he says, handing Nodin a piece of paper with the temple's address. "You navigate."

This proves easy for Nodin. The Outback has a GPS. He plugs in the address and we follow directions to the highway.

I'm surprised Johannesburg is such a metropolis. I'm not sure what I expected, but definitely not the countless tall buildings emitting a sea of twinkling white lights, made more spectacular by the New Year's fireworks blazing across the sky. One blue-lit building towers over the rest, reminding me of photos I've seen of the Space Needle in Seattle. The major highway we're on intersects with several others as we wind past downtown.

It's a long, tense drive to the Nan Hua Temple, but we make it in a little less than two hours. It wasn't supposed to take that long, but with the winding, unfamiliar roads in the dark, we were lucky it didn't take longer. Baron did a great job driving on the left side of the road, but it was nerve-wracking.

When I see the grandeur of the temple, I gasp. This isn't some quaint little building. It's a compound with gracefully arched rooftops scooping up to meet tall peaks. We hoist our luggage over our shoulders. It's two thirty-six in the morning when we walk up the steps to its twelve-foot tall, ornate doors.

"Do we just walk in?" I whisper.

"Their website said they were open twenty-four hours a day, seven days a week. I checked," says Nodin.

Baron pulls one of the doors and it opens easily, spilling forth warm light from inside. "Let's go," he says.

Inside is an explosion of warm reds and golds. Enormous, intricately carved columns flank the entranceway and lead us into a large, oval room. Hallways shoot off from this main room like arms, two on each side. There is a shuffle of feet, and an Asian man appears from a hallway on the left.

"Good morning," he says in a low voice. He's wearing an orange robe, and looks exactly like every picture of the Dalai Lama I've seen. But bald, and with a rounder face.

"Good morning," we say, then Nodin steps forward. "I think someone is expecting us. We're supposed to ask for Master Tran."

He bows. "You have found him," he says with a little smile. "Follow me." He turns and walks to a different hallway on the right.

Baron hooks arms with Mapiya and we follow. The hallway is long and only lit by intermittent sconces hanging on the walls. Our footsteps echo tiny shuffles all around us. We arrive at a door, which Master Tran opens and gestures for us to go in. We enter the dimly lit room and see two guys sitting on mats. Their eyes light up when they see us and they jump to their feet.

"G'Day," the younger one says as he rushes to greet us.

He actually said G'Day. I'm dying.

"I'm Aadam. Good to meetcha." He points next to us, where two other bags are against the wall. "Setcha bags down." He looks like a surfer, with spikey blonde hair, blue eyes, freckles and classic beach clothes.

The taller one introduces himself. "Nice to meet you. I'm Aren." He's got a full beard, and his long, dark hair is pulled up into a bun. His dark brown, almond-shaped eyes exude kindness and warmth. I see that his left arm is completely sleeved in tribal tattoos. When he moves to shake hands with me, his eyes catch above my head and follow all around me, his mouth slightly open in surprise.

"I take it you work with energy, too," I say, smiling.

"It's impressive, isn't it?" Baron says to Aren.

"Can't say I've ever seen one quite like that," Aren says.

I silently applaud myself for understanding what sounded like *cahnt sigh I've evah seen wone qwaht layk thaht*. Most luscious accent, ever.

I lean closer to Baron and whisper, "Why are Aren and I not having an energy reaction like you and I have?"

"He must not be able to receive energy the way I can, so your energy isn't recognizing him."

The door shuts behind us and I see Master Tran has left us alone. "S-alright. He'll be back in the morning to take us to Keb," Aren says. "You can sleep if you want." He gestures to a stack of mats and folded blankets. "Restrooms are just outside on the left."

"How long have you guys been here?" I ask Aadam.

"I hopped a plane from Cape Town to Jo'Burg early this morning and waited for his flight to get in." Aadam gestures to Aren. "We got here together around six this afternoon."

"Cape Town?" Baron says. "Africa?"

"He goes to university there," Aren says. "He's doing his doctorate work in astrophysics."

I whip my head in Aadam's direction. "Doctorate work? But how old are you?"

Aadam blushes. "Fifteen. Don't worry. I get that look a lot."

So our Aussie rune lives in Africa and is some sort of boy-genius.

Baron and Aren are completely consumed in a conversation about energy and wander to the other side of the room. At this distance, our energy reaction is a mere annoying staccato. It's nice to be within sight of Baron, yet not inside the violent plasma globe.

I get a mat and blanket for myself and Mapiya and set them next to Aadam's. Nodin puts his mat next to mine. It's late and we should be exhausted from travelling, but the buzz of excitement is too much. We can't stop talking and getting to know each other.

Aadam is a catacomb of scientific knowledge. With his bubblegum face and Mapiya-like enthusiasm, he rambles like a professor, an astrophysics avalanche spilling out of his mouth.

I can picture him pushing dark-rimmed glasses up on his nose. His whole being strikes me as a contrast, and I'm sort of fascinated with him. He's only fifteen, yet has authored a book on antimatter—whatever the hell that is—which is evidently so groundbreaking, it's being used in universities.

Baron walks over and asks Mapiya if she'll speak to Aren about her ability. He leads her over to him and returns to us alone.

"Is Aren a shaper too?" I ask him.

"Aren," Baron says with awe, "is amazing. He is a shaper, but he doesn't have the ability to harness or pull energy from sources." He shoots me a glance in recognition of conversation regarding my lack of energy reaction with Aren. "He has to work with kinetic energy already in motion at the time he's using it, like wind. He can concentrate energy flux and control pulse lengths in a way that scientists know is possible—"

"On paper," Aadam says, interrupting. "But nothing's been designed yet to test it at the distances he can do it."

"I'm not sure I understand," I say.

"I don't have the ability to keep the energy I propel focused," Baron says. "Once it leaves my hands, it's out of my control. It loses its strength, scatters and reacts to the laws of velocity and momentum. In other words, it's like throwing a snowball. It doesn't matter that I can throw it with the velocity of a rocket. It's still a friggin' snowball. But Aren can focus that energy at massive megawatt pulses over infinite distances."

"And this is going to…?"

"Well," Aadam says, "basically it's goin' to send a focused mega-blast of energy into space and nudge an asteroid off its future collision course with Earth."

"Wait, if scientists already know about this asteroid, why can't they do something about it?"

"To construct a satellite to travel to this asteroid would be a tremendous feat. But then to ever-so-gently push it off its trajectory without bursting it into a thousand smaller rocks would take technology we don't have yet."

"I have another question," I say. "Why didn't we—" I gesture to those of us who flew in from the U.S, "—know any of this the last time there was a warning?"

Aadam grins. "Simple. There hasn't been a warning in nearly two hundred years."

"Two hundred years?" I almost shout. "What happened? Why did the warnings stop?"

He shrugs. "The gods were displeased. Humans weren't holding up their end of the deal."

"I bet that's the real reason the Tabari lost their rune," I say.

Nodin nods. "And now?" he asks Aadam.

"Now, evidently we're doing something right. At least enough to receive warnings again."

"So you've always known you are a rune," Nodin says to Aadam.

He nods and looks around the room. "Which is why those of us who weren't aware had to be…awakened, I guess is the best word."

"What was the last warning? What did the runes stop?" I ask.

Aadam's blue eyes sparkle. "I've heard this story from my grandpa my whole life. Four runes. It took four to turn what would've been a cataclysmic eruption into one that barely bothered nearby buffalo herds."

My eyes grew wide. "Which volcano?"

"More like supervolcano. The Yellowstone Caldera. Had it blown at full strength, it would've buried the surrounding states in three feet of ash and affected the weather for a decade. The loss of animal, plant and human life would've been catastrophic."

Aren returns with Mapiya and they sit on their mats with the rest of us.

"And exactly where does Keb fit in with the Order?" Nodin asks, scrubbing his fingers through his goatee.

"Keb is a channeler," Aren says.

"Like me?" I ask, sitting up straight. I'd do anything to meet another channeler.

"Keb channels seismic energy," Aren says. "Like from faults and tectonic movement. Organic Earth energy. Baron will take what the two of you channel, combine them into a single wavelength and propel it. I will keep it moving in a focused column."

"And Mapiya?" Nodin asks.

"She's going to alter the infrared waves so no one sees the enormous blazing light this will produce. If the blast isn't concealed, millions of people will witness it," Aren says.

"The bringer of light and dark," I say, and that reminds me of something.

I grab my iPhone from my bag and ask Aren and Aadam how their names are spelled, explaining Baron's earth symbol tattoos and how our names correspond. I find that Aadam's name means metal and Aren's means wood. We already know Mapiya is linked to the fire symbol since her name means Seven Rays Sun. That leaves water.

"How am I the water sign? The name Devi has nothing to do with water."

"What does your name mean?" Aadam asks.

"It's Hindu and means Goddess of Earth and life," I say.

Nodin nods, "Yeah, life. Devi, you channel life energy, and how is it able to travel to you?"

Water, I realize with a shiver.

"What about you?" Aadam asks Nodin. "What's your ability?"

"I'll make sure no one gets in our way," Nodin says. "I can manipulate people."

"He's already come in handy," Baron says. "He's the reason Mapiya is here."

I look around at all of us and am floored by what we'll be doing. The power in just one of us is astounding enough, but all of us together? Mind-boggling.

The six of us sit in the circle and talk for hours. Nodin and Mapiya nod off eventually, but the rest of us are up until the sunrise streams through windows.

"I don't mean to scare you, mate," Aadam says to Nodin, "but I've lived in South Africa long enough to know you have to be careful out here. Not so much in the cities, but when we get out into the bush, you need to cover yourself."

"What are you talking about?" Nodin asks.

"Witchcraft. Some indigenous peoples hunt albinos for their body parts. They think there's magic in them. They will straight up kill you."

Terror harpoons me from all directions. I look at Nodin and his posture changes, riddled with tension and fear.

"What about her? Is she in danger?" Baron asks, gesturing to me.

"No. They won't bother with yellow-hairs."

"Well, maybe we shouldn't go out there. Maybe we should stay in the city, or here," I say, panic rising in my throat.

"You are safe on Mahtembo land," Master Tran says.

I hadn't heard him enter the room.

"No need to worry as long as you stay with them." He pushes a cart in the room. "Breakfast. I will return for you in half an hour. Be ready to leave, please." He bows on his way out.

Starving, we quickly encircle the cart and find warm flat bread, a rice dish that resembles grits, dates, milk, tea and something that looks like creamed spinach. We eat, savoring the rich, earthy flavors. Afterward, we take turns in the restroom to freshen up, and change into fresh clothes. Knowing it'll be hot as hell and we're going somewhere with no air conditioning, I change into shorts and a tank top.

Not long after that, Master Tran enters with a smile. "Hello. I take you now. Bring your things."

We grab our bags and follow him into the entranceway where we were last night, but this time a hundred pairs of shoes line the walls. I can hear the monotone hum of a large amount of people chanting at once.

"Morning prayer," Master Tran says.

It's the most stilling, harmonious sound I've ever heard. I feel Baron sidle up next to me and lean his face near mine, a mischievous grin on his face.

He whispers, "Do I get a New Year's kiss?"

I smile. "Happy New Year," I say quietly, and peck him on the lips.

Master Tran leads us out the back door, where we descend another long set of stairs and follow along a paved walkway to a garage, which he opens to reveal a large, black SUV with tinted windows. He opens the back and we pile our bags inside, although some of us will have to carry smaller bags in our laps.

When we're all situated, Master Tran climbs in the driver's seat and we head down a long driveway that leads to a street and then a highway.

I'm sitting behind Aren and see he has a tattoo on the back of his neck. It's that symbol I always see on the signs of yoga studios. I come to the conclusion he's a yogi.

I watch out the window as the landscape blurs past. Larger, industrial buildings intermixed with primitive shacks. Signs with words in both a foreign language and English.

Wowza, I'm in Africa.

A large billboard approaches and its image catches my eye, instantly filling me with terror. The photo is of an albino woman with short, tight curls of reddish hair. She's crying and holding out the stump that's left of her arm. A black woman sits next to her, comforting her. The sign reads: *Every Human Deserves to Feel Safe.*

A muffled half-sob, half-whimper leaves my throat. Mapiya's tiny fingers press into my arm. She hums softy, and I recognize the tune of the prayer she sang to me the night before we left.

Master Tran looks at us in the rearview mirror. "It is okay," he says, reminding me of his words at the temple. "You are safe among the Mahtembo."

The others glance around in confusion, which reassures me that no one else noticed the sign. I'm sure as hell not going to tell Nodin about it. I force a laugh and say, "I must look as nervous as I feel."

I have no idea how long we've been driving, because I have zero cell reception and I chose not to wear my watch on the trip. We exit the highway and turn right on a wide, dirt road. Master Tran slows down and the SUV bounces around for a good twenty minutes before the road evens out.

We're in an area with more trees now and it gets denser the further we drive. I feel more vulnerable here, like albino hunters could jump out any minute and we'd be trapped. I'm incredibly nervous to meet the Mahtembo tribe and Keb, but even more than that, I wonder if I will know someone else in the tribe. Someone like…my father.

I wring my sweaty hands.

We take a left and travel another ten, fifteen minutes until the trees open up and I see miles of open grassland. We go up a big hill and when we come down, I see them: Mahtembo children, maybe thirty of them, jumping up and down and cheering. Both girls and boys are stark naked, skin black as night, with big smiles full of luminous white teeth.

"They very excited by visitors," Master Tran says with a grin. He turns right by a large boulder and travels slowly through the field to another group of trees, the children following. He parks and announces, "We're here."

Doors open and we pile out. We are instantly engulfed by a sea of curious children and barking dogs who jump up to greet us as heartily as the children.

I notice a few children glancing toward a group of trees, when a tower of a human steps out from the leafy camouflage. She looks like a statue chiseled out of polished obsidian. Her hair is cropped short. She wears a thin, red cloth around her chest and waist and her dark skin shines in the sun, accentuating her incredible physique.

"Keb," Master Tran says with a grin, walking toward the most intimidating woman I've ever seen.

26
FAMILY SECRETS

Master Tran beckons us over to Keb and we all introduce ourselves to the last rune. She's built like a basketball player with her chiseled features and broad, muscular shoulders, yet somehow retains femininity.

Despite the sense of authority and power that exudes from her, I'm put at ease by her friendly smile and warm handshake. She speaks English beautifully, in a smooth, velvety voice, though her thick accent chops words into concise blocks. I like how she pronounces our names "de-VEE" and "no-DEN."

Mapiya steps forward, her head turning to face all of us. "Lights," she says, then repeats it several times with a look of wonder on her face.

"What is it, Mapiya?" I ask.

"It's us." Baron makes a triangle shape, first to Keb, then me, then to himself. "Can't you feel it? There's an undercurrent."

When he says it, I do. The hum has intensified. It's like sitting in an idling monster truck.

Baron clarifies, "My energy is reacting to hers much like ours reacts. She's a channeler too."

Oh, special. A little energy threesome, I think. I know it's irrational and ridiculous, but I'm a tiny bit jealous. I don't like someone else having this connection with him, much less a striking woman like Keb.

Master Tran asks Aren and Baron to help him unload the luggage. The children grab what bags they can lift and begin walking toward the field beyond the trees. The dogs follow along, tails wagging.

Keb beckons us to follow. "Come. Your father waits to see you."

I freeze and grab Nodin's wrist. We look at each other in disbelief.

"I take you to him," Keb says.

With each step my heart beats harder and faster. I cling to Nodin, my breath coming in short bursts. I'm thankful Mapiya is led by Aadam, because I can hardly trust myself to walk at the moment.

The village comes into view, and I notice carvings and simple paintings of elephants on huts and tall poles scattered throughout, and the sights slam me with déjà vu. This isn't the scratch 'n sniff version of my memories that have teased me all these years. This is In Your Face, full infusion of stimuli that's both new and familiar.

The dust kicking up from our feet grits against my teeth. The smell of straw and herbs and dirt tumbles me down a rabbit hole to the past, where I'm just a toddler. The sounds of the children giggling and talking enthusiastically in their native tongue, a language I don't understand, speaks to me. The colors in the paintings and on the clothes and embellishments of the people are so vivid it hurts my eyes.

I'm home, I think, and that thought surprises, scares, and thrills me at the same time.

The huts are round, the circumferences brightly painted from top to bottom with shapes and symbols, some animal and astronomical, others representations of people or perhaps a story. We're approaching a large hut toward the back, but just before we reach it, Keb motions for us to wait. She walks the rest of the way and steps inside.

I'm shaking. I glance at Nodin and see his pulse pounding in his neck.

Keb comes out the hut, followed by Ashon, our father, and then the air is depleted of oxygen.

I see where Nodin gets his height. Long hair and a beard frames his face. It's white, but from Albinism, not old age. His lean body is loosely clothed in a faded shirt and baggy shorts. Pale skin is covered in the blue highways of underlying veins. His eyes reflect his pain as he struggles to hold back tears.

I hear a whimper come from Nodin, all our emotions

threatening to break him. Nodin takes a step forward, then another, and then he's running to our father.

It seems I can do nothing but cry as I watch as the nearly identical men run to each other and embrace. I feel Baron nudge me forward, but for some reason I'm frozen. Only when I see Ashon looking at me with an outstretched arm, eyes sorrowful and pleading, am I able to move my legs forward.

He releases Nodin and looks as if he might crumble as fresh tears pour down his face. He wraps his arms around me in a bear hug, lifting me right off the ground. "My Devi, mi sita, mi sita, my beautiful girl," he says over and over, squeezing me so tight I can't breathe, but I don't care. He sets me down and cups my face. "Your mother would be so proud. *So proud*," he says, and pulls Nodin close again. "*Barandi Lanka. Barandi Lanka.* I am whole again."

The others join us, and introductions are made. Only then do I notice we've gathered quite a crowd, including adults.

The men wear nothing except strips of red cloth about their waists, but it's the women who are a sight to behold. Their right eyes are ornately decorated as I saw in my dream, but it is a hundred times more striking in person. The colors are vibrant, almost luminous against their dark skin, each with their own unique design. Their sarong-type, red wrap only covers their left breast.

Their other breast being exposed is uncomfortable and a bit distracting, but with so many women around, I find myself becoming desensitized quickly. I can't speak for the guys. I wonder why Keb doesn't dress this same way or have a decorated eye.

The seven of us follow Ashon to his hut. It's much roomier inside than it appeared from the outside, with colorful pillows lining the circumference of the room. A few pieces of pottery are under the only window, and a small mattress is tucked on the opposite side with a single pillow atop. We gather on the floor in a circle, sitting on pillows or the ground. I sit next to Baron, Mapiya on his left, Nodin on my right.

With the seven of us finally together, there is something

titillating in the air. Impending excitement whirled with trepidation.

Ashon steps outside and calls over a boy, speaking with him in the Mbala language.

I can't believe that's our father, right there, close enough to touch.

I watch him move and speak, the realization that he's my father hitting me in waves. Although he resembles Nodin, I recognize myself in his face, too. I think I have his delicate features. Do I resemble my mother? I try and remember the details of her face from my dream, but all I remember are her eyes, wide with terror.

A few moments later, the boy returns with cups and a carafe of water. "We're waiting on one more," Ashon says. "The boy will be back with Sahr in a moment." His accent is a mixture of what's left from his days as a Maz from Mexico and his African home for the past twenty years.

"Sahr is my father. Also our shaman," Keb says.

"Yes," Ashon says. "For the Mahtembo, the shaman acts as chief. Sahr has been chief many years." He looks at me and Nodin. "He knew your mother well. But I will let him explain the rest."

As if waiting for his cue, a shadow blocks the entrance. The shaman is tall and shiny-bald, with dark skin that hangs from weary bones. He enters with the assistance of an elaborately decorated walking stick.

Ashon speaks softly to him in Mbala and Sahr sits, joining our circle, folding his long legs in front of him. He looks directly at me and I notice his eyes are two different colors, one light blue, one dark brown.

He wears a bracelet with white bones, which he shakes three times in the center of our circle. Keb explains this is to clear negative energy. Keb adds that Sahr only speaks Mbala, but she will gladly translate.

Again, as if on cue, Sahr begins to speak. He has no front teeth. I recognize his voice.

Keb translates: "Your mother's soul is brightly lit. The gods chose her to bring you both here, a new home when your old one is no longer safe. Her death split my heart. But I know her spirit will not end, so I do not grieve for long. I see Bahtmi in Tembo. And I see Bahtmi in you."

Sahr is looking at me as Keb translates this. The hut is silent.

Tears unexpectedly spring in my eyes. "Her name is Bahtmi?" My mother. A woman I'll never know. "What does Tembo mean?"

"Her spirit has continued in the elephants," Keb explains. I nod because I know it's true.

I gaze into Sahr's sage eyes again. "You were at my naming ceremony," I whisper. "You wore the bear mask. You spoke my name."

"You remember that night?" Ashon asks, eyes wide.

Keb translates to Sahr, who breaks into a huge grin, wrinkling his face like a prune. He speaks and Keb translates:

"Me and Bahtmi give you that. We want you and Nodin to know who you are. We want you to know where you come from. We tell you many things. We bring you here."

"You did that?" I ask, bewildered. "You gave me the reoccurring dream? And the visions in my tree?"

Keb translates and Sahr nods enthusiastically.

"I remember everything about that night up until the screaming starts and you and Bahtmi run away," I say to Ashon. "What happened?"

Ashon's face drops and he stares at the dirt floor.

"That's the night our mother died, isn't it?" Nodin says, and Ashon nods, his chin trembling with emotion.

"Do you want me to...?" Keb asks tenderly.

Ashon shakes his head. "I'll tell them." He lifts his eyes to ours. "The Tabari knew where we were. It didn't take long for them to figure out you had been moved to another rune tribe, and after that, well, it was just process of elimination. Paytah had arranged—"

"Who's Paytah?" Nodin asks.

"Your Lyriad." He sees our confusion and elaborates,

"Runes must have mentors. Sometimes it is an uncle or grand-father. Paytah was chosen by the gods to protect you two. It's an enormous honor."

Lyriad. I remember that word from Mealy's journal, I think. Our guide when we fled Mexico.

We nod and Ashon continues.

"Paytah had spoken to our neighboring tribes." He points left and right. "The Bewa and the Zuni. He had meetings with their chiefs and befriended their families. They agreed to guard the land and keep the Tabari from getting through to us." He pauses and lowers his voice. "But the Tabari learned of the albino black market and met with the leader of a tribe who hunts white-hairs. The Tabari told the hunter a mystical al-bino with more potent powers was living on Mahtembo land. He said the hunter could have me if he caught me, but he'd also get a large sum of money if he brought back the albino's young children and handed them over."

"Why wasn't Paytah at risk? He's Maz, right?" Nodin says.

"Paytah is a half-breed. His hair was...*is* light, but his skin is not."

"So we were being hunted like animals," Nodin says in a heavy voice.

Ashon nods. "The rune who channels the spirit world is the calling of all callings, for not a single Order can be car-ried out without this rune. The spirit energy is integral to the Order. When Sahr was given your name in a vision quest, Devi, that's when we knew you were this rune. The naming ceremony was supposed to be a special occasion. A celebra-tion. Nodin and I were painted as an extra precaution because we knew we were at risk. Our mistake was not realizing how close this risk was."

His words move through me like a slithery eel: *Not a single order can be carried out without this rune.*

"The hunters are stealthy and know the woods. They got to our land without the Bewa or Zuni knowing. They attacked us that night. We separated as we had planned if under attack. The women took you both and hid you quickly. I ran with your mother in the other direction, hoping to confuse them. As we neared a hut, a hunter jumped from behind it, blocking us. He drew his bow and let an arrow fly. I thought I was a dead man." His voice cracks with emotion. "Until Bahtmi jumped in front of me and took the arrow through her chest."

His head drops, and tears fall into his lap. I hear Nodin sniffling. "Paytah came running and shot an arrow through the hunter's head," Ashon says. "We picked up Bahtmi's body and ran inside the hut."

He takes a moment and wipes his eyes. "Paytah was never the same. He blamed himself for not protecting us. After that night, the hunters were tenacious and ruthless. We knew it was only a matter of time. We knew it wasn't safe here anymore and I was afraid they would find you. We came to the decision to put you up for adoption. It was the only way to really hide you, to keep you from the Tabari. Paytah oversaw everything. I couldn't bring myself to do it. He made sure he approved of who adopted you. And I never saw him again."

Not a word is uttered. The hut is silent for several minutes, until Baron asks, "Where did Paytah go?"

Ashon shrugs. "I don't know. He was broken. A Lyriad without someone to protect."

"Are you still hunted?" Nodin asks Ashon.

He shakes his head. "Paytah spread word that I'd died of a fatal arrow wound that night. I hid for months, never outside the hut without cover, until allies confirmed the hunt was off."

"What about the Tabari? They knew you were in Africa." I ask.

"That threat is long gone," Ashon says. "Without you two, I am nothing to the Tabari. They've been looking elsewhere for nearly two decades. They probably don't look anymore."

"That's not true, actually," Baron says. "They've never stopped. Let's hope they stopped looking here."

I think of the man I detected in Ben's mind. The man who watches me. A dull panic weights me to the floor.

27
THE SPY

We only leave Ashon's hut to be shown where to take care of bathroom needs. It's pretty awful, just a hole in the ground behind some trees. A bowl of water with berries floating in it sits on a tree stump adjacent to the hole. This is where we wash our hands.

"The berries have germ killing properties," Keb says.

I ask her why the women decorate their right eyes and leave their right breasts exposed. She says they believe the right side is the portal to the spirit world.

"Why don't you do it?" I ask.

"I don't need a door. I am a door."

Chills prickle my arms.

We have an amazing stew for lunch made of sweet potatoes, turnips, carrots and rice, served on large leaves. The day flies by and soon the sun is setting in graceful smears of lavender. The hut is a cacophony of yawns after our bellies are filled with more stew for dinner. Ashon takes us to two empty huts near Keb's, where we'll sleep. Aadam and Aren claim the one nearest Keb's. It takes some convincing, but I talk Nodin into letting Baron and I stay in the other hut with Mapiya.

"I'm a basket case and you're going to put Baron just out of my reach?" I say. "You can feel how painful it is for us. Give me this one thing, Nodin. This is about our energy reaction. Nothing else," I say, and I mean it. I gesture to Mapiya, who's holding Baron's arm and lower my voice. "Besides, Mapiya will be with us."

Nodin rolls his eyes and joins Aren and Aadam in their hut. I exhale, relieved.

We are given blankets, which we make into little pallets, padding the dirt floor as much as possible. It gets cool outside quickly. We huddle in the darkness of our surprisingly warm hut and, although exhausted, I'm having trouble falling asleep. This time, it's not because I'm lying next to Baron. Not that I don't think about him still, but I just met my father for the first time, and the Order is just days away.

I toss and turn for a bit, then dig through my bag to find the hematite skull.

"What are you doing?" Baron whispers, careful not to wake Mapiya.

"It's a hematite skull," I whisper back. "It helps me relax and sleep."

"Hematite?" he asks. "Where did you get it?"

"From Joe. The man who lives in our old house."

Baron launches to his feet, alarm in his eyes. "Oh no."

"What?"

"Hematite is a powerful conductor. It makes your mind vulnerable, like an open tunnel. They call it the Spy. Why did he give it to you?"

"He collects all kinds of random crap. It was just a friendly gesture. I'm sure of it," I say, dropping it back in my luggage. "He told me it helps ground you to Earth and protects the wearer."

He huffs. "No, it doesn't. Hematite doesn't do that at all."

I'm confused and Baron is scaring me. "Stop it. Joe wouldn't do that. He wouldn't have any reason to do that."

"What do you know about this guy?" Baron demands.

"I…uh…not a whole lot, I guess," I say. "He's just this lonely guy. But he's always been ni—"

"We have to get rid of it. Immediately." Baron leaves our hut and returns with Keb.

I wait in stupefied silence.

"I will take it to the temple tonight," Keb says. "Master Tran will make it go away."

"Tonight? How are you getting there tonight?" I ask.

"I run," she says in a deep, authoritative voice. She holds out her hand and I place the skull in her palm.

"What the hell?" I ask as she leaves. "You stay here with Mapiya," I say to Baron. "I'll be right back."

I duck behind a hut near Keb's and watch her under the bright moonlight as she attaches a knife to her calf and pulls a strap across her chest. A small pouch rests against her back.

Hearing a dog bark, I glance away for two seconds and she's gone. Disappeared into the darkness.

"Do not worry about Keb," a voice says from behind me and I jump. It's Ashon. "She can navigate these forests as well as the animals, and she is as fast as them too." He rests a hand on my shoulder. "I wish I could be of more help to you and your brother. If your Lyriad, Paytah, were here, he'd know what to do about this man who gave you the hematite. I agree with Baron. He's probably a Tabari mystic."

Ashon told us our Lyriad was someone chosen by the gods to protect and guide us. I wish he'd been around to tell me Joe was working for the Tabari, though I still can't picture Joe that way. It doesn't seem right.

"Do you think Paytah is still in Africa?" I ask.

Ashon leans against the hut and considers my question. "I don't know. What does a Lyriad do without the runes he was chosen to guide? How does he make new meaning of his life? I've been asking myself these questions for nearly twenty years."

I look into the woods where Keb disappeared.

"She will return by tomorrow. Now go get some sleep, Devi."

I wake up the next morning, not quite believing I'm on the floor of a hut in Africa, just days away from saving mankind from an asteroid. Immediately my mind is reeling, overwhelmed by all that has happened the last few days and all that awaits us. I look over at Mapiya, who exudes joy even in her sleep. I feel Baron's hand in mine and I turn to my other side and watch the slow rise and fall of his chest.

Five more days, and we can be together, I think.

Sleeping next to him with the intent of actual sleep is surprisingly peaceful, like being in a boat gently rocking in the waves.

I stretch and yawn, enjoying the silence until Mapiya is awake. I speak to her in hushed tones, but Baron wakes as well. We take turns changing into fresh clothes in the hut before leaving to visit the gross-hole-bathroom. Just as we round a hut, we see Nodin and Aadam heading our way.

Everyone is in summer clothes because of the searing heat. Everyone but Nodin, who's in jeans and a long-sleeved hoodie.

"Nodin," I say. "The term 'Africa hot' exists for a reason. Wear summer clothes for Pete's sake. No one will make fun of you here."

His face reddens. My father walks up and tells us to follow him for breakfast, linking arms with Mapiya to lead her.

"Where's Aren?" I ask Aadam.

"Doing yoga."

Ashon asks me to walk with him. "The Tabari might have a mystic," he says, "but we have our shaman. I will speak with Sahr about the man and his hematite when Keb returns. He will know what to do."

I'm reminded of my dream as we are led into a clearing where the Mahtembo gather around a fire. Two women are tending to a large pot on the fire. A boy brings a stack of leaves and passes one to each of us. When the food is ready, we take turns spooning the contents of the pot onto our leaves.

Ashon explains it is cassava, a millet porridge sweetened with mashed banana. We sit back in our circle and eat. It's delicious.

As we eat and smaller conversations begin to break out, Ashon stands and approaches, gesturing to the ground between me and Baron. "Can I sit here?"

I nod, and Baron scoots over.

Ashon sits close, his shoulder almost touching mine, and says quietly, "You seem worried, mi sita."

I don't look up from my food. "Am I that transparent?"

"You show your emotions on your face, just like your mother did."

I stop chewing. *Mother.* Sadness quells my appetite.

"I know you're scared." He pauses. "That's to be expected. But what you need to remember is, whether you realize it or not, you've been preparing for this your whole life."

We lock eyes.

"Each of you was chosen by the gods for a reason." Ashon puts a hand on my shoulder. "Trust your gift. Trust your purpose." He stands, kisses me on the top of my head and leaves to sit by Nodin, no doubt delivering a similar pep talk.

I'm beyond grateful for his words of confidence. Lord knows I need it. We all do.

Aren arrives, slick with sweat. He gets his food and takes the still-vacant spot next to me.

"How was yoga?" I ask him.

He grins. "Harmonizing and transcendent."

"Wow, those are big words to describe stretching," I say, teasing.

Aren chuckles. "Stretching, huh? If you'd like to *stretch* with me sometime, let me know. We'll see what words you use afterward."

I throw back my head in laughter.

Baron gets our attention and gestures to Nodin.

I look over and grin when I see a beautiful Mahtembo girl with an eye decorated in stunning shades of yellow paying extra attention to him. He's paying attention right back. I don't think I've ever seen my brother being flirtatious. It's endearing, and entertaining.

After we finish eating, Ashon hands us all small sticks. "To brush your teeth," he says, rubbing a tooth with the end of his.

"Is Keb back yet?" I ask, following suit.

"Not yet, but she will be soon. Do not worry, Devi. Keb does not get caught."

"Caught?" Being caught hadn't even crossed my mind. I was more concerned with a lion attack or something. "Caught by whom?"

"To get to the temple, she has to pass through the land of three hostile villages."

I stop brushing and put my head in my hands. "I can't believe she'd put herself in that kind of danger for this."

"She'll be all right, Devi," Aren says. "If they're not worried, we shouldn't be." He stands. "We need to practice working together today."

"But we're not all here," Aadam says.

"S'alright. We'll work with what we have," Aren says. "Is there somewhere we can go with less of an audience?"

Ashon nods. "I'll take you to the river. You will have privacy there."

28
SCARS RUN DEEP

The river is about a mile away. I walk next to Aadam, who leads Mapiya.

"Lightning," she says. Before I can ask her what she means, I see a bolt spear down from dark clouds in the distance.

"How did you know?" I ask her.

"I felt it coming." Her head sways slightly from side to side, milky eyes roaming.

The storm looks far away, but grey clouds spread across the sky like spilled paint.

"You think it's going to storm today?" I say loudly, so Ashon can hear from where he's walking with Nodin.

He peers up at the clouds. "No. It moves west."

That is my father, I think for the hundredth time. I have to swallow the fact down. The concept is surreal. I want to feel more connected to him, but he is a stranger to me.

Nodin acts as though they have formed an instant bond. *Am I that bad at letting people in?* I try to tell myself it is just the suddenness, but the truth is, I do not know how to act toward this man.

Aadam helps Mapiya navigate over a large root that passes across the trail. I move forward and take her other arm to help.

"You have a lot of friends at college?" I ask Aadam.

He grins. "Yeah. Why, you think I sit alone in my dorm, masterminding time travel?"

Mapiya giggles.

"Kinda." I shoot him a smile so he knows I'm teasing. "But I mean because you're younger than everyone else. Weren't you scared at first? Like no one would take you seriously?"

He seems to consider this, then shrugs. "No, not really. I'm just myself. And when I'm myself, the important things seem to fall into place. Everything else is just nuts and cake."

"Nuts and cake? I like that."

"Right? The trivial stuff doesn't really matter, does it?"

"I guess not."

"Nuts and cake," Mapiya says. Her face is beaded with sweat, reminding me how hot it is. My shirt is glued to my body.

We arrive at the river and Ashon points upstream. "You can cross there, where it is shallow. On the other side, it is open just past the trees. Return on the same path when you're finished. I'll go back and wait for Keb."

We cross the river where he told us, stopping only to cool off, splashing water against our flushed skin. As soon as we touch ground on the other side, I feel the calling vibrating up my legs. I know where to go. Ahead of me is a large tree split into four thick trunks that splay out from its center.

"There," I say and start walking. The others follow.

The energy reverberates in my bones, luring me, calling me. I arrive at its trunk and lay my hand on the bark, faintly aware of Nodin rushing to my side to support me.

It's night, and I sit across from Sahr under a full moon. In front of him on the dirt is a pile of different colored crystals beside a bowl of burning sage. He looks at me with his different colored eyes and smiles his toothless smile, then gestures behind me.

I look and see Bahtmi. My heart grows twice its size. She sits next to me and touches my cheek. Her amber eyes tell me everything of her sorrow, filled with the same pain as Ashon's.

I lay my head in her lap, silently crying while she rocks me gently and strokes my hair.

Sahr waves his hand over the burning sage and the smoke wafts under my nose. It is the smell I remember from my naming ceremony. I stare ahead of me at the pile of crystals and notice one of them is a large sphere of hematite.

The Spy, I think.

Baron was right. The hematite makes it possible for Sahr to visit my dreams and give me knowledge through the trees.

Bahtmi nudges me up from her lap and braids my hair, like she does in my other dream. It's so maternal and loving, it makes me ache. When she finishes the braid, Sahr reaches over and taps her knee.

Bahtmi kisses my temple and whispers in my ear, "Tell Nodin I love him with all my heart and soul. I am very proud of both of you."

Then she's gone.

My eyes open, the smell of sage still lingering in my nose. Nodin is watching me with intensity, sweat beaded on his brow as he supports my upper body in his arms.

I tell him the cliff notes of my vision and relay Bahtmi's message. His cheeks flush with emotion as he helps me stand upright.

Baron is ten feet away, shaping the energy he pulled from me. Aren is by his side, waiting to take it from him. Across the grove, Aadam sits, taking painstaking notes on what we're doing. Not far from him is Mapiya, waiting with that content, confident expression she always has. *Little Buddha.*

Searing heat washes over me and I see Baron has shaped my energy into a dense, hot ball. Sweat drips off his chin as he leans back and hurls it with a growl. It whistles toward the clouds with furious intent.

Aren bends his knees, like he's supporting a tremendous weight. His body is so rigid he looks like a wax figure of himself. His hands are up, palms out to the sky as he directs the energy in a tight column. It emits light so bright, I have to cover my eyes, but as quickly as it appears, it is gone.

Mapiya is no longer smiling. She looks angry, almost possessed, with her eyes rolled up in her head as she conceals the red-hot energy. The air is eerily void of sound and seems charged with static electricity.

Baron wipes sweat from his brow with the back of his hand, and we exchange looks with the others, awestruck.

After about two minutes, Aren drops his arms to his side with a grunt. Mapiya's eyes roll back, but they are wide and wild with frenzy. Her hands flail, feeling the space around her, and she screams.

"She doesn't know where she is," Nodin cries as he bolts toward her. He wraps his arms around her little body, holding her still. I watch his eyes close as he forces a calm energy to melt over them, easing Mapiya out of her trance-like state.

In seconds she's alert and aware again. Her blind eyes swim back and forth and she smiles. Nodin releases her and collapses.

"Nodin," I shout, rushing to his side.

Baron cups his head and repeats his name a few times, but Nodin doesn't respond. His face is red as an apple.

"He needs water, fast," Baron says.

"What's happening? What's wrong with him?" I ask, high pitched and panicked.

"I don't know. Maybe the heat got to him," Baron says.

Aren runs toward the river, returning quickly with his own soaking wet shirt balled in his hands. I notice he's got the rune spiral symbol tatted on his back. He bends over Nodin, patting cool water on his forehead. Nodin moans but doesn't open his eyes. Aren squeezes water from the shirt, letting it drip on his neck.

"I need to cool his body. Get his shirt off," Aren says, and pulls Nodin to a sitting position.

Nodin is completely limp, hunched forward, head hanging. Baron helps support his body while Aren removes his hoodie.

Everyone freezes into statues at the sight of Nodin's flesh.

His body is covered in scars, hundreds of them, long and short, covering his stomach and arms. Bright ones blemish his flesh, glowing red against the ivory backdrop.

Then I realize the real reason he's been so careful to hide his skin all these years.

Nodin is a cutter.

I back away, moaning, a visceral reaction welling up inside me like a tsunami.

Nodin makes a noise and his eyes flutter open. He looks around at us and his hand goes to his chest. Realizing he's shirtless, his eyes bulge with panic.

I collapse on him, throwing my arms on his shoulders, holding him tight. "It's okay, it's okay," I murmur. "It's not your fault, it's okay."

His blue eyes search deep into mine. "I don't do it anymore. I swear it. Not in a very long time."

I hug him tighter.

"Can I have my shirt?" he asks meekly. Aren hands it to him, I help him to his feet and he puts it back on.

Everyone is still crowded around him in a concerned silence.

"I'm fine, really," he says, a weak smile on his face. "It's history. I learned to get rid of the emotions in more productive ways years ago. Unfortunately, my scars will always reflect my past."

Baron puts his hand on Nodin's shoulder. "It's alright, man. We all have our struggles. There's no shame in that."

Nodin nods.

"Overheating won't be a problem again. You have nothing to hide anymore," I say, looking straight into his eyes so he knows I mean it. I know it'll be an adjustment for him, though. Hiding is all he's ever known.

We head back to the village, Aren and I flanking Nodin protectively. I hear Mapiya giggling at something Aadam says. They get along quite well, being the youngest of the group. He's taken sole ownership of the role of leading her, which I think is immensely sweet.

As we near the village, Baron and I drop to the back of the group. He takes my hand in his. I'm arcing and, just as a precaution, I hasten our pace until we are just steps behind Nodin. I begin to arc with him, too.

He seems fine. He's worried about Ama, the yellow-eyed girl, knowing about his scars. I didn't realize she meant that much to him. Maybe that's because he's fighting it, for fear he'd have to share that part of himself.

My brother reminds me of myself more than I'd like to admit. We've both been guilty of avoiding intimacy to keep part of us hidden.

I walk faster, pulling Baron with me, ahead of the group and away from Nodin's thoughts. We enter the village and our energy throttles into high gear.

Keb is back.

Relief spreads through my muscles, relaxing them.

I see Keb standing with Ashon, and Ama waiting for Nodin. As we get closer, thoughts other than Baron's invade my mind. I see myself from across the clearing and realize it's Keb I'm sensing. She has something for me. Something Master Tran handed her in an envelope.

Something from Ben. My throat tightens.

29
Ashes

Keb doesn't give me the envelope for several brutal hours. She waits until I'm alone, on my way back from the gross-hole-bathroom. She calls me over just outside her hut.

"This is for you. A message sent to the temple."

I take it and ask what Master Tran did with the skull.

She smiles. "He gave it to a friend who leaves for Germany in the morning."

I want to read Ben's message in private, so I thank her for all she did and walk to my hut. I lean against the outside wall, open the envelope and read:

> *I think you may be in danger. I detected someone watching you. When I tracked him down, I found his property burned to the ground. The police say no bodies were found inside. I believe he's on the run, possibly coming to you. Look at the address on the police report. I'm sorry you have to find out this way.*

I turn the page and see it's the police report. I don't have to look at the address, recognizing the black and white photo.

Our old house. Joe's house. Burned to the ground. All of it. Even my tree.

I crumble into a heap on the ground, moaning like a wounded animal, my sadness and confusion spilling out of me.

Joe was the man Ben sensed watching me. Baron and Ashon were right. He gave me the hematite skull so he'd be able to read me after Ben started blocking me. *How could I be so stupid? How could I be so fucking gullible?*

The reality of how unsafe I've been all those years in his house hits me hard in the gut and I'm shaking.

Keb kneels beside me. "Child, what is the matter?"

"Get Nodin," I croak. "Please, get Nodin."

She returns with him and I hand the crumpled pages to Nodin. His face grimaces in anger as he reads.

Baron rushes up beside us and Nodin hands the pages to him. "Joe," he says in explanation.

"I fucking knew it," Baron says. He sits next to me on the ground and puts an arm around my shoulders, comforting me.

"The tree's gone," I say, looking up at Nodin with teary eyes.

His shoulders sag with the weight of my emotions.

"I don't understand," I say. "If his goal was to find us, why didn't he just take us years ago, in Odessa? It would've been so easy." I choke back a sob. "And why set the fire?"

"I don't know why he burnt everything down. I don't understand that either." Nodin is pacing. "What if the Tabari were waiting? What if they were content knowing where we were, just waiting for a sign the Order had begun?"

"Why would they do that?" Baron asks.

"Think about it. If they captured us before that, they'd obviously be holding us against our will," Nodin says. "And if they lost us to the Order, we'd have a chance to escape them and they'd have to find us all over again. But Joe is a mystic. He knew of your dream and your visions in the tree. He knew a rune summoning was imminent. So they watched. And they waited. And they plan to take us after the Order is carried out."

A full-body shudder rattles me and Baron holds me tighter. I think of the tree of life charm and promise myself to flush it down the toilet when I get my hands on it back home. *If* I get back home. All those hours I spent with Joe. I trusted him. And it was all a filthy fucking ruse to spy on me. I want to vomit.

It's been two days since I read the letter from Ben, but the shock and pain are in my bones, festering, burning, punishing me for being so blind.

We've been sleeping, eating, and practicing in an endless cycle, waiting for those first early hours of January seventh. It's crucial we become intimately familiar with each other's abilities and how they work. No glitches, no surprises.

Keb channels by sitting with her palms pressed to the ground on either side of her legs, although getting into position is all I've witnessed since we work simultaneously.

Nodin hasn't overheated again, partially from dressing less like an Eskimo, partially from knowing what to expect and standing a safe distance from the energy. After supporting me at the tree, he stands with Mapiya, away from the heat, ready to ease her transition back to awareness.

Aadam calculated Sirius will be in line with the Alta Stones at exactly two in the morning, which means we only have tomorrow and the next day to prepare. By sunrise on the seventh, our job will be done.

I lie in the hut wide awake after a full day's practice. Mapiya and Baron sleep, so exhausted they have both collapsed fully clothed. I want to collapse and sleep too.

Instead I think of our mother, who sacrificed her life protecting Ashon, and ultimately us. I think of the tremendous burden Nodin carried while protecting me from knowing what I am, all the while grappling with his own crippling struggles. I think about how naïve I was for trusting Joe, and how much danger I've put us in as a result. *I led the Tabari straight to Africa.* Anguish swirls in my gut like a virus, a sickness I need to purge before I can heal.

I sit up quietly so I don't wake Mapiya, and jostle Baron's chest. His eyes bolt open.

"What's wrong?" he asks.

"Nothing," I whisper. "Come outside with me. I need to talk."

He follows me out. I take his hand and lead him away from the huts, toward the trees. When we get somewhere secluded, I turn and look at him, his face softly lit by the moon. My lips tremble as I fight a total breakdown. His body is warm and solid and I need that. I need something to lean on.

Baron holds me tight, whispering reassuring words in my ear. The hug is comforting, but I need more, and at this moment the consequences no longer matter. In fact, I welcome them. *I dare them.* I want the energy to bash me. I want to be punished.

My mouth finds the warmth of his skin, the salted-caramel taste of him an elixir. I kiss along his collar bone to the hollow of his neck.

"Devi," he says. It's both a warning and a plea.

"Shut up." I pull his mouth to mine and then I'm lost, tumbling weightlessly with the intensity of our kiss.

We're breathless, our energy throbbing in our veins. I run my hands under his shirt and trace a red ray slowly down to his navel. I hook a finger in his waistband and tug him to me, our lips a millimeter apart, and undo the button of his jeans.

He grasps my wrists. His green eyes smolder, but he shakes his head no.

"Please," I whisper. "Right now. Don't stop no matter what." I twist from his grasp and tug at his zipper.

He closes his eyes and grabs my hands again, holding them to my sides firmly.

"We can't risk this three days away," he whispers, his body rigid, caging his undoing.

"We'll stop if we need to," I say, pressing against him.

"Last time we tried that, you got a cannonball to the chest," he says. "Is that what you want? A repeat of that?"

"Yes," I whisper. *I deserve it.*

"Devi." He pulls my arms around his waist. "I know what you're doing and this isn't the answer."

My body goes lax in defeat.

"What's going on with you? What's wrong?" he says, and then the floodgates open.

"I haven't even tried to bond with my father, but I do love him, so much, and I'm not cold or unfeeling," I sob. "I feel so damn much but I don't know how to show it, and I'm pissed I trusted Joe and he's after us and it's all my fault, and my tree is gone, I can't seem to get ahold of myself, which makes me feel like a weak idiot, and—"

Baron cups my chin, forcing me to look at him. "Don't be ridiculous. No one blames you for anything. And you've known your father for a couple days, in the midst of incredibly stressful conditions. There'll be time to get closer to him. You're being way too hard on yourself. Besides, I don't feel like you were ever cold with me. On the contrary, you're quite warm." He smiles a little and pulls me against him.

His words comfort. But excess guilt burns in my veins. I have one final confession. Something I've felt increasingly terrible about.

"That's only because I knew for a fact I could trust you." I hesitate, then let it out. "I arc every time we touch."

He stills.

"I'm so sorry I didn't tell you right away." I try to meet his eyes, but he stares past me. "I was in a different place a few months ago. So much had been kept from me, I didn't know who to trust. I didn't want to look like a fool again. I was afraid if I told you, Ben could find out." I place my hands on his shoulders. "I'd never do it again."

"You know what I'm thinking now?" Baron asks.

I nod with renewed anxiety. "You're surprised and hurt. You have every right to be." I start to pull away, but he doesn't let me.

"It's okay." He sighs. "I get it."

"You forgive me?" I ask, but I already know the answer. He understands. *He trusts me.*

Baron smiles his crooked smile and shakes his head, tucking my hair behind my ears. "Of course I do. Let's get back," he says, and buttons his jeans. "Besides, you've officially drained me of all my willpower for one night. And no, that's not a challenge."

We walk back to the hut. I'm overwhelmed with exhaustion and relief, and collapse on my pallet with my hand curled in Baron's. Sleep comes easily this time.

30
January 5, 2011

I awake, unsure for a moment of my surroundings. An arm tightens around me, and something scruffy nuzzles the back of my neck. Our temporary hut.

The ground is hard and cool but Baron is warm. I nudge closer.

Tomorrow, we leave well before sunrise for the Wonderboom Preserve two hours away. We need the extra time there to see what surroundings we're dealing with, and Aadam needs the day to set up his measuring instruments so we will be exactly where we need to be at the precise moment. Master Tran will pick us up and take us to the front gates of the preserve. The rest is up to us.

I feel bad for Nodin because he has become quite attached to Ama, and now must leave her to do something incredibly dangerous. I watch them sit together while we eat breakfast. It warms me to my toes to see Nodin smile. The sight of the two of them together is a beautiful juxtaposition, like a human yin-yang, jet black and ivory white.

Baron arrives, fills his leaf with cassava and sits next to me. We look at each other in surprise.

"What the hell?" I wince. "Why is the reaction so strong?"

Energy is whipping around us, lashing me from left to right so hard it hurts. He rests his knee against mine and it calms a little. Baron calls Keb over and she notices the same thing. The hum between the three of us is downright throttling.

"Our abilities are getting stronger. Peaking," she says, without an ounce of concern.

I'm envious she had a father to mentor her about the Order.

Baron leaves for the gross-hole-bathroom, and Aren strolls by with his leaf of cassava. As usual, he arrives later than the rest of us because of his morning yoga. He is soaked in sweat, and it occurs to me I've never seen his hair out of a bun.

"How long is your hair?" I ask.

He takes it down for me. Wavy hair with intermittent thin dreadlocks falls to the bottom of his shoulder blades.

"Cool," I say and he twists it back up in a bun. I point to his dreads. "Do those things smell? I heard they smell."

Aren laughs and shakes his head. "Do you want to sniff them and let me know? I mean, we've been out here for days with nothing but swims in the river. I imagine you smell, too."

Giggles bubble out my chest and I shake my head.

He laughs also, then his smile fades and he studies me. "I feel different today," he confesses. "Stronger. Like I could focus the energy of the sun all the way across the galaxy." His gaze lowers. "I guess it's time. Our abilities are heightening."

"Yeah, Baron and I noticed it too."

He nods and points to Aadam, who is pacing furiously and talking to himself like a mad scientist on crack. We find it difficult not to laugh, but then it dawns on me he's not with Mapiya. I look around and don't see her, but she was awake when I left the hut. I excuse myself from Aren and run to look for her.

I find her sitting in our hut, rocking and whispering, eyes rolled almost all the way back. I drop to my knees beside her, almost scared to interrupt whatever's going on, but too worried not to.

I put my hand on her shoulder and whisper her name. The halting ceases and her eyes roll forward. "Mapiya?" I say again.

"Ben sees Joe. He's in Africa. He speaks to a dark man. We are in danger." Her voice is monotone and void of emotion.

Goosebumps prickle my scalp and neck. Before I can even think how to respond, she's back in her cheerful Buddha way.

"Hi, Devi," she says.

"Hi, Mapiya. How did you know I was here?"

"I see your light," she says. "I'm hungry. Can we go eat?"

"Yeah. Yeah, sure we can." I take her arm and lead her to the fire.

When she's settled and eating, I pull Baron, Aren, Nodin and Ashon aside and tell them what Mapiya said.

Ashon clutches his head. "Not again, please, not again."

Nodin puts an arm around his shoulder.

"We need a plan," Aren says. "But first, we need to get out of plain sight."

"Calmly," Baron says. "The last thing we need is panic."

We all agree, although I think that ship has sailed, at least in my case. We gather Mapiya and Aadam and explain the risk of albino hunters has risen *slightly*, so we need to go inside our huts.

Aadam's eyes are wild with worry, but Mapiya just seems a bit confused. We spend the day talking, packing a few necessities for our morning departure and jumping at every little sound.

I awake with a start the next morning.

We will be saving humankind from the catastrophic effects of an asteroid collision in less than twenty-four hours. I replay Ashon's words over and over, clinging to them, white knuckled. *Trust your gift. Trust your purpose.*

I peer through the darkness of our hut, first to my left at Mapiya, and then to my right at Baron. They're both awake, too.

"Nervous?" I ask, and they both nod.

"Me too." I swallow hard and squeeze Baron's hand. His energy webs through mine, viscous like lava, warming me from the inside out.

A wild, blond tuft of hair leans in our doorway. "Time to go, mates," Aadam says.

Elephants trample the butterflies in my stomach. We hurry to Ashon's hut, where we've planned to meet. Upon entering, I see all the others are here already, but when I see Nodin I let out a little shriek.

What little skin is showing on his face and hands is painted black. Memories from my naming ceremony flash in front of eyes, filling me with sadness and dread.

"We have to keep him safe," Ashon says.

I nod and remind myself to be strong. *Breathe, Devi.*

We go in pairs to the gross-hole-bathroom and then await Master Tran. Ashon hands Baron two black duffle bags.

"One has food and water, the other has supplies," Ashon says, although I can't imagine any of us will be able to eat today.

As we sit and wait, it occurs to me I'm arcing with all the others, but I'm not touching Baron. My energy's intensity is off the charts.

Ama appears in the doorway, her eyes never leaving Nodin's as she announces Master Tran has arrived. Ashon hugs us with tears in his eyes. We promise him we'll be back tomorrow safely and file out of the hut, Nodin deliberately last. I glance back and see he's hugging Ama tight.

The drive is long and quiet, filled with trepidation and anxiety. We're like seven superheroes being forced to take a cab to save the day. Our abilities are peaking to unfathomable heights. I fight hard not to arc with the others, their nervous thoughts too much for me.

Aadam is so antsy he's twitching and talking to himself, muttering calculations. I can almost hear the power emanating from Aren and Baron. Nodin is slumped against the door, saturated with our nervousness and fear. Keb's presence is like a fierce dragon, pumped and ready for battle. And then there's Mapiya, sitting in silent contentment, milky eyes wandering. I can't help but wonder what she's seeing.

Roughly two hours later, we arrive at the preserve's entrance, unmanned due to the early hour. The first signs of sunrise fan brilliant yellow across the horizon. We exit the SUV and gather near a large, metal gate emblazoned with the words: *Wonderboom Preserve. Hours 8:00am – 10:00pm. Day fee: 80 R per carload.*

"I pick you up here tomorrow morning," Master Tran says. He wishes us a safe journey and bows before leaving, seeming surprisingly unconcerned. How is everyone around us so sure everything will go as planned? I wish I felt their same certainty. Stones and gravel pop under his retreating tires, and then silence.

We climb over the gate, all of us working together to guide Mapiya to the other side, and gaze upon the rolling hills outstretched in front of us.

"Where do we go from here?" Aren asks, his arm linked with Mapiya's. His voice sounds loud and out of place.

"This way," Keb says, and we follow her.

We walk for quite some time. The sun crawls further from its horizon nest, heating the day. We share the duty of carrying the duffel bags and take breaks for water. Highways of sweat streak down Nodin's black-painted face.

After a mild descent, Aadam points to the largest hill across the meadow. "There," he says and we start walking faster.

"Wait," Aren's voice calls from behind us.

Mapiya's eyes are rolled up, her hands clenched in fists at her stomach as she rocks back and forth.

My pulse quickens as I walk toward her, the others close behind. When she speaks, I hear Ben's voice simultaneously because I'm arcing with her.

"They're coming."

My stomach is in my throat. "Who?" I manage to choke out, but the answer is rhetorical. We all know who and we're all thinking the same thing. *How do they know we're here?*

"No matter what happens, even if we're being bloody shot at, we do not stop the Order," Aren says.

My mind is a cacophony of everyone's panicked thoughts, heightening my own to near hysteria. I try putting my hands over my ears to shut them out. Nodin's whole body is sagging with our cumulative fear.

I grab his hand and we walk fast ahead of the others. Distancing ourselves from them is a matter of sanity at this point.

We reach a large hill that Keb and Baron help Mapiya up. At the top we can now see an enormous boulder, at least thirty feet high.

"There's its twin." Aadam points to the other side of the peak. He takes off his backpack and removes a folded telescope and other measuring devices, one of which he uses to inspect the boulder closest to us.

"I have a problem," he says. "I didn't know the rocks were this tall and smooth. I can't get to the top. I need this—" he holds up one of his savant-physicist instruments, "up there." He points to the top of the boulder.

Baron gets rope out of the supply bag and walks past Aadam, grabbing the instrument. "Got it," he says.

Using the rope, he fastens the instrument to his back and then climbs the boulder. I don't know how he's doing it. There are seemingly no foot or hand holds, yet he's scaling it with the fluidity and grace of, well, the offspring of Spiderman and a ballet dancer.

A few harrowing minutes later, Baron reaches the top and follows Aadam's instructions on where to mount it. To get down, he slides on his ass, leaving the rock surface about halfway down, but landing on his feet and tucking into a roll. He strolls over to the supply bag, retrieves binocular and says, "Now we watch and wait."

I turn in a circle, surveying the hilltop. "Where's the Wonderboom tree? I don't see it."

"There." She points down in the valley below. "See that large mound of foliage? That's all one tree. It's more than a thousand years old."

I gaze at it. "But how am I going to channel down there if the action is up here?"

Mapiya answers. "You, Bear and Keb go to the tree. Bear will throw your channeled energy to Aren up here."

"How will we know it's time to start?" Baron asks.

"I will flash light three times, a three-two-one countdown, when Aadam tells me to," Mapiya says.

"With what light?" Nodin asks.

"I will make light," she says.

The bringer of light and dark.

"Flash another when it's time for me to throw to Aren," Baron says.

She nods. "Got it."

We glance around at each other. "That should work," Aadam says, scribbling furiously in his notebook. "Yes. That should work."

At eleven that night, Baron, Keb and I head to the Wonderboom tree. It's dark, and with the moon our only light we practically slide down the hilltop. Once on level ground, we let Keb take the lead. Her powerful legs glide over the terrain smooth as a panther. Even Baron has trouble keeping up with her confident stride and I trip every two seconds.

Down here, off the hilltop where we could see around us for miles, I feel more vulnerable. Practically running, we arrive at the tree about forty minutes later. It's much further than it looks from the hilltop. There's a low fence surrounding the circumference of the tree, which we easily climb.

As we go under the tree's monstrous canopy, I gasp at its vast infrastructure. "Wow, this is…"

"Epic," Baron says.

We choose a location with a break in the branches so Baron has an uninterrupted line to Aren.

"How much longer?" I ask.

Keb peers at the full moon. She holds first one, then two fingers horizontal between the moon and the horizon, measuring. "About two hours."

We wait, sitting in eerie silence, watching for any suspicious movement.

31

JANUARY 7, 2011
1:58 A.M.

The moon is much lower in the sky than when we first arrived. I glance at Keb and raise my brows.

"Any minute," she mouths.

I nod and try to settle my trembling muscles. I look at the chosen spot on my tree again, and my eyes notice something through the leaves.

Several figures are standing still as statues on the other side of the low fence. At least fifty of them surround us. A panicked sound escapes my throat.

Keb looks at me and I point. She nods.

I open my mouth to scream for Baron when a flash of light beams from the hilltop. Aren's words come back to me: *do not stop the Order no matter what.*

I am nothing but energy and terror and light.

"Three," Baron calls.

Keb readies herself to channel seismic energy, sitting with her palms flat against the dirt. But I'm frozen.

"Two."

I dash to the trunk.

"One."

I place my hand on its bark and an ocean of energy charges through me like an angry, rogue wave. I collapse to the ground and fight to keep my palm against the trunk. I feel Baron pulling energy from me in swift torrents before I'm lost in a vision.

I'm a child, trembling with fear, huddled on the ground just outside our hut. Lightning blazes across the boiling sky. I squeeze my eyes shut and count, awaiting the thunder. When I get to three, it claps with such ferocity I feel it in my bones. The skies open up and I'm pelted with warm rain. It smells like wet straw. I whimper and pull my knees to my chest.

I hear someone calling my name and see a figure running to me. It's our Lyriad, our guide, our Paytah.

I jump up and leap into his arms. He holds me and tells me it's okay, and that thunder can't hurt me. I am comforted.

He rushes me to shelter and sets me down in front of him. Lightning claps again, followed quickly by a crash of thunder.

I look down, wringing my hands. "I'm scared," I say.

He takes my small, pudgy hands in his. "Don't be. I'm here. I will always protect you."

I shake my head, sadness swelling in my gut. "I lost my Lyriad."

"You sure about that?" He tilts my chin up to his face and I am shocked to the core.

"Joe!" I gasp, consciousness streaming back. *Joe Bridle.*

I search in the darkness for Keb and Baron. Keb is near me, still sitting on the ground. I know she's finished channeling because I see Baron condensing our combined amount of energy. He growls with effort, pressing and forming it smaller and smaller. The orb glows like a bowling ball of fire.

Another light flashes from the hilltop and on cue he heaves his whole body into his throw. The glowing ball leaves his hand, emitting a sound like a race car speeding by. Baron falls to his knees.

Keb and I run and huddle next to him, taking in the hilltop and the figures surrounding us. A brief flash of red-orange light fills the sky, then disappears as it rockets into space under Mapiya's concealment.

Aren has estimated it will take about three minutes for the energy to reach the asteroid. *We're almost done.*

I visualize wax-figure Aren on his haunches, focusing the comet-like ball of energy into space. Possessed-looking

Mapiya with her eyes rolled up, concealing the blast's light. Aadam, sweat dripping down his freckled cheeks, peering through his telescope. And Nodin, ready by Mapiya's side.

To keep from going insane, I count in my head. *One-one-thousand, two-one-thousand...*until I reach three minutes.

It's over.

We did it.

It's done.

But we can't celebrate yet. We're not alone.

We're clinging to each other, struggling for breath, waiting to be taken or attacked or whatever horrors the hunters have in store for us. The figures don't move, so we stay huddled and silent. My brain is grappling with the information I know Sahr gave me.

Joe is our Lyriad, Paytah. He didn't disappear, he's been protecting us all along.

In a tumble of whisper-panicked words, I tell Keb and Baron my vision.

"Paytah's alive?" Keb whispers, her mouth hanging open.

The figures begin to move, but not toward us. Grunts and cries sing through the air.

What's happening?

An arrow whirs past me, sticking in the ground at my feet. Survival instincts kick in, and I dive to the dirt, yelling to Baron and Keb to move around. It will make us harder to hit.

We dart and roll for several panicked minutes, but no other arrows come our way. For a second, it seems to quiet down, and then the figures begin to collectively move toward us. I suppress a scream and we back up to the tree's trunk.

They cross over the fence and under the canopy of branches. Terror is the only thing driving me, the only thing pushing blood through my veins, the only thing I breathe. I consider the possibility that Baron could take energy from me and blast them, but even if I could concentrate enough to channel right now, there's not enough time, and there's too many of them.

"Stay away from us," Baron shouts, shielding me and Keb.

"Wait," Keb says, squinting.

I squint too, and can see now they are short, Neanderthal-looking men. They have overhanging brows and under bites, and bright yellow paint glows against their coal black faces and chests. It's the only thing on their bodies, aside from a small string of reeds around their waists.

Keb speaks to them in frightened bursts of Mbala.

One of them answers in a gravelly voice.

Keb turns to me with wide eyes and a half-smile of relief. "These are Bewa. Paytah sent them to protect us. They're *fighting* the albino hunters."

A Bewa steps forward and says something to Keb.

"The hunters got to the others," she translates, eyes wide.

"Nodin," I scream, and we sprint toward the hill.

I'm so fucking terrified for my brother and the others, the adrenaline enables me to keep up with Keb.

My terror is mixed with fury. *This* is what trusting my purpose got me? What if they hurt Nodin? *What if they kill him?* I can't consider that possibility one more second or I'll go insane, so I use the anger and fear to run faster. Dirt kicks up from Keb's heels, hitting me in my eyes and mouth, but I don't care. Nothing short of a train can stop me.

The Bewa run with us, crouched low, daunting in their girth and numbers, like a herd of buffalo ready to kill. I feel as though we're moving in slow motion, like those dreams where a person can't run fast enough, and their muscles are moving through molasses.

Nodin has to be okay.

We reach the other Bewa who tried to stave off the albino hunters from getting to the hilltop. I run up the hill, sliding and falling, hardly aware my knees bleeding. I scream for Aren because he's the only one up there I think can help Nodin and then—*BAM*—I bang into something so hard, I'm thrown back on my ass.

It's Aren. Temporary relief washes over me.

"He's gone," he says, answering my unspoken question.

I die inside. *Nodin.*

"Gone where?" I demand.

"They dragged him off the mountain. We tried to follow but they were too fast." His eyes are vacant and look through me, not at me.

I turn and run down the hill toward the Bewa. I run right to the first Bewa I come to, my fists pounding his chest. "How could you let them get to Nodin?" I scream.

"Devi," Keb's voice booms. "The hunters found us long before the Bewa arrived. They were hiding, waiting." She walks closer and lowers her voice. "Some Bewa have already gone on search for them."

I back away from the wide-eyed Bewa I'd attacked. "Find him. *Find him,*" I demand with authority I didn't know I was capable of.

Keb shouts Mbala words and the Bewa scatter like ninjas into the trees. Keb crouches, about to take off, and I say, "I'm going with you."

She looks down at me and shakes her head.

"You'll have to knock me unconscious to stop me," I threaten.

For a terrifying second, I think she's considering it, but then she gestures me to stay near her. We take off running in the dark, the landscape a blur in my peripheral as we hunt the hunters.

We're crouching low, which burns my thighs like a bitch, but I don't dare fall behind. The Bewa are camouflaged and silent in the trees, stopping periodically to inspect a footprint or bent twigs.

Ten minutes later, or an hour, or six, the Bewa come across a camp. They hold out their hands, gesturing for us to stay back and be quiet. Through the trees, I see the orange flicker of a small fire. I shadow Keb closer in and we are just on the other side of the trees from the fire when something catches my eye.

I strain harder and it comes into focus: a totem pole. I dare to inch past Keb. The pole is thick, not like ones I've seen in books. This one is the width of a door. In the flickering fire, I can make out intricate designs etched on its surface, and I see something else. *Rope.* I move around the trees to get a view of the front and that's when I see him.

Nodin is suspended by his wrists with rope, his feet barely grazing the ground. The rope coils inside the mouth of a carved lion high on the totem. Nodin's hands, dripping blood, dangle outside the lion's mouth like its latest kill. His head droops and his body hangs limp, unconscious. There are four hunters on the other side of the fire.

A primal sound threatens to erupt from my chest and I clamp my hand over my mouth to stop it. I see Keb signal the Bewa and they're moving in.

Like panthers, they creep between the trees and surround the hunters, arrows loaded. I watch in a daze as Keb confirms their position, then steps closer to the camp, shouting at the hunters in another language. Her voice is authoritative as she points at Nodin, her height a menacing shadow in the darkness.

Chaos ensues as the hunters draw arrows and hatchets, screaming at her. The only hunter wearing an elaborate necklace of bones, presumably the leader, turns a loaded arrow at Nodin. I collapse against a tree trunk.

The Bewa move in closer, making their numbers apparent, but instead of intimidating the hunters, it heightens the screaming and tension. The threat seems to excite the hunters.

I squeeze my eyes shut and pray. I don't know to what or who, but I'm frantic, desperate, begging for my brother's life. Keb bellows again and my eyes pop open, instinctively searching for Nodin, to make sure he's okay. I see my first sign of hope: his eyes open for just a second, peering at the leader, and then close again.

He's not unconscious.

I force myself up onto shaky legs and touch Keb's shoulder. She tilts her head down to me and I whisper, "Keep them busy. Nodin's conscious."

She nods once, then peers toward the nearest Bewa and pushes her palm down and back, a signal I assume means to hold off.

I cover my mouth with my hands, praying Nodin can use his gift to manipulate the feelings of the leader before he releases his arrow. Keb's voice is lower, calm, attempting to dial down the tension. Roughly half the Bewa retreat into the trees.

Nodin's eyes are closed, but his brows are furrowed in concentration.

The hunters are ready to defend, standing with bent knees, nostrils flaring, weapons raised. I watch the leader with bated breath, and almost faint with relief when I see his shoulders relax just a tad. His bow dips an inch, and then another.

Yes, yes, it's working.

His shoulders sag. The hunter shakes his head, as if foggy. He is confused.

Come on, Nodin, a little more.

The leader turns his arrow on one of his own tribe mates next to him and shouts at his men. They stare at him. He yells again, louder this time, his voice booming through the camp as he inches the tip of his arrow against his comrade's temple. The rest of the hunters drop their weapons.

Keb shouts to the Bewa on her right and they crouch low and move inside the camp.

Two Bewa approach the totem pole; one acts as a ladder for the other, enabling access to where Nodin's hands are bound. The Bewa retrieves a sheathed knife from his hip and chops swift and hard. Nodin collapses in a heap with a moan. The Bewa scoop him up and pull him into the cover of the trees.

They hand Nodin to Keb, who helps support his exhausted body as we retreat. Most of the Bewa fall behind, making sure we're not followed. The rest run ahead, leading the way.

After roughly thirty minutes of our thigh-screaming, lung-burning night dash, the Bewa determine we're out of danger and stop to rest. Keb hands a leather pouch of water, borrowed from a Bewa, to Nodin, who drips some over his face before drinking. Nodin's eyes are shallow and red, his face gaunt.

I lean next to him, taking a hand in mine. "You're okay now. It's all over," I say.

32
SACRIFICES

The sun is breaking on the horizon when we meet the others on the hilltop. We run to each other, whooping and hollering, hugs and high-fives abounding as we celebrate our successful fulfillment of the Order.

But I can't help feeling uneasy, and almost let down.

What we did was mind-numbingly unbelievable, yet it was over so quickly, without ceremony. No one will ever know the seven of us *sent energy into space and moved an asteroid.*

My eyes meet Aadam's and I ask if he's sure we succeeded.

"We followed the instructions to a T, but I'll be able to confirm it when I get back to the university's radio telescope and do some final measurements."

I feel someone tugging my sleeve. It's Baron. I dissolve into him, relief pouring off me in waves. And then I see someone standing sheepishly beyond our group. It's Ben. I rush to him and jump into his arms.

"You're here? How are you here?" I squeeze his shoulders to make sure he's real.

"I followed him." He points to someone sitting against the other Twin Alter boulder, but it's too far to make out who it is. He holds out a hand. "Come with me."

As we get closer, I see it's Joe, otherwise known as Paytah. He's holding a bloody hand over his opposite shoulder. I sink to my knees.

"I'm okay," he says, seeing my worried glance. He squints with that tilt of his head I've seen a thousand times before. "Are you okay?"

I nod, too overwhelmed to form words.

"Devi," Ben says, kneeling next to us. "I have something to tell you." He gestures to Joe. "He's my father."

"*What?* I thought your father died in a plane crash before you were born?"

"So did I. That's what I've always been told," Ben says. "But I knew this person—" he gestures to Joe, "—as my uncle. You can imagine my surprise when I finally caught up to the person I *thought* was going to South Africa to harm you and saw it was my Uncle Joe. Not to mention he was living in your old house."

"That's when I knew I had to tell him the truth," Joe says. "Not long after Ashon and I moved you and your brother here to the Mahtembo tribe, I met and fell in love with a woman from Bronkhorstspruit, named Natalie. Months later, we found out she was pregnant. The night of your naming ceremony, when the hunters attacked and Bahtmi lost her life, I realized how dire our circumstances were.

"Ben was born a month later. I knew I had to get all of us out of South Africa, away from the hunters and hidden from the Tabari, but I also knew they'd find you again, unless I split us up. I didn't even want Natalie and Ben near me, for fear they'd meet the same fate as your mother. I arranged the adoption to hide you and Nodin, but I was never far away." He glances at Ben. "I moved Nat and Ben to Oklahoma. Near enough to be a part of his life, but far enough to keep them safe."

"But why pretend to be his uncle?"

Joe's eyes are heavy with sadness as he grasps Ben's wrist. "I'd rather be an uncle he saw sometimes, than have to explain why I wasn't around as a father. I had no choice. It was a sacrifice I had to make to keep you safe. The Lyriad resolve doesn't compromise. It's in my blood, and in his." He gestures to Ben.

I look from one to the other. "Ben is a Lyriad, too?"

He and Ben both nod. "The Lyriad DNA is strong," Joe says. "He was born to protect and guide, although he didn't understand why he felt compelled to protect you and Nodin until I explained it to him last night."

The hair stands up on my arms. It makes so much sense,

the protectiveness and the connection he's always had with me. The brotherly friendship he and Nodin share. I smile at Ben with a new depth of affection.

"What about buying our old house?" I ask.

"When your parents put the house up for sale, I knew I had to live there. I had to protect your gift," he says.

"Why did it burn down?" I ask him.

"Before you got rid of the hematite—"

"I'm sorry," I say, interrupting. "We had no idea you were using it to help."

"It's okay, you had no way of knowing. Before you got rid of it, I was able to learn the Tabari mystic was sensing your where-abouts. I suspected they found you through me, so I burned everything that could connect us to keep them from learning anything else." He shrugs. "I guess I was too late. They knew you came here, and sparked interest among the albino hunters again to make sure they got you and Nodin this time."

"How did they find out? I was being blocked by Ben."

"When you left for Africa, I couldn't block you as well." Ben shrugs. "They got in."

"Where's A—I mean, your dog?" I say to Joe.

A tired smile widens across his face. "Safe and sound."

"What happened to you?" I gesture to his shoulder wound. My eyes scan his face and Ben's and the similarities are aston-ishing. They have the same face shape. Same smile. Ben didn't inherit his father's white hair, which I'd always assumed was grey due to age, but he did get Joe's half-breed tan skin.

"Eh, just a scrape," he says with a shrug.

"From a hunter's arrow," Ben says. "When he first arrived at Mahtembo, they were already attacking."

Dread harpoons my spine. "Is Ashon safe?"

Paytah nods. "Everybody is fine, thanks to the Bewa."

Nodin approaches, his face hollow from exhaustion, bright red cuts circling his wrists from the ropes. "I'm told you are Paytah and I have a lot to thank you for."

"Nodin," Paytah says, his eyes desperate and reaching, his chin quivering with emotion.

Only then does it hit me how immensely important we are to him.

Four hours later, we're back on Mahtembo land. Ama rushes to meet Nodin. They fall into each other, a tangle of dark and light. He holds her face and kisses her.

Ashon brushes past them and almost falls over with relief at the sight of all of us. We hug tight and, for the first time since we arrived, I call him Father. He beams at me, then reaches for Nodin.

I walk to Keb and Baron and stand between them. Our energy threesome has decreased, barely detectable anymore. Even the reaction between me and Baron is subdued to an almost imperceptible vibration.

Aadam sidles up to us with a grinning Mapiya on his arm, his freckled face carefree and smiling. "See? Nuts and cake, mates."

I glance over at Aren. "You did good," I say.

He nods. "It's all the stretching," he says with a sideways grin, and I laugh.

That evening, there's a celebration at the clearing. The men play drums while the women and children do a celebratory dance. Keb joins the women and we watch her powerful body move with mesmerizing rhythm and grace. Sahr appears out of nowhere and sits next to Ashon, Ben and Joe, grinning and clapping with the beat. The night is haunting in its resemblance to the night we were attacked, but this time it has a happy ending.

We sit around the fire long after the celebration dwindles to a close, after all the stew is consumed and the rest of the Mahtembo people go to their huts. Aadam pokes the fire with a stick and tiny embers fly around us like fireflies. Aren is telling Mapiya jokes and she is rolling around the dirt ground in a fit of giggles. I look around at all these beautiful people and realize I never need to be jealous of Nodin again. I have a place in this world now, one that makes sense and has purpose. I have found my people.

I lay my head on Baron's shoulder. I'm not arcing anymore. Not even a little.

I ask him something that's been on my mind since we met with Mealy. "Has this changed how you think of God?"

He doesn't hesitate. "Only in that I had to reconcile with the idea that energy can have intelligence. I still think there's a higher power, or a knowing energy, with which we flow. But I believe it's not a person or a soul, and whether or not we believe in it has no bearing on life or afterlife."

I glance at Joe and remember what he told me about religion giving people what they need: faith that there's a plan.

I realize energy is Baron's story, just as much as Christianity is to Mom and Dad, or Judaism, Islam, Animism and Buddhism are to others. Joe is right. We need to believe we're not alone and there's a purpose to our existence. What matters is not what our story is, but rather that we have one.

In the two days that follow, Aadam returns to school in Cape Town and Aren flies back home to England. It is harder than I could ever imagine saying goodbye to them, but we promise to keep in touch weekly via phone, email or Skype. Knowing this helps, but not much. They are my family now.

The evening before the rest of us leave for the airport, Nodin approaches me outside my hut.

"I need to talk to you," he says.

"What is it?" I notice he's wearing a short sleeved shirt, probably borrowed from Ben. His scars, red and striking against his pale skin, are fully visible. I'm proud of him, but more than that I'm elated he's not hiding anymore.

He hesitates, swallowing hard. "I'm not leaving with you. I'm staying here with Ama and Ashon."

Although I have realized that he is in love, I'm stunned by his decision. "But...but what about school? What about—"

He puts his hand on my shoulder and smiles. "I don't care. It'll work itself out."

I've never seen him this content. This is where he belongs and there's nothing I can do to change it. Come to think of it, I wouldn't change it if I could. I want him to have this. He's waited his whole life to be free of protecting me and of his secret. Free to be. As have I.

"I have lots of work to do here," he says.

At first I'm not sure what he means, and then I remember the billboard with the dismembered albino woman, and pride fills me to the point I could burst into a million pieces.

As the sun sets in an explosion of pinks and lavenders, I know I can't leave without saying goodbye to the one person who's been an intrinsic part of this from the beginning. I ask Ashon where Sahr's hut is. He points into the trees.

I walk down a crude trail worn by decades of Sahr's footsteps. Flanking the path are tall poles etched and painted with elephants.

Sahr's hut is smaller than the others and encircled with river rocks. The distinct smell of sage burns my nose as I approach the opening of a doorway. It feels like home. I lean down and am about to say his name when a bony hand reaches out of the shadows and takes mine, guiding me inside where the only light comes from burning embers of a little nest of sage and crystals in the middle of the dirt floor. We sit across from each other.

"I wait fah yoo long tine," Sahr says in broken English.

My jaw drops.

He puts his finger to his lips. "Shhh. It ouwa seecket."

"I just... I couldn't leave without saying thank you for all you've done. For the dream and the visions, for leading us here, and for the time with Bahtmi."

His huge, toothless grin wrinkles his face and he puts a palm to his chest. "A dahtah to Bahtmi ees dahtah to Sahr." He reaches over the pile of smoldering sage and takes my hands. "Dees nawt gootbye, deBI."

I know it's not. Not really. As long as there is sage to burn and crystals to utilize, my mother and Sahr will always be with me.

The next morning, we say our final goodbyes. Keb's eyes are wet with emotion and for some reason this surprises me. Not that she's sad, but that she is showing it. She's so stoic and strong, and that speaks so much to the beautiful contradiction that is Keb. I will miss her tremendously.

It takes me a long time to let go of Nodin. My brother, my twin, the person to whom I am infinitely connected. Life will be strange without him. "What about Mom and Dad?" I ask. "What do I tell them?"

"I'll handle it," he says, and I know he will.

Ashon holds my shoulders and looks deep into my eyes. "My Devi, mi sita, I will not be whole until I see you again."

Me either, I think and hug him hard.

Master Tran drives me, Mapiya, Ben, Baron and Joe to the temple where we retrieve our Outback and head to the airport. We check our luggage and wait for Joe and Ben's flight, which leaves first, eventually connecting to Tulsa, Oklahoma.

"Where will you live now?" I ask Joe.

He crosses his arms. "Now that I'm no longer needed to protect the tree for you, I think I'll spend some time in Oklahoma." He looks across the terminal at where Ben is sitting, and a smile crinkles his eyes. "I've got a lot of catching up to do. And then I'm moving my family closer to you and Nodin."

"You are?" I'm surprised by the relief I feel at this news.

Joe nods and tilts his head. "The threat from the Tabari will always be part of your lives. But so will me and Ben." He puts his hand on my shoulder and squeezes.

Forty-five minutes later, Baron, Mapiya and I leave for our long journey home, on the same flight, because we can. Our energy is no longer a concern, and I'm elated by this for more reasons than flying.

I use the flight to talk to Mapiya. *Really* talk. I want to know about her friends, her family, what her favorite animal is...everything. Because I'm done not connecting with people.

We land in Midland almost twenty-eight hours later and stay in Nodin's apartment one night to rest before driving Mapiya home safe to her father as we promised. We meet him in the same spot, same Exxon, and my eyes are wet when they drive away. *Bye, little Buddha.*

The entire drive to Baron's home in Ardmore, we talk and laugh and enjoy spending time together without the fear and anxiety of the Order looming over our heads. It's the most fulfilled I've ever felt. The most complete. The most grounded. The most happy.

During the drive, I receive a text from Aadam.

> Apophis has been taken off the Torino Impact Hazard
> Scale "due to a slight variation in its trajectory."
> Thought you'd want to know. -A

Epilogue
Two years later
June 23, 2013

I'm sitting on the banks of a river, my feet dangling in the cool water. The ground beneath me rumbles violently. I look at the water churning and undulating like a giant snake, black and boiling.

I yank my feet out and run as fast as I can, but the water level is rising over the bank, chasing me. It gets fuller and taller, and my feet are slapping in the soaked grass. The powerful water is reaching my knees, pulling me under, choking me.

I'm tumbling in the frigid waves, disoriented as objects scrape my face and body. I'm desperate, struggling to find the surface when I slam into something with bull-meets-matador velocity. It's large and unmoving, so I cling with all my strength.

I feel parts of it in the darkness above me, and I move along it surface, pulling myself in the direction I hope is up. I gulp whale-sized breaths when my head breaks the surface.

It is a tree that saved me. Above me are four thick branches reaching toward the sky.

I awake with a gasp and glance at Baron. His eyes are wide, chest heaving. He looks confused, startled and…

Chills prickle my scalp and arms. This isn't my nightmare. It's Baron's. I'm arcing for the first time in more than two years.

We've received a warning.

It will take four of us.

Acknowledgements

I'm obsessed with acknowledgement pages. I hungrily flip to them, sometimes even before I've read the book. I'm fascinated by the veritable village it takes to go from an idea in a writer's brain to a finished, published product.

When I first began this journey, it was an isolating, solo endeavor. But over time, I accumulated wonderful souls who cared about this crazy writing thing I was doing, and invested their time and energy to support me. I found my village, and I've been waiting a long time to thank them.

First and foremost, my husband, Jim. There were many days when the only thing that kept me going was his unyielding belief in me. He may be the slowest reader in the world, but he's also the most supportive, and he has an eagle eye for inconsistencies.

My sons, Draden and Sawyer, for being tolerant of the gazillion hours I spend at the computer, for keeping me rooted inside the mind of a child – a magical place where anything's possible, and for putting up with being called by my character's names more times than I'd like to admit. But especially for that time I overheard you tell some friends your mom is a writer and my heart burst with pride.

My family and friends, whose encouragement and support still astound me. My beta readers, who were both honest and careful with my words. Robyn, for being my touchstone, therapist, sounding board, pseudo-agent and crème-de-le-crème of best friends. Mandi, my book whisperer, who consumed an inordinate amount of tacos with me while poring over edits, plot twists and character development, and whose invaluable advice changed everything for me, more than once.

To the blogging community and fellow authors: although I've never met any of you in person, yet, you were, and continue to be, an intrinsic part of this journey. Thank you for your encouragement, for inspiring me with your words, for your generous assistance, and for graciously lending your blogs to help market this book. Katie Cross, you deserve a medal for being so patient with my near-daily onslaught of questions. I'm immensely grateful for your advice and guidance.

A special thanks to my editors, Rebecca T. Dickson and Bailey Karfelt, who helped carve my pile of sand into a castle, and who were patient and kind to this rookie. The miraculous Jenny Zemanek, who made me the most delicious cover I've ever seen, and didn't yell at me when I completely changed direction midway. For design elements, typesetting, and formatting, I was incredibly fortunate to work with the wicked-talented Jeff Johnston, Chris Bell, and Kella Campbell, respectively.

Thank you, village. You helped this writer fulfill a dream and I love you for it.

To the moon and stars.